William Carleton

Amusing Irish Tales

Fourth Edition

William Carleton

Amusing Irish Tales
Fourth Edition

ISBN/EAN: 9783337242244

Printed in Europe, USA, Canada, Australia, Japan

Cover: Foto ©Andreas Hilbeck / pixelio.de

More available books at **www.hansebooks.com**

AMUSING IRISH TALES

BY

WILLIAM CARLETON

*Author of " The Colleen Bawn," " Traits and Stories of the
Irish Peasantry," " The Fawn of Springvale," " The Squanders
of Castle Squander," " Fardarougha the Miser,"
&c., &c.*

FOURTH EDITION

LONDON
SIMPKIN, MARSHALL, HAMILTON, KENT & CO
GLASGOW: THOMAS D. MORISON

EDITORIAL NOTE.

WILLIAM CARLETON, the unrivalled delineator of the habits and character of his countrymen, was born at Prillisk, in the county of Tyrone, in the year 1798. His father was a small farmer. Both father and mother were persons of greatly superior mind ; and although not highly educated they were better informed than most of their class, and were rich in natural endowments, so that the son had considerable privileges, both in the matter of mental inheritance and early associations. The father was endowed with such a marvellous memory, that it is said he could repeat the greater part of the bible by heart. He was also a walking repertory of legendary lore, and could tell tales from year's end to year's end. His mother was noted for her beautiful voice, and talent in the realms of song.

William was intended for a priest, and had begun the preliminary studies required to fit him for entering Maynooth. At this critical period of his early career, his father died, and immediately the son abandoned all thought of the church ; which would make it appear, that to take this step had been more the wish of his father than of himself. Some years afterwards he left the Roman Catholic Church and joined the Church of England.

Of an imaginative and sanguine temperament, he was, through a perusal of Gil Blas, fired with a desire to see the world and seek his fortune away from the quiet vale where he had been nurtured. His first effort only resulted in obtaining a situation as tutor, at a very poor salary, in a farmer's house. Soon tired of this uncongenial drudgery, he threw up the situation and started for Dublin, in which city he found himself without any definite plan for the future in his mind, and with the sum of two shillings and ninepence in his pocket. Here again he had to reconcile himself for some time to the uncongenial labours of tutor.

Ultimately, while still resident in Dublin, he became acquainted with the Rev. Cæsar Otway. At this gentleman's suggestion young Carleton wrote a tale for one of the magazines, which attracted general notice. This formed the second turning point in the young man's life, and showed to himself and friends where his *forte* lay. From this period a long stream of writings came from the talented author's pen, both through separate volumes and through the magazine press. In all, the volumes he became author of amounted to over forty in number. Many of his novels and tales exhibit singular power and talent, and have universally been acknowledged as giving true and faithful representations of the social life of his countrymen. William Carleton died in 1869 at the age of seventy-one.

The tales contained in this volume are selected from several of the distinguished author's numerous works. These latter, as already intimated, amount to a very considerable number. It will be observed that those given in the following pages are all of an amusing and humorous nature, it being chiefly on that ground that they have been selected. At the same time, they will be found rich descriptively of the manners, customs, sympathies, and ideas of the Irish people. The native habits and tastes of any people form an interesting study, and in such matters the Irish are quite as attractive as any of the other modern nations—in temperament and character they are as strongly distinctive as each of the three sister peoples. The Irish have been distinguished for their warm-hearted, affectionate disposition, capable of great goodness, faithful to trust, and grateful for kindness and sympathy received. And no doubt through increased industry and improved laws these beautiful traits of character will aid in forming a distinguished future for them as a people.

CONTENTS.

—:o:—

AMUSING IRISH TALES.

BUCKRAM-BACK,

The Country Dancing Master.

ONE of the most amusing specimens of the Irish dancing-master, that I ever met, was the person who went under the nickname of Buckram-Back. This man had been a drummer in the army for some time, where he had learned to play the fiddle ; but it appears that he possessed no relish whatever for a military life, as his abandonment of it without even the usual form of a discharge or furlough, together with a back that had become cartilaginous from frequent flogging, could abundantly testify. It was from the latter circumstance that he had received his nickname.

Buckram-Back was a dapper light little fellow, with a rich Tipperary brogue, crossed by a lofty strain of illegitimate English, which he picked up whilst abroad in the army. His habiliments sat as tight upon him as he could readily wear them, and were all of the shabby-genteel class. His crimped black coat was a closely worn second-hand, and his crimped face quite as much of the second-hand as

the coat. I think I see his little pumps, little white stockings, his coaxed drab breeches, his hat, smart in its cock
but brushed to a polish, and standing upon three hairs,
together with his tight questionable-coloured gloves, all
before me. Certainly he was the jauntiest little cock
living—quite a blood, ready to fight any man, and a great
defender of the fair sex, whom he never addressed except
in that high-flown bombastic style so agreeable to most of
them, called by their flatterers the complimentary, and by
their friends the fulsome. He was in fact a public man,
and up to everything. You met him at every fair, where
he only had time to give you a wink as he passed, being
just then engaged in a very particular affair ; but he would
tell you again. At cock-fights he was a very busy personage, and an angry bettor from half-a-crown downwards.
At races he was a knowing fellow, always shook hands
with the winning jockey, and then looked pompously about,
that folks might see he was hand and glove with people
of importance. The house where Buckram-Back kept his
school, which was open only after the hours of labour, was
an uninhabited cabin, the roof of which, at a particular spot,
was supported by a post that stood upright from the floor.
It was built upon an elevated situation, and commanded a
fine view of the whole country for miles about it. A
pleasant sight it was to see the modest and pretty girls,
dressed in their best frocks and ribbons, radiating in little
groups from all directions, accompanied by their partners
or lovers, making way through the fragrant summer fields,
of a calm cloudless evening, to this happy scene of innocent
amusement.

And yet what an epitome of general life, with its
passions, jealousies, plots, calumnies, and contentions, did
this tiny segment of society present ! There was the
shrew, the slattern, the coquette, and the prude, as sharply
marked within this their humble sphere, as if they appeared

on the world's wider stage, with half its wealth and all its temptations to draw forth their prevailing foibles. There too was the bully, the rake, the liar, the coxcomb, and the coward, each as perfect and distinct in his kind as if he had run through a lengthened course of fashionable dissipation, or spent a fortune in acquiring his particular character. The elements of the human heart, however, and the passions that make up the general business of life, are the same in high and low, and exist with impulses as strong in the cabin as in the palace. The only difference is, that they have not equal room to play.

Buckram-Back's system, in originality of design, in comic conception of decorum, and in the easy practical assurance with which he wrought it out, was never equalled, much less surpassed. Had the impudent little rascal confined himself to dancing as usually taught, there would have been nothing so ludicrous or uncommon in it; but no; he was such a stickler for example in everything, that no other mode of instruction would satisfy him. Dancing! why, it was the least part of what he taught or professed to teach.

In the first place, he undertook to teach every one of us —for I had the honour of being his pupil—how to enter a drawing-room " in the most fashionable manner alive," as he said himself.

Secondly. He was the only man, he said, who could in the most agreeable and polite style teach a gintleman how to salute, or, as he termed it, how to shiloote, a leedy. This he taught, he said, with great success.

Thirdly. He could taich every leedy and gintleman how to make the most beautiful bow or curchy on airth, by only imitating himself—one that would cause a thousand people if they were all present, to think that it was particularly intended only for aich o' themselves!

Fourthly. He taught the whole art o' courtship wid all

peliteness and success, accordin' as it was practised in Paris
durin' the last saison.

Fifthly.   He could taich them how to write love-letthers
and valentines accordin' to the Great Macademy of com-
pliments, which was supposed to be invinted by Bonaparte
when he was writing love letthers to both his wives.

Sixthly.   He was the only person who could taich the
famous dance called Sir Roger de Coverly, or the Helter-
Skelter Drag, which comprehended widin itself all the
advantages and beauties of his whole system—in which
every gintleman was at liberty to pull every leedy where
he plaised, and every leedy was at liberty to go wherever
he pulled her.

With such advantages in prospect, and a method of
instruction so agreeable, it is not to be wondered at that
this establishment was always in a most flourishing condition.   The truth is, he had it so contrived that every
gentleman should salute his lady as often as possible, and
for this purpose actually invented dances, in which not only
should every gentleman salute every lady, but every lady,
by way of returning the compliment, should render a
similar kindness to every gentleman.   Nor had his male
pupils all this prodigality of salutation to themselves, for
the amorous little rascal always commenced first and ended
last, in order, he said, that they might *cotch* the manner
from himself.   " I do this, leedies and gintlemen, as your
moral (model), and because it's part o' *my* system—ahem !"

And then he would perk up his little hard face, that
was too barren to produce more than an abortive smile,
and twirl like a wagtail over the floor, in a manner that
he thought irresistible.

Whether Buckram-Back was the only man who tried to
reduce kissing to a system of education in this country, I
do not know.   It is certainly true that many others of his
stamp made a knowledge of the arts and modes of court-

ship, like him, a part of the course. The forms of love letters, valentines, &c., were taught their pupils of both sexes, with many other polite particulars, which it is to be hoped have disappeared for ever.

One thing, however, to the honour of our country-women we are bound to observe, which is, that we do not remember a single result incompatible with virtue to follow from the little fellow's system, which, by the way, was in *this* respect peculiar only to himself, and not the general custom of the country. Several weddings, unquestionably, we had, more than might otherwise have taken place, but in no one instance have we known any case in which a female was brought to unhappiness or shame.

We shall now give a brief sketch of Buckram-Back's manner of tuition, begging our readers at the same time to rest assured that any sketch we could give would fall far short of the original.

"Paddy Corcoran, walk out an' 'inther your drawin'-room ;' an' let Miss Judy Hanratty go out along wid you, an' come in as Mrs. Corcoran."

"Faith, I'm afeard, master, I'll make a bad hand of it ; but, sure, it's something to have Judy here to keep me in countenance."

"Is that by way of compliment, Paddy ? Mr. Corcoran, you should ever an' always spaik to a leedy in an alablasther tone ; for that's the cut."

[*Paddy and Judy retire.*

"Mickey Scanlan, come up here, now that we're braithin' a little ; an' you Miss Grauna Mulholland, come up along wid him. Miss Mulholland, you are masther of your five positions and your fifteen attitudes, I believe ?" "Yes, sir." "Very well, Miss. Mickey Scanlan—ahem—*Misther* Scanlan, can *you* perform the positions also, Mickey ?"

"Yes, sir ; but you remember I stuck at the eleventh altitude."

"Attitude, sir—no matther. Well, Misther Scanlan, do you know how to shiloote a leedy, Mickey?"

"Faix, it's hard to say, sir, till we try; but I'm very willin' to larn it. I'll do my best, an' the best can do no more."

"Very well—ahem! Now merk me, Misther Scanlan; you approach your leedy in this style, bowin' politely, as I do. Miss Mulholland, will you allow me the honour of a heavenly shiloote? Don't bow, ma'am; you are to curchy, you know; a little lower *eef* you plaise. Now you say, 'Wid the greatest pleasure in life, sir, an' many thanks for the feevour.' *(Smack).* There, now, you are to make another curchy politely, an' say, 'Thank you, kind sir, I owe you one.' Now, Misther Scanlan, proceed."

"I'm to imitate you, masther, as well as I can, sir, I believe?"

"Yes, sir, you are to imitate *me*. But hould, sir; did you see me lick my lips or pull up my breeches? Be gorra, that's shockin' unswintemintal. First make a curchy, a bow I mane, to Miss Grauna. Stop again, sir; are you going to sthrangle the leedy? Why, one would think that it's about to teek laive of her for ever you are. Gently, Misther Scanlan; gently, Mickey. There—well, that's an improvement. Practice, Misther Scanlan, practice will do all, Mickey, but don't smack so loud, though. Hilloo, gintlemen! where's our drawin'-room folks? Go out, one of you, for Misther and Mrs. Paddy Corcoran."

Corcoran's face now appears peeping in at the door, lit up with a comic expression of genuine fun, from whatever cause it may have proceeded.

"Aisy, Misther Corcoran; an' where's Mrs. Corcoran, sir?"

"Are we both to come in together, masther?"

"Certainly: turn out both your toses—turn them out, I say."

"Faix, sir, it's aiser said than done wid some of us."

"I know that, Misther Corcoran; but practice is every-thing. The bow legs are strongly against you, I grant. Hut tut, Misther Corcoran—why, if your toes wor where your heels is, you'd be exactly in the first position, Paddy. Well, both of you turn out your toses; look street forward; clap your caubeen—ahem!—your castor under your ome (arm), an' walk into the middle of the flure, wid your head up. Stop, take care o' the post. Now, take your caubeen, castor I mane, in your right hand; give it a flourish. Aisy, Mrs. Hanratty—Corcoran I mane—it's not *you* that's to flourish. Well, flourish your castor, Paddy, and thin make a graceful bow to the company. Leedies and gintlemen"—

"Leedies and gintlemen"—

"I'm your most obadient sarvint"—

"I'm your most obadient sarwint."

"Tuts man alive! that's not a bow. Look at this: *there's* a bow for you. Why, instead of meeking a bow, you appear as if you wor goin' to sit down with an embargo (lumbago) in your back. Well, practice is every thing; an' there's luck in leisure."

"Dick Doorish, will you come up, and thry if you can meek anything of that treblin' step. You're a purty lad, Dick; you're a purty lad, Misther Doorish, with a pair o' left legs an you, to expect to larn to dance; but don't dispeer, man alive, I'm not afeard but I'll make a graceful slip o' you yet. Can you meek a curchy?"

"Not right, sir, I doubt."

"Well, sir, I know that; but, Misther Doorish, you ought to know how to meek both a bow and a curchy. Whin you marry a wife, Misther Doorish, it mightn't come wrong for you to know how to taich her a curchy. Have you the *gad* and *suggaun* wid you?" "Yes, sir." "Very well, on wid them; the suggaun on the right foot, or what ought to be the right foot, an' the gad upon what ought to be the

left. Are you ready?" "Yes, sir." "Come, then, do as I
bid you. Rise upon suggaun an' sink upon gad ; rise upon
suggaun an' sink upon gad ; rise upon——Hould, sir ;
you're sinkin' upon suggaun an' risin' upon gad, the very
thing begad you ought *not* to do. But, God help you !
sure you're left-legged. Ah, Misther Doorish, it 'ud be a
long time before you'd be able to dance Jig Polthogue or
the College Hornpipe upon a drum-head, as I often did.
However, don't despeer, Misther Doorish : if I could only
get you to know your right leg—but God help you ! sure
you hav'n't such a thing—from your left, I'd make something of you yet, Dick."

The Irish dancing-masters were eternally at daggers-
drawn among themselves ; but as they seldom met, they
were forced to abuse each other at a distance, which they
did with a virulence and scurrility proportioned to the
space between them. Buckram-Back had a rival of this description, who was a sore thorn in his side. His name was
Paddy Fitzpatrick, and from having been a horse-jockey,
he gave up the turf, and took to the calling of a dancing-
master. Buckram-Back sent a message to him to the
effect that "if he could not dance Jig Polthogue on the
drum-head, he had better hould his tongue for ever." To
this Paddy replied, by asking if he was the man to dance
the Connaught Jockey upon the saddle of a blood horse,
and the animal at a three-quarter gallop.

At length the friends on each side, from a natural love
of fun, prevailed upon them to decide their claims as follows : Each master with twelve of his pupils, was to dance
against his rival with twelve of his ; the match to come off
on the top of Mallybeny hill, which commanded a view of
the whole parish. I have already mentioned that in
Buckram-Back's school there stood near the middle of the
floor a post, which, according to some new manœuvre of
his own, was very convenient as a guide to the dancers

when going through the figure. Now, at the spot where this post stood it was necessary to make a curve, in order to form part of the figure of eight, which they were to follow ; but as many of them were rather impenetrable to a due conception of the line of beauty, he forced them to turn round the post, rather than make an acute angle of it, which several of them did. Having premised thus much, we proceed with our narrative.

At length they met, and it would have been a matter of much difficulty to determine their relative merits, each was such an admirable match for the other. When Buckram-Back's pupils, however, came to perform, they found that the absence of the post was their ruin. To the post they had been trained—accustomed ; with *it* they could dance ; but wanting that, they were like so many ships at sea without rudders or compasses. Of course a scene of ludicrous confusion ensued, which turned the laugh against poor Buckram-Back, who stood likely to explode with shame and venom. In fact he was in an agony.

"Gintlemen, turn the post!" he shouted, stamping upon the ground, and clenching his little hands with fury ; "leedies, remimber the post! Oh, for the honour of Kilnahushogue don't be bate. The post, gintlemen! leedies the post, if you love me. Murdher alive, the post!"

"Be gorra, masther, the jokey will distance us," replied Bob Magawly ; "it's likely to be the *winnin'-post* to him, any how."

"Any money," shouted the little fellow, "any money for long Sam Sallaghan ; he'd do the post to the life. Mind it, boys dear, mind it or we're lost. Divil a bit they heed me : it's a flock of bees or sheep they are like. Sam Sallaghan, where are you? The post, you blackguards!"

"Oh, masther dear, if we had even a fishin'-rod or a crowbar, or a poker, we might do yet. But, anyhow, we had betther give in, for it's only worse we're gettin'."

3

At this stage of the proceedings, Paddy came over, and making a low bow, asked him, " Arra, how do you feel, Misther Dogherty ?" for such was Buckram-Back's name.

" Sir," replied Buckram-Back, bowing low, however, in return, " I'll take the shine out of you, yet. Can you shiloote a leedy wid me—that's the chat ! Come, gintlemen, show them what's betther than fifty posts—shiloote your partners like Irishmen. Kilnahushogue for ever ! "

The scene that ensued baffles all description. The fact is, the little fellow had them trained, as it were, to kiss in platoons, and the spectators were literally convulsed with laughter at this most novel and ludicrous character that Buckram-Back gave to his defeat, and the ceremony which he introduced. The truth is, he turned the laugh completely against his rival, and swaggered off the ground in high spirits, exclaiming, " He know how to shiloote a leedy ! Why the poor spalpeen never kissed any woman but his mother, an' her only when she was dyin'. Hurra for Kilnahushogue ! "

Such is a slight sketch of an Irish dancing-master, which if it possesses any merit at all, is to be ascribed to the circumstance that it is drawn from life, and combines, however faintly, most of the points essential to the truest conception of the character.

MARY MURRAY,

The Irish Match-Maker.

OUR readers are not to understand that in Ireland there exists, like the fiddler or dancing-master, a distinct character openly known by the appellation of match-maker. No such thing. On the contrary, the negotiations they undertake are all performed under false colours. The business, in fact, is close and secret, and always carried on with the profoundest mystery, veiled by the sanction of some other ostensible occupation.

One of the best specimens of the kind we ever met was old Mary Murray. Mary was a tidy creature of middle size, who always went dressed in a short crimson cloak, much faded, a striped red and blue drugget petticoat, and a heather-coloured gown of the same fabric. When walking, which she did with the aid of a light hazel staff hooked at the top, she generally kept the hood of the cloak over her head, which gave to her whole figure a picturesque effect ; and when she threw it back, one could not help admiring how well her small but symmetrical features agreed with the dowd cap of white linen, with a plain muslin border, which she wore. A pair of blue stockings and sharp-pointed shoes, high in the heels, completed her dress. Her features were good-natured and Irish, but over the whole countenance there lay an expression of quickness and sagacity, contracted no doubt by an habitual exercise of penetration and circumspection. At the time I saw her she was very old, and I believe had the reputation of being the last in that part of the country who was known to go about from house to house spinning on the distaff, an instrument which has now passed away, being more conveniently replaced by the spinning wheel.

The manner and style of Mary's visits were different from those of any other who could come to a farmer's house, or even to an humble cottage, for to the inmates of both were her services equally rendered. Let us suppose, for instance, the whole female part of a farmer's family assembled of a summer evening about five o'clock, each engaged in some domestic employment : in runs a lad who has been sporting about, breathlessly exclaiming, whilst his eyes are lit up with delight, " Mother, mother, here's Mary Murray comin' down the boreen !" " Get out, avick : no, she's not." " Bad

cess to me but she is; that I may never stir if she isn't.
Now!" The whole family are instantly at the door to see
if it be she, with the exception of the prettiest of them all,
Kitty, who sits at her wheel, and immediately begins to
croon over an old Irish air, which is sadly out of tune;
and well do we know, notwithstanding the mellow tones
of that sweet voice, why it is so, and also why that youthful
cheek, in which health and beauty meet, is the colour of
crimson.

"*Oh, Vara, acushula, cead millia failte ghud?* (Mary,
darling, a hundred thousand welcomes to you!) Och,
musha, what kep' you away so long, Mary? Sure you
won't have us this month o' Sundays, Mary!" are only a
few of the cordial expressions of hospitality and kindness
with which she is received. But Kitty, whose cheek but a
moment ago was carmine, why is it now pale as the lily?

"An' what news, Mary," asks one of her sisters: "sure
you'll tell us everything: won't you?"

"Throth, avilish, *I have no bad news*, any how—an' as to
tellin' you *all*— Biddy, *lhig dumh*, let me alone. No, I have
no bad news, God be praised, *but good news*."

Kitty's cheek is again crimson, and her lips, ripe and red
as cherries, expand with the sweet soft smile of her country,
exhibiting a set of teeth for which many a countess would
barter thousands, and giving out a breath more delicious
than the fragrance of a summer meadow. Oh, no wonder,
indeed, that the kind heart of Mary contains in its recesses
a message to her as tender as ever was transmitted from
man to woman.

"An', Kitty acushla, where's the welcome from *you*, that's
my favourite? Now don't be jealous, childre; sure you all
know she is, an' ever an' always was."

"If it's not upon my lips, it's in my heart, Mary, an' from
that heart you're welcome."

She rises up and kisses Mary, who gives her one glance

of meaning, accompanied by the slightest imaginable smile, and a gentle but significant pressure of the hand, which thrills to her heart, and diffuses a sense of ecstasy through her whole spirit. Nothing now remains but the opportunity, which is equally sought for by Mary and her to hear without interruption the purport of her lover's communication, and this we leave to lovers to imagine.

In Ireland, however odd it may seem, there occur among the very poorest classes some of the hardest and most penurious bargains in match-making than ever were heard of or known. Now, strangers might imagine that all this close higgling proceeds from a spirit naturally near and sordid, but it is not so. The real secret of it lies in the poverty and necessity of the parties, and chiefly in the bitter experience of their parents, who, having come together in a state of destitution, are anxious, each as much at the expense of the other as possible, to prevent their children from experiencing the same privation and misery which they themselves felt. Many a time have matches been suspended, or altogether broken off, because one party refuses to give his son "*a slip of a pig*," or another his daughter "a pair of blankets;" and it was no unusual thing for a match-maker to say, "Never mind; I have it all settled *but the slip*." One might naturally wonder why those who are so shrewd and provident upon this subject do not strive to prevent early marriages where the poverty is so great. So unquestionably they ought, but it is a settled usage of the country, and one, too, which Irishmen have never been in the habit of considering as an evil. We have no doubt that if they once began to reason upon it as such, they would be very strongly disposed to check a custom which has been the means of involving themselves and their unhappy offspring in misery, penury, and not unfrequently in guilt itself.

Mary, like many others in this world who are not con-

scious of the same failing, smelt strongly of the shop; in
other words her conversation had a strong matrimonial
tendency. No two beings ever lived so decidedly antithetical
to each other in this point of view as the match-maker and
the *Keener.* Mention the name of an individual or a family
to the keener, and the medium through which her memory
passes back to them is that of her professed employment—
a mourner at wakes and funerals.

"Don't you know young Kelly of Tamlaght?"

"I do, avick," replies the keener, "and what about him?"

"Why he was married to-day mornin' to ould Jack
M'Cluskey's daughter."

"Well, God grant them luck an' happiness, poor things!
I do indeed remimber his father's wake an' funeral well—
ould Risthard Kelly of Tamlaght—a dacent corpse he made
for his years, an' well he looked. But indeed I *knewn* by
the colour that sted in his cheeks, and the limbs remaining
soople for the twenty-four hours afther his departure, that
some of the family 'ud follow him afore the year was out,
an' so she did. The youngest daughter, poor thing, by
raison of a could she got, over-heatin' herself at a dance,
was stretched beside him that very day was eleven months;
an' God knows it was from the heart my grief kem for *her*
—to see the poor han'some colleen laid low so soon. But
whin a gallopin' consumption sets in, avourneen, sure we all
know what's to happen. In Crockaniska churchyard they
sleep—the Lord make both their beds in heaven this day."

The very reverse of this, but at the same time as inveter-
ately professional, was Mary Murray.

"God save you, Mary."

"God save you kindly, avick. Eh, let me look at you.
Aren't you red Billy M'Guirk's son from Ballagh?"

"I am, Mary. An', Mary, how is yourself and the world
gettin' an?"

"Can't complain, dear, in such times. How are yez all

at home, alanna?" "Faix middlin' well, Mary, thank God
an' you. You hard of my grand-uncle's death, big Ned
M'Coul?"

"I did, avick, God rest him. Sure it's well I remimber
his weddin', poor man, by the same atoken that I know one
that helped him an wid it a thrifle. He was married in a
blue coat an' buskins, an' wore a scarlet waistcoat that you'd
see three miles off. Oh, well I remimber it. An' whin he
was settin' out that mornin' to the priest's house, ' Ned,' says
I, an' I fwhishspered him, ' dhrop a button on the right
knee afore you get the words said.' ' *Thighum*,' said he,
wid a smile, an' he slipped ten thirteens into my hand as he
spoke. ' I'll do it,' said he, ' and thin a fig for the fairies !'*
—because, you see if there's a button of the right knee left
unbuttoned, the fairies—this day's Friday, God stand betune
us and harm !—can do neither hurt nor harm to sowl or
body, an' sure that's a great blessin', avick. He left two fine
slips o' girls behind him."

"He did so—as good-lookin' girls as there's in the parish."

"Faix, an' kind mother for them, avick. She'll be
marryin' agin, I'm judgin', she bein' sich a fresh good-lookin'
woman."

"Why, it's very likely, Mary."

"Throth it's natural, achora. What can a lone woman
do wid such a large family on her hands, widout having
some one to manage it for her, an' prevint her from bein'
imposed on? But indeed the first thing she ought to do is
to marry off her two girls widout 'oss of time, in regard that
it's hard to say how a stepfather an' thim might agree; and
I've often known the mother herself, when she had a fresh
family comin' an her, to be as unnatural to her fatherless
childre as if she was a stranger to thim, and that the same
blood didn't run in their veins. Not saying that Mary
M'Coul will or would act that way by her own ; for indeed

* Such is the superstition.

she's come of a kind ould stock, an' ought to have a good
heart.   Tell her, avick, when you see her, that I'll spind a
day or two wid her—let me see—the day after to-morrow
will be Palm Sunday—why, about the Aisther holidays."

"Indeed I will, Mary, with great pleasure."

"An' fwhishsper, dear, just tell her that I've a thing to
say to her—that I had a long dish o' discoorse about her
wid *a friend o' mine*.   You won't forget, now ? "

"Oh, the dickens a forget ! "

"Thank you, dear : God mark you to grace, avourneen !
When you're a little oulder, maybe I'll be a friend to you
yet."

This last intimation was given with a kind of mysterious
benevolence, very visible in the complacent shrewdness of
her face, and with a twinkle in the eye, full of grave humour
and considerable self-importance, leaving the mind of the
person she spoke to in such an agreeable uncertainty as
rendered it a matter of great difficulty to determine whether
she was serious or only in jest, but at all events throwing
the onus of inquiry upon him.

The ease and tact with which Mary could involve two
young persons of opposite sexes in a mutual attachment,
were very remarkable.   In truth, she was a kind of matrimonial incendiary, who went through the country holding
her torch now to this heart and again to that—first to one
and then to another, until she had the parish more or less
in a flame.   And when we consider the combustible materials of which the Irish heart is composed, it is no wonder
indeed that the labour of taking the census in Ireland in-
creases at such a rapid rate, during the time that elapses
between the period of its being made out.   If Mary, for
instance, met a young woman of her acquaintance acci-
dentally—and it was wonderful to think how regularly
these accidental meetings took place—she would address
her probably somewhat as follows :—

" Arra, Biddy Sullivan, how are you, a-colleen ? "

" Faix, bravely, thank you, Mary.   How is yourself ? "

" Indeed, thin' sorra a bit o' the health we can complain of, Bhried, barrin' whin this pain in the back comes upon us. The last time I seen your mother, Biddy, she was complainin' of a *weid*.* I hope she's betther, poor woman?"

" Hut ! bad scran to the thing ails her ! She has as light a foot as e'er a one of us, an' can dance ' Jackson's mornin' brush' as well as ever she could."

" Throth, an' I'm proud to hear it. Och ! och ! ' Jackson's mornin' brush' ! and it was she that *could* do it. Sure I remimber her wedding-day like yestherday. Ay, far an' near her fame wint as a dancer, an' the clanest-made girl that ever came from Lisbuie Like yestherday do I remimber it, an' how the squire himself an' the ladies from the Big House came down to see herself an' your father, the bride and groom—an' it wasn't on every hill head you'd get sich a couple—dancin' the same ' Jackson's mornin' brush.' Oh ! it was far and near her fame wint for dancin' that,—An' is there no news wid you, Bhried, at all at all ? "

" The sorra word, Mary : where 'ud I get news? Sure it's yourself that's always on the fut that ought to have the news for *us*, woman alive."

" An' maybe I have too. I was spaikin' to a friend o' mine about you the other day."

" A friend o' yours, Mary ! Why, what friend could it be ? "

" A friend o' mine—ay, an' of yours too. Maybe you have more friends than you think, Biddy—and kind ones too, as far as wishin' you well goes, 't any rate. Ay have you faix, an' friends that e'er a girl in the parish might be proud to hear named in the one day wid her. Awouh ! "

" Bedad we're in luck, thin, for that's more than I knew of. An' who may these great friends of ours be, Mary ? "

---

* A feverish cold.

"Awouh ! Faix, as dacent a boy as ever broke bread the same boy is, 'and,' says he, 'if I had goold in bushelfuls, I'd think it too little for that girl ;' but poor lad, he's not aisy or happy in his mind in regard o' that. 'I'm afeared,' says he, 'that she'd put scorn upon me, an' not think me her aiquals. An' no more I am,' says he again, 'for where, afther all, would you get the likes o' Biddy Sullivan ?'— Poor boy ! throth my heart aches for him ! "

"Well, can't you fall in love wid him yourself, Mary, who-ever he is ? "

"Indeed, an' if I was at your age, it would be no shame to me to do so ; but, to tell you the thruth, the sorra often ever the likes of Paul Heffernan came acrass me."

"Paul Heffernan ! Why, Mary," replied Biddy, smiling with the assumed lightness of indifference, "is that your beauty ? If it is, why, keep him, an' make much of him."

"Oh, wurrah ! the differ there is between the hearts an' tongues of some people—one from another—an' the way they spaik behind others' backs ! Well, well, I'm sure that wasn't the way he spoke of you, Biddy, an' God forgive you for runnin' down the poor boy as you're doin'. Trogs ! I believe you're the only girl would do it."

"Who, me ! I'm not runnin' him down. I am neither runnin' him up nor down. I have neither good nor bad to say about him—the boy's a black stranger to me, barrin' to know his face."

"Faix, an' he's in consate wid you these three months past, an' intends to be at the dance on Friday next, in Jack Gormly's new house. Now, good-bye, alanna ; keep your own counsel till the time comes, an' mind what I said to you. It's not behind every ditch the likes of Paul Heffernan grows. *Bannaght lhath !* My blessin' be wid you ! "

Thus would Mary depart just at the critical moment, for well she knew that by husbanding her information and leaving the heart something to find out, she took the most effectual steps to excite and sustain that kind of interest which is apt ultimately to ripen, even from its own agitation, into the attachment she is anxious to promote.

The next day, by a meeting similarly accidental, she comes in contact with Paul Heffernan, who, honest lad, had never probably bestowed a thought on Biddy Sullivan in his life.

"*Morrow ghud*, Paul !—how is your father's son, ahager ?"

"*Morrow ghutcha*, Mary !—my father's son wants nothin' but a good wife, Mary."

"An' it's not every set day or bonfire night that a good wife is to be had, Paul—that is, a *good* one, as you say ; for, throth, there's many o' them in the market, sich as they are. I was talkin' about you to a friend of mine the other day— an' trogs, I'm afeard you're not worth all the abuse we gave you."

"More power to you, Mary ! I'm oblaged to you. But who is the friend in the manetime ? "

"Poor girl ! Throth, when your name slipped out an her, the point of a rush 'ud take a drop of blood out o' her cheek, the way she crimsoned up. 'Ah, Mary,' says she, "if ever I know you to braith it to man or mortual, my lips I'll never open to you to my dyin' day.' Trogs, when I looked at her, an' the tears standin' in her purty black eyes, I thought I didn't see a betther favoured girl, for both face and figure, this many a day, than the same Biddy Sullivan."

"Biddy Sullivan ! Is that long Jack's daughter of Carga ? "

"The same. But, Paul avick, if a syllable o' what I tould you—"

"Hut, Mary ! honour bright ! Do you think me a *stag*, that I'd go and inform on you."

"Fwhishsper, Paul : she'll be at the dance on Friday next in Jack Gormly's new house. So *bannagh lhath*, an' think o' what I bethrayed to you."

Thus did Mary very quietly and sagaciously bind two young hearts together, who probably might otherwise have never for a moment even thought of each other. Of course, when Paul and Biddy met at the dance on the following Friday, the one was the object of the closest attention to the other ; and each being prepared to witness strong proofs of attachment from the opposite party, everything fell out exactly according to their expectations.

Sometimes it happens that a booby of a fellow, during his calf love, will employ a male friend to plead his suit with a pretty girl, who, if the principal party had spunk, might be very willing to marry him. To the credit of our fair country-women, however, be it said, that in scarcely one instance out of twenty does it happen, or has it ever happened, that any of them ever fails to punish the faint heart by bestowing the fair lady upon what is called the blackfoot or spokesman whom he selects to make love for him. In such a case it is very naturally supposed that the latter will speak two words for himself and one for his friend, and indeed the result bears out the supposition. Now, nothing on earth gratifies the heart of the established match-maker so much as to hear of such a disaster befalling a spoony. She exults over his misfortune for months, and publishes his shame to the uttermost bounds of her own little world, branding him " as a poor pitiful creature, who had not the courage to spaik up for himself, or—to employ them that could." In fact, she entertains much the same feeling against him that a regular physician would towards some weak-minded patient, who prefers the knavish ignorance of a quack to the skill and services of an able and educated practitioner.

Characters like Mary are fast disappearing in Ireland ; and indeed in a country where the means of life were generally inadequate to the wants of the population, they were calculated, however warmly the heart may look back upon the memory of their services, to do more harm than good, by inducing young folks to enter into early and improvident marriages. They certainly sprang up from a state of society not thoroughly formed by proper education and knowledge—where the language of a people, too, was in many extensive districts in such a state of transition as in the interchange of affection to render an interpreter absolutely necessary. We have ourselves witnessed marriages where the husband and wife spoke the one English and the other Irish, each being able with difficulty to understand the other. In all such cases Mary was invaluable. She spoke Irish and English fluently, and indeed was acquainted with every thing in the slightest or most remote degree necessary to the conduct of a love affair, from the first glance up until the priest had pronounced the last words—or, to speak more correctly, until "the throwing of the stocking."

Mary was invariably placed upon the *hob*, which is the seat of comfort and honour at a farmer's fireside, and there she sat neat and tidy, detailing all the news of the parish, telling them how such a marriage was one unbroken honeymoon—a sure proof, by the way, that she herself had a hand in it—and again, how another one didn't turn out well, and she said so; "there was always a bad dhrop in the Haggarties; but, my dear, the girl herself was *for* him; so as she made her own bed, she must lie in it, poor thing. Any way, thanks be to goodness, I had nothing to do wid it."

Mary was to be found in every fair and market, and always at a particular place at a certain hour of the day, where the parties engaged in a courtship were sure to meet her on these occasions. She took a chirping glass, but never so as to become unsteady. Great deference was paid to everything she said; and if not conceded to her, she extorted it with a high hand. Nobody living could

drink a health with half the comic significance that Mary
threw into her eyes when saying, " Well, young couple,
here's everything as you wish it."

Mary's motions from place to place usually were very
slow, and for the best reason in the world—she was
frequently interrupted.   For instance, if she met a young
man on her way, ten to one but he stood and held a long
and earnest conversation with her ; and that it was both
important and confidential, might easily be gathered from
the fact, that whenever a stranger passed, it was either
suspended altogether, or carried on in so low a tone as to
be inaudible.   This held equally good with the girls.
Many a time have I seen them retracing their steps, and
probably walking back a mile or two, all the time engaged
in discussing some topic evidently of more than ordinary
interest to themselves.   And when they shook hands and
bade each other good-bye, heavens ! at what a pace did the
latter scamper homewards across fields and ditches, in
order to make up for the time she had lost !

BOB PENTLAND,

The Irish Smuggler;

OR,

THE GAUGER OUTWITTED.

THAT the Irish are a ready-witted people, is a fact to the
truth of which testimony has been amply borne both by
their friends and enemies.   Many causes might be brought
forward to account for this questionable gift, if it were our
intention to be philosophical ; but as the matter has been
so generally conceded, it would be but a waste of logic to
prove to the world that which the world cares not about,
beyond the mere fact that it is so.   On this or any other

topic one illustration is worth twenty arguments, and, accordingly, instead of broaching a theory we shall relate a
story.

Behind the hill or rather mountain of Altnaveenan lies
one of those deep and almost precipitous valleys, on which
the practised eye of an illicit distiller would dwell with delight, as a topography not likely to be invaded by the un-
hallowed feet of the gauger and his red-coats. In point of
fact, the spot we speak of was from its peculiarly isolated
position nearly invisible, unless to such as came very close
to it. Being so completely hemmed in and concealed by
the round and angular projections of the mountain hills,
you could never dream of its existence at all, until you
came upon the very verge of the little precipitous gorge
which led into it. This advantage of position was not,
however, its only one. It is true, indeed, that the moment
you had entered it, all possibility of its being applied to the
purposes of distillation at once vanished, and you consequently could not help exclaiming, "what a pity that so
safe and beautiful a nook should not have a single spot on
which to erect a still-house, or rather on which to raise a
sufficient stream of water to the elevation necessary for the
process of distilling." If a gauger actually came to the
little chasm, and cast his scrutinizing eye over it he would
immediately perceive that the erection of a private still in
such a place was a piece of folly not generally to be found
in the plans of those who have recourse to such practices.

This absence, however, of the requisite conveniences was
only apparent, not real. To the right, about one hundred
yards above the entrance to it, ran a ledge of rocks, some
fifty feet high, or so. Along the lower brows, near the
ground, grew thick matted masses of long heath, which
covered the entrance to a cave about as large and as high
as an ordinary farm-house. Through a series of small
fissures in the rocks which formed its roof, descended a

stream of clear soft water, precisely in body and volume
such as was actually required by the distiller ; but, unless
by lifting up this mass of heath, no human being could for
a moment imagine that there existed any such grotto, or
so unexpected and easy an entrance to it.   Here there was
a private still-house made by the hand of nature herself,
such as no art or ingenuity of man could equal.

Now it so happened that about the period we write of,
there lived in our parish two individuals so antithetical to
each other in their pursuits of life, that we question
whether throughout all the instinctive antipathies of nature
we could find any two animals more destructive of each
other than the two we mean—to wit, Bob Pentland, the
gauger, and little George Steen, the illicit distiller.   Pentland was an old, staunch, well-trained fellow, of about fifty
years or more, steady and sure, and with all the characteristic points of the high-bred gauger about him.   He was a
tallish man, thin but lathy, with a hooked nose that could
scent the tread of a distiller with the keenness of a slew-
hound ; his dark eye was deep-set, circumspect, and roguish
in its expression, and his shaggy brow seemed always to be
engaged in calculating whereabouts his inveterate foe, little
George Steen, that eternally blinked him when almost in
his very fangs, might then be distilling.   To be brief,
Pentland was proverbial for his sagacity and adroitness in
detecting distillers, and little George was equally proverbial for having always baffled him, and that, too, sometimes under circumstances where escape seemed hopeless.

The incidents which we are about to detail occurred at
that period of time when the collective wisdom of our
legislators thought it advisable to impose a fine upon the
whole townland in which the Still, Head, and Worm, might
be found ; thus opening a door for knavery and fraud, and,
as it proved in most cases, rendering the innocent as liable
to suffer for an offence they never contemplated as the

guilty who planned and perpetrated it. The consequence of such a law was, that still-houses were always certain to be erected either at the very verge of the neighbouring districts, or as near them as the circumstances of convenience and situation would permit. The moment of course that the hue-and-cry of the gauger and his myrmidons was heard upon the wind, the whole apparatus was immediately heaved over the *mering* to the next townland, from which the fine imposed by parliament was necessarily raised, whilst the crafty and offending district actually escaped. The state of society generated by such a blundering and barbarous statute as this, was dreadful. In the course of a short time, reprisals, lawsuits, battles, murders, and massacres multiplied to such an extent throughout the whole country, that the sapient senators who occasioned such commotion were compelled to repeal their own act as soon as they found how it worked. Necessity, together with being the mother of invention, is also the cause of many an accidental discovery. Pentland had been so frequently defeated by little George, that he vowed never to rest until he had secured him ; and George on the other hand frequently told him—for they were otherwise on the best terms—that he defied him, or as he himself more quaintly expressed it, " that he defied the devil, the world, and Bob Pentland." The latter, however, was a very sore thorn in his side, and drove him from place to place, and from one haunt to another, until he began to despair of being able any longer to outwit him, or to find within the parish any spot at all suitable to distillation with which Pentland was not acquainted. In this state stood matters between them, when George fortunately discovered at the hip of Altnaveenan hill the natural grotto we have just sketched so briefly. Now, George was a man, as we have already hinted, of great fertility of resources ; but there existed in the same parish another distiller who outstripped him in that

4

far-sighted cunning which is so necessary in misleading or circumventing such a sharp-scented old hound as Pentland. This was little Mickey M'Quade, a short-necked squat little fellow with bow legs, who might be said rather to creep in his motion than to walk. George and Mickey were intimate friends, independently of their joint antipathy against the gauger, and, truth to tell, much of the mortification and many of the defeats which Pentland experienced at George's hands, were *sub rosa*, to be attributed to Mickey. George was a distiller from none of the motives which generally actuate others of that class. He was in truth an analytic philosopher —a natural chemist never out of some new experiment—and we have reason to think might have been the Kane, or Faraday, or Dalton, of his day, had he only received a scientific education. Not so honest Mickey, who never troubled his head about an experiment, but only thought of making a good running, and defeating the gauger. The first thing of course that George did, was to consult Mickey, and both accordingly took a walk up to the scene of their future operations. On examining it, and fully perceiving its advantages, it might well be said that the look of exultation and triumph which passed between them was not unworthy of their respective characters.

" This will do," said George. " Eh—don't you think we'll put our finger in Pentland's eye yet ? " Mickey spat sagaciously over his beard, and after a second glance gave one grave grin which spoke volumes. " It'll do," said he ; "but there's one point to be got over that maybe you didn't think of ; an' you know that half a blink, half a point, is enough for Pentland."

" What is it ? "

" What do you intend to do with the smoke when the fire's lit ? There'll be no keepin' *that* down. Let Pentland see but as much smoke risin' as would come out of an ould woman's dudeen, an' he'd have us."

George started, and it was clear by the vexation and dis-
appointment which were visible on his brow that unless this
untoward circumstance could be managed, their whole plan
was deranged, and the cave of no value.

"What's to be done?" he inquired of his cooler companion.   "If we can't get over this, we may bid good-bye to it."

"Never mind," said Mickey; "I'll manage it, and *do*
Pentland still."   "Ay, but how?"

"It's no matter.   Let us not lose a minute in settin' to
work.   Lave the other thing to me; an' if I don't account
for the smoke without discoverin' the entrance to the still,
I'll give you lave to crop the ears off my head."

George knew the cool but steady self-confidence for which
Mickey was remarkable, and accordingly without any further
interrogatory, they both proceeded to follow up their plan
of operations.

In those times when distillation might be truly considered
as almost universal, it was customary for farmers to build
their out-houses with secret chambers and other requisite
partitions necessary for carrying it on.   Several of them had
private stores built between false walls, the entrance to which
was only known to a few, and many of them had what
were called *Malt-steeps* sunk in hidden recesses and hollow
gables, for the purpose of steeping the barley, and afterwards
of turning and airing it, until it was sufficiently hard to be
kiln-dried and ground.   From the mill it was usually con-
veyed to the still-house upon what were termed *Slipes*, a
kind of car that was made without wheels, in order the
more easily to pass through morasses and bogs which no
wheeled vehicle could encounter.

In the course of a month or so, George and Mickey,
aided by their friends, had all the apparatus of keeve, hogs-
head, &c., together with Still, Head, and Worm, set up and
in full work.

"And now, Mickey," inquired his companion, "how will

you manage about the smoke? for you know that the two
worst informers against a private distiller, barrin' a *stag*, is
a smoke by day, an' a fire by night."

"I know that," replied Mickey; "an' a rousin' smoke
we'll have for fraid a little puff wouldn't do us. Come,
now, an' I'll show you."

They both ascended to the top, where Mickey had closed
all the open fissures of the roof with the exception of that
which was directly over the fire of the still. This was at
best not more than six inches in breadth, and about twelve
long. Over it he placed a piece of strong plate-iron perfor-
ated with holes, and on this he had a fire of turf, beside
which sat a little boy who acted as a vidette. The thing
was simple but effective. Clamps of turf were at every side
of them, and the boy was instructed, if the gauger, whom
he well knew, ever appeared, to heap on fresh fuel, so as to
increase the smoke in such a manner as to induce him to
suppose that *all* he saw of it proceeded merely from the
fire before him. In fact, the smoke from the cave below
was so completely identified with and lost in that which
was emitted from the fire above, that no human being could
penetrate the mystery, if not made previously acquainted
with it. The writer of this saw it during the hottest process
of distillation, and failed to make the discovery, although
told that the still-house was within a circle of three hundred yards, the point he stood on being considered the
centre. On more than one occasion has he absconded from
home, and spent a whole night in the place, seized with that
indescribable fascination which such a scene holds forth to
youngsters, as well as from his irrepressible anxiety to hear
the old stories and legends with the recital of which they
generally pass the night.

In this way, well provided against the gauger—indeed
much better than our readers are yet aware of, as they shall
understand by and by—did George, Mickey, and their

friends, proceed for the greater part of a winter without a
single visit from Pentland. Several successful runnings
had come off, which had of course turned out highly profitable, and they were just now preparing to commence
their last, not only for the season, but the last they should
ever work together, as George was making preparations to
go early in the spring to America. Even this running was
going on to their satisfaction, and the singlings had been
thrown again into the still, from the worm of which projected the strong medicinal *first-shot* as the doubling commenced—this last term meaning the spirit in its pure and
finished state. On this occasion the two worthies were
more then ordinarily anxious, and certainly doubled their
usual precautions against a surprise, for they knew that
Pentland's visits resembled the pounces of a hawk or the
springs of a tiger more than any thing else to which they
could compare them. In this they were not disappointed.
When the doubling was about half finished he made his
appearance, attended by a strong party of reluctant soldiers
—for indeed it is due to the military to state that they
never took delight in harassing the country people at the
command of a keg-hunter, as they generally nicknamed
the gauger. It had been arranged that the vidette at the
iron plate should whistle a particular tune the moment that
the gauger or a red-coat, or in fact any person whom he
did not know, should appear. Accordingly, about eight
o'clock in the morning they heard the little fellow in his
highest key whistling up that well-known and very significant old Irish air called " Go to the devil an' shake yourself"—which in this case was applied to the gauger in any
thing but an allegorical sense.

" Be the pins," which was George's usual oath, " be the
pins, Mickey, it's over with us—Pentland's here, for there's
the sign."

Mickey paused for a moment and listened very gravely ;

then squirting out a tobacco spittle, " Take it easy," said he ; " I have half a dozen fires about the hills, any one as like this as your right hand is to your left. I didn't spare trouble, for I knew that if we'd get over *this* day, we'd be out of his power."

"Well, my good lad," said Pentland, addressing the vidette, " what's this fire for ? "

" What is it for, is it ? "

" Yes ; if you don't let me know instantly, I'll blow your brains out, and get you hanged and transported afterwards."

This he said with a thundering voice, cocking a large horse pistol at the same time.

" Why, sir," said the boy, " it's watchin' a still I am : but be the hole o' my coat if you tell upon me, it's broilin' upon these coals I'll be soon."

" Where is the still, then ? An' the still-house, where is it ? "

" Oh, begorra, as to where the still or still-house is, they wouldn't tell *me* that."

" Why, sirra, didn't you say this moment you were watching a still ? "

" I meant, sir," replied the lad, with a face that spoke of pure idiocy, " that it was the gauger I was watchin', an' I was to whistle upon my fingers to let the boy at that fire on the hill there above know he was comin'."

" Who told you to do so ? "

" Little George, sir, an' Mickey M'Quade.'

" Ay, ay, right enough there, my lad—two of the most notorious schemers unhanged they are both. But now, like a good boy, tell me the truth, an' I'll give you the price of a pair of shoes. Do you know where the still or still-house is ? Because if you do, an' won't tell me, here are the soldiers at hand to make a prisoner of you ; an' if they do, all the world can't prevent you from being hanged, drawn, and quartered."

"Oh, bad cess may seize the morsel o' me knows that ; but if you'll give me the money, sir, I'll tell you who can bring you to it, for he tould me yestherday mornin' that he knew, an' offered to bring me there last night, if I'd steal him a bottle that my mother keeps the holy water in at home, tal he'd put whiskey in it."

"Well, my lad, who is this boy ?"

"Do you know ' Harry Neil, or Mankind,' * sir ? "

"I do, my good boy."

"Well, it's a son of his, sir ; an' look, sir : do you see the smoke farthest up to the right, sir ? "

"To the right ?   Yes."

"Well, 'tis there, sir, that Darby Neil is watchin' ; and he *says* he knows."

"How long have you been watching here ? "

"This is only the third day, sir, for *me,* but the rest, them boys above, has been here a good while."

"Have you seen nobody stirring about the hills since you came ? "

"Only once, sir, yesterday, I seen two men, havin' an empty sack or two, runnin' across the hill there above."

At this moment the military came up, for he had himself ran forward in advance of them, and he repeated the substance of his conversation with our friend the vidette.   Upon examining the stolidity of his countenance, in which there certainly was a woful deficiency of meaning, they agreed among themselves that his appearance justified the truth of the story which he told the gauger, and upon being still further interrogated. they were confirmed that none but a stupid lout like himself would entrust to his keeping any secret worth knowing.   They now separated themselves into as many detached parties as there were fires burning on the hills about them, the gauger himself resolving to

---

* This was a nickname given to Harry, who was a cooper, and made the necessary vessels for distillers.

make for that which Darby Neil had in his keeping, for he could not help thinking that the vidette's story was too natural to be false. They were just in the act of separating themselves to pursue their different routes, when the lad said,

"Look, sir! look, sir! bad scran be from me but there's a still any way. Sure I often seen a still : that's just like the one that Philip Hagan the tinker mended in George Steen's barn."

"Hollo, boys," exclaimed Pentland, "stoop! stoop! they are coming this way, and don't see us: no, hang them, no! they have discovered us now, and are off towards Mossfield. By Jove this will be a bitter trick if they succeed ; confound them, they are bent for Ballagh, which is my own property; and may I be hanged but if we do not intercept them it is I myself who will have to pay the fine."

The pursuit instantly commenced with a speed and vigour equal to the ingenuity of this singular act of retaliation on the gauger. Pentland himself being long-winded from much practice in this way, and being further stimulated by the prospective loss which he dreaded, made as beautiful a run of it as any man of his years could do. It was all in vain, however. He merely got far enough to see the Still, Head, and Worm, heaved across the march ditch into his own property, and to reflect after seeing it that he was certain to have the double consolation of being made a standing joke of for life, and of paying heavily for the jest out of his own pocket. In the meantime, he was bound of course to seize the still, and report the caption ; and as he himself farmed the townland in question, the fine was levied to the last shilling, upon the very natural principle that if he had been sufficiently active and vigilant, no man would have attempted to set up a still so convenient to his own residence and property.

This manœuvre of keeping in reserve an old or second

set of apparatus, for the purpose of acting the lapwing and misleading the gauger, was afterwards often practised with success; but the first discoverer of it was undoubtedly Mickey M'Quade, although the honour of the discovery was attributed to his friend George Steen. The matter, however, did not actually end here, for in a few days afterwards some malicious wag—in other words, George himself—had correct information sent to Pentland touching the locality of the cavern and the secret of its entrance. On this occasion the latter brought a larger military party than usual along with him, but it was only to make him feel that he stood in a position, if possible, still more ridiculous than the first. He found indeed the marks of recent distillation in the place, but nothing else. Every vessel and implement connected with the process had been removed, with the exception of one bottle of whisky, to which was attached by a bit of twine the following friendly note :—

"MR. PENTLAND, SIR—Take this bottle home and drink your own health. You can't do less. It was distilled *under your nose*, the first day you came to look for us, and bottled for you while you were speaking to the little boy that made a hare of you. Being distilled then under your nose, let it be drunk in the same place, and don't forget while doing so to drink the health of   G. S."

The incident went abroad like wildfire, and was known everywhere. Indeed for a long time it was the standing topic of the parish ; and so sharply was it felt by Pentland that he could never keep his temper if asked, "Mr. Pentland, when did you see little George Steen?"—a question to which he was never known to give a civil reply.

TOM GRESSIEY,

The Irish Senachie,

OR,

THE ORIGIN OF THE NAME OF GORDON.

THE most accomplished Senachie that ever came within
our observation, was a man called Tom Gressiey, or Tom
the Shoemaker.   He was a very stout well-built man, about
fifty years of age, with a round head, somewhat bald, and
an expansive forehead that argued a considerable reach of
natural intellect.   His knowing organs were large, and projected over a pair of deep-set lively eyes, that scintillated
with strong twinklings of humour.   His voice was loud, his
enunciation rapid, but distinct ; and such was the force and
buoyancy of his spirits, added to the vehemence of his
manner, that altogether it was impossible to resist him.
His laughter was infectious, and so loud that it might be
heard of a calm summer evening at an incredible distance.
Indeed, Tom possessed many qualities that rendered him a
most agreeable companion ; he could sing a good song for
instance, dance a hornpipe as well as any dancing-master,
and we need not say that he could tell a good story.   He
could also imitate a Jew's harp or trump upon his lips, with
his mere fingers, in such a manner that the deception was
complete ; and it was well known that flocks of the country
people used to crowd about him for the purpose of hearing
his performance upon the ivy leaf, which he played upon
by putting it in his mouth, and uttering a most melodious
whistle.   Altogether, he was a man of great natural powers,
and possessed such a memory as the writer of this never
knew any other human being to be gifted with.   He not
only remembered everything he saw or was concerned in,
but everything he heard also.   His language, when he spoke

Irish, was fluent, clear, and sometimes eloquent ; but when he had recourse to the English, although his fluency remained, yet it was the fluency of a man who made an indiscriminate use of a vocabulary which he did not understand. His pedantry on this account was highly ludicrous and amusing, and his wit and humour surprisingly original and pointed. He had never received any education, and was consequently completely illiterate, yet he could repeat every word of Gallaher's Irish Sermons, Donlevy's Catechism, Think well on't, the Seven Champions of Christendom, and the substance of Postorini's and Kolumb Kill's Prophecies, all by heart. Many a time have we seen him read, as he used to call it, one of Dr. Gallaher's Sermons out of the skirt of his big-coat ; a feat which was looked upon with twice the wonder it would have produced had he merely said that he repeated it. But to read it out of the skirt of his coat ! Heavens, how we used to look on with awe and veneration, as Tom, in a loud rapid voice, "rhymed it out of him," for such was the term we gave to his recital of it ! His learning, however, was not confined to mere English and Irish, for Tom was also classical in his way, and for want of a better substitute it was said could serve mass, which must always be done in Latin. Certain it was that he could repeat the *De profundis* and the *Dies Iræ*, in that language. We need scarcely add, that in these learned exhibitions he dealt largely in false quantities, and took a course for himself altogether independent of syntax and prosody; this, however, was no argument against his natural talents, or the surprising force of his memory.

Tom was a great person for attending wakes and funerals, where he was always a busy man, comforting the afflicted relatives with many learned quotations, repeating *ranns*, or spiritual songs, together with the *De profundis* or *Dies Iræ*, over the corpse, directing even the domestic concerns, paying attention to strangers, looking after the pipes and tobacco, and in fact making himself not only generally useful, but essentially necessary to them, by his happiness of manner, the cordiality of his sympathy, and his unextinguishable humour.

At one time you might see him engaged in leading a Rosary for the repose of the soul of the departed, or singing the Hermit of Killarney, a religious song, to edify the company ; and this duty being over, he would commence a series of comic tales and humorous anecdotes, which he narrated with an ease and spirit that the best of us all might envy. The Irish heart passes rapidly from the depths of pathos to the extremes of humour ; and as a proof of this, we can assure our readers that we have seen the nearest and most afflicted relatives of the deceased carried away by uncontrollable laughter at the broad, grotesque, ludicrous farce of his narratives.

The last night we ever had the pleasure of being amused by Tom, was at a wake in the neighbourhood ; for it somehow happened that there was seldom either wake or dance within two or three miles of us that we did not attend ; and, God forgive us ! when old Poll Doolin was on her death-bed, the only care that troubled us was an apprehension that she might recover, and thus defraud us of a right merry wake ! Upon the occasion we allude to, it being known that Tom Gressiey would be present, of course the house was crowded. And when he did come, and his loud good-humoured voice was heard at the door, heavens ! how every young heart bounded with glee and delight !

The first thing he did on entering was to go where the corpse was laid out, and in a loud rapid voice repeat the *De profundis* for the repose of her soul, after which he sat down and smoked a pipe. Oh, well do we remember how the whole house was hushed, for all was expectation and interest as to what he would do or say.

After narrating a legend of St. Patrick, he passed at once

into a different spirit. He and Frank Magavren marshalled their forces, and in a few minutes two or three dozen young fellows were hotly engaged in the humorous game of "Boxing the Connaughtman." Boxing the Connaughtman was followed by the "Standing Brogue" and the "Sitting Brogue," two other sports practised only at wakes. And here we may remark generally, that the amusements resorted to on such occasions are never to be found elsewhere, but are exclusively peculiar to the house of mourning, where they are benevolently introduced for the purpose of alleviating sorrow. Having gone through a few more such, Tom took a seat, and addressing a neighbouring farmer as follows :—

"Jack Gordon, do you know the history of your own name, and its original fluency?"

" Indeed no, Tom, I cannot say I do."

" Well, boys, if yez derogate your noise a little, I'll tell yez the origin of the name of Gordon. It's only about ould Oliver Crummle whose tongue is on the look for a drop of wather ever since he went to the lower storey :—"

The hum of general conversation now gradually subsided into silence, and every face assumed an expression of curiosity and interest, with the exception of Jemsy Baccagh, who was rather deaf, and blind George M'Girr, so called because he wanted an eye ; both of whom, in high and piercing tones, carried on an angry discussion touching a small lawsuit that had gone against Jemsy in the Court Leet, of which George was a kind of rustic attorney. An outburst of impatient rebuke was immediately poured upon them from fifty voices. " Whist wid yez, ye pair of devil's limbs, an' Tom goin' to tell us a story. Jemsy, your sowl's as crooked as your lame leg, you sinner ; an' as for blind George, if roguery 'ud save a man, he'll escape the devil yet. Tarenation to yez, an' be quiet till we hear the story."

" Ay," said Tom, "Scriptur says that when the blind

leads the blind, both'll fall into the ditch ; but God help the
lame that have blind George to lead them ; we may easily
guess where he'd guide them to, especially such a poor
innocent as Jemsy there." This banter, as it was not intended to give offence, so was it received by the parties to
whom it was addressed, with laughter and good humour.

"Silence, boys," said Tom ; " I'll jist take a dhraw of the
pipe till I put my mind in a proper state of transmigration
for what I was goin' to narrate."

He then smoked on for a few minutes, his eyes com-
placently but meditatively closed, and his whole face
composed into the philosophic spirit of a man who knew and
felt his own superiority, as well as what was expected from
him. When he had sufficiently arranged the materials in
his mind, he took the pipe out of his mouth, rubbed the
shank-end of it against the cuff of his coat, then handed it
to his next neighbour, and having given a short preparatory
cough, thus commenced his legend :—

"You must know that afther Charles the First happened
to miss his head one day, havin' lost it while playin' a game
of 'Heads an' Points' with the Scotch, that a man called
Nolly Rednose, or Oliver Crummle, was sent over to Ireland
wid a parcel of breekless Highlanders an' English Bodaghs,
to subduvate the Irish, an' as many of the Prodestans as
had been friends to the late king, who were called Royalists.
Now, it appears by many learned transfigurations that
Nolly Rednose had in his army a man named Balgruntie,
or the Hog of Cupar ; a fellow who was as coorse as sackin',
as cunnin' as a fox, an' as gross as the swine he was named
afther. Rednose, there is no doubt of it, was as nate a hand
at takin' a town or castle as ever went about it; but then,
any town that didn't surrendher at discretion was sure to
experience little mitigation at his hands ; an' whenever he
was bent on wickedness, he was sure to say his prayers at
the commencement of every siege or battle—that is, that

he intended to shew no marcy in—for he'd get a book, an'
openin' it at the head of his army, he'd cry, 'Ahem, my
brethren, let us praise God by endeavourin' till sing sich or
sich a psalm;' an' God help the man, woman, or child, that
came before him afther that. Well an' good: it so happened
that a squadron of his psalm-singers were despatched by
him from Enniskillen, where he stopped, to rendher assistance to a party of his army that O'Neil was leatherin' down
near Dungannon, an' on their way they happened to take
up their quarthers for the night at the Mill of Aughentain.
Now, above all men in the creation, who should be
appointed to lead this same squadron but the Hog of
Cupar. 'Balgruntie, go off wid you,' said Crummle, when
administering his instructions to him; 'but be sure that
whenever you meet a fat royalist on the way, to pay your
respects to him as a Christian ought,' says he ; 'an' above all
things, my dear brother Balgruntie, *don't neglect your devotions*, otherwise our arms can't prosper, and be sure,' says he,
with a pious smile, 'that if they promulgate opposition, you
will make them bleed anyhow, either in purse or person ;
or if they provoke the grace of God, take a little from them
in both ; an' so the Lord's name be praised, yeamen.'

  "Balgruntie sang a psalm of thanksgivin' for bein' elected
by his commander to sich a holy office, set out on his march,
an' the next night he an' his choir slept in the mill of Aughentain, as I said. Now, Balgruntie had in this same congregation of his a long-legged Scotchman named Sandy Saveall, which name he got, by way of etymology, for his charity ;
for it appears by the historical elucidations that Sandy was
perpetually rantinizin' about sisterly affection an' brotherly
love : an' what shewed more taciturnity than anything else
was, that while this same Sandy had the persuasion to
make every one believe that he thought of nothing else, he
shot more people than any ten men in the squadron. He
was indeed what they call a dead shot, for no one ever knew

him to miss any thing he fired at. He had a musket that would throw point blank an English mile, an' if he only saw a man's nose at that distance, he used to say that, with aid from above, he could blow it for him with a leaden hankerchy, mainin' that he could blow it off his face wid a musket bullet; and so by all associations he could, for indeed the faits he performed were very insinivating an' problematical.

" Now, it so happened, that at this period there lived in the castle a fine wealthy ould royalist, named Graham or Grimes, as they are often denominated, who had but one child, a daughter, whose beauty an' perfections wor mellifluous far an' near over the country, an' who had her health drunk, as the toast of Ireland, by the Lord-Lieutenant in the Castle of Dublin, undher the sympathetic appellation of ' the Rose of Aughentain.' It was her son that afterwards ran through the estate, and was forced to part wid the castle ; an' it's to him the proverb colludes which mentions ' ould John Grame, that *swallied* the castle of Aughentain.'

" Howsomever, that bears no prodigality to the story I'm narratin'. So what could you have of it, but Balgruntie, who had heard of the father's wealth, and the daughter's beauty, took a holy hankerin' afther both ; an' havin' as usual said his prayers and sung a psalm, he determined for to clap his thumb upon the father's money, thinkin' that the daughter would be the more aisily superinduced to folly it. In other words, he made up his mind to sack the castle, carry off the daughter an' marry her righteously, rather, he said, through a sincere wish to bring her into a state of grace by a union with a God-fearin' man, whose walk he trusted was Zion-ward, than from any cardinal detachment for her wealth or beauty. He accordingly sent up a file of the most pious men he had, picked chaps, with good psalm-singin' voices and strong noses, to request that John Graham

would give them possession of the castle for a time, an'
afterwards join them at prayers, as a proof that he was no
royalist, but a friend to Crummle and the Commonwealth.
Now, you see, the best of it was, that the very man they
demanded this from, was commonly denominated by the
people as 'Gunpowder Jack,' in consequence of the great
signification of his courage ; an', besides, he was known to
be a member of the Hell-fire Club, that no person could
join that hadn't fought three duels, and killed at least one
man ; and in ordher to show that they regarded neither
God nor hell, they were obligated to dip one hand in blood
an' the other in fire, before they could be made members of
the club. It's aisy to see, then, that Graham was not likely
to quail before a handful of the very men he hated wid all
the vociferation in his power, an' he accordingly put his
head out of the windy, an' axed them their tergiversation
for being there.

"'Begone about your business,' he said ; 'I owe you no
regard. What brings you before the castle of a man who
despises you ? Don't think to determinate me, you cant-
ing rascals, for you can't. My castle's well provided wid
men an' ammunition an' food ; an' if you don't be off, I'll
make you sing a different tune from a psalm one.' Bedad
he did plump to them, out of the windy.

"When Crummle's men returned to Balgruntie in the
mill, they related what had tuck place, and he said that
afther prayers he'd sind a second message in writin', an' if
it wasn't attended to, they'd put their trust in God, an' storm
the castle. The squadron he commanded was not a
numerous one, an' as they had no artillery, an' were surrounded by enemies, the takin' of the castle, which was a
strong one, might cost them some snufflication. At all
events, Balgruntie was bent on makin' the attempt,
especially afther he heard that the castle was well vittled,
an' indeed he was meritoriously joined by his men, who

5

piously licked their lips on hearin' of such glad tidins.
Graham was a hot-headed man, without much ambidex-
terity or deliberation, otherwise he might have known that
the bare mintion of the beef and mutton in his castle was
only fit to make such a hungry pack desperate. But be
that as it may, in a short time Balgruntie wrote him a
letter demandin' of him, in the name of Nolly Rednose an'
the Commonwealth, to surrendher the castle, or if not, that,
ould as he was, he would make him as soople as a two-year
ould.   Graham, after readin' it, threw the letter back to
the messengers, wid a certain recommendation to Balgruntie
regarding it ; but whether the same recommendation was
followed up and acted on so soon as he wished, historical
retaliations do not inform.

"On their return, the military narrated to their commander the reception they resaved a second time from
Graham, an' he then resolved to lay regular siege to the
castle ; but as he knew he could not aisily take it by
violence, he determined, as they say, to starve the garrison
leisurely and by degrees.   But, first an' foremost, a thought
struck him, an' he immediately called Sandy Saveall behind the mill-hopper, which he had now turned into a pul-
pit for the purpose of expoundin' the word, an' givin' ex-
hortations to his men.

" 'Sandy,' sis he, 'are you in a state of justification to-
day ? '

" 'Towards noon,' replied Sandy, 'I had some strong
wrestlings with the enemy : but I am able, under praise, to
say that I defated him in three attacks, and I consequently
feel my righteousness much recruited.   I had some whole-
some communings with the miller's daughter—a comely
lass, who may yet be recovered from the world, and led out
of the darkness of Aigyp, by a word in saison.'

" 'Well, Sandy,' replied the other, 'I lave her to your own
instructions ; there is another poor benighted maiden, who

is also comely, up in the castle of that godless sinner, who belongeth to the Perdition Club; an' indeed, Sandy, until he is somehow removed, I think there is little hope of plucking her like a brand from the burning.'

"He serenaded Sandy in the face as he spoke, an' thin cast an extemporary glance at the musket, that was as much as to say, ' can you translate an insinivation?' Sandy concocted a smilin' reply, an' takin' up the gun, rubbed the barrel, an' patted it as a sportsman 'ud pat the neck of his horse or dog, wid reverence for comparin' the villain to either one or the other.

"'If it was known, Sandy,' said Balgruntie, ' it would harden her heart against me; an' as he is hopeless at all events, bein' a member of that Perdition Club '———

"'True,' said Sandy, ' but you lave the miller's daughter to me?'

"'I said so.'

"'Well, if his removal will give you any consolidation in the matther, you may say no more.'

"'I could not, Sandy, justify it to myself to take him away by open violence, for you know that I bear a conscience if anything too tendher an' dissolute. Also I wish, Sandy, to presarve an ondeniable reputation for humanity; an', besides, the daughter might become as reprobate as the father, if she suspected me to be personally consarned in it. I have heard a good deal about him, an' am sensibly informed that he has been shot at twice before, by the sons, it is thought, of an enemy that he himself killed rather significantly in a duel.'

"'Very well,' sis Sandy; ' I would myself feel scruples; but as both our consciences is touched in the business, I think I am justified. Indeed, captain, it is very likely afther all that we are but mere instruments in it, an' that it is through us that this ould unrighteous sinner is to be removed by a more transplendant judgment.'

"Begad, neighbours, whin a rascal's bent on wickedness, it is aisy to find cogitations enough to back him in his villany. And so was it wid Sandy Saveall and Balgruntie.

"That evenin' ould Graham was shot through the head standin' in the windy of his own castle, an' to extenuate the suspicion of such an act from Crummle's men, Balgruntie himself went up the next day, beggin' very politely to have a friendly explanation wid Squire Graham, sayin' that he had harsh orders, but that if the castle was peaceably delivered to him, he would, for the sake of the young lady, see that no injury should be offered either to her or her father.

"The young lady, however, had the high drop in her, and becoorse the only answer he got was a flag of defiance. This nettled the villain, an' he found there was nothin' else for it but to place a strong guard about the castle, to keep all that was in, in—and all that was out, out.

"In the meantime the very appearance of the Crum-wellians in the neighbourhood struck such terror into the people, that the country, which was then only very thinly inhabited, became quite desarted, an' for miles about the face of a human bein' couldn't be seen, barrin' their own, sich as they were. Crummle's thrack was always a bloody one, an' the people knew that they were wise in putting the hills and mountain passes between him and them. The miller and his daughter bein' encouraged by Sandy, staid principally for the sake of Miss Graham ; but except them, there was not a man or woman in the barony to bid good-morrow to, or say Salvey Dominey. On the beginnin' of the third day, Balgruntie, who knew his officialities extremely well, and had sent down a messenger to Dungannon to see whether matters were so bad as they had been reported, was delighted to hear that O'Neill had dis-appeared from the neighbourhood. He immediately informed Crummle of this, an' tould him that he had laid

siege to one of the leadin' passes of the north, an' that, by
gettin' possession of the two castles of Aughentain and
Augher, he could keep O'Neill in check, an' command that
part of the country. Nolly approved of this, an' ordhered
him to proceed, but was sorry that he could send him no
assistance at present; 'however,' said he, 'wid a good
cause, sharp swords, an' aid from above, there is no fear of
us.'

"They now set themselves to take the castle in airnest.
Balgruntie an' Sandy undherstood one another, an' not a
day passed that some one wasn't dropped in it. As soon
as ever a face appeared, pop went the deadly musket, an'
down fell the corpse of whoever it was aimed at. Miss
Graham herself was spared for good reasons, but in the
coorse of ten or twelve days she was nearly alone. Ould
Graham, though a man that feared nothing, was only
guilty of a profound swagger when he reported the strength
of the castle and the state of the provisions to Balgruntie
an' his crew. But above all things, that which eclipsed
their distresses was the want of wather. There was none
in the castle, an' although there is a beautiful well beside
it, yet, *fareer gair*, it was of small responsibility to thim.
Here, thin, was the poor young lady placed at the marcy of
her father's murdherer; for however she might have doubted
in the beginnin' that he was shot by the Crumwellians, yet
the death of nearly all the servants of the house in the same
way was a sufficient proof that it was like masther like man
in this case. What, however, was to be done? The whole
garrison now consisted only of Miss Graham herself, a fat
man-cook advanced in years, who danced in his distress in
ordher that he might suck his own perspiration, and a little
orphan boy that she tuck undher her purtection. It was a
hard case, an' yet, God bless her, she held out like a man.

"It's an ould sayin' that there's no tyin' up the tongue of
Fame, an' it's also a true one. The account of the siege

had gone far an' near in the counthry, an' none of the Irish
no matter what they were, who ever heard it, but wor sorry.
Sandy Saveall was now the devil an' all. As there was no
more in the castle to shoot, he should find something to
regenerate his hand upon : for instance, he practised upon
three or four of Graham's friends, who undher one pretence
or other were seen skulkin' about the castle, an' none of
their relations dar come to take away their bodies in ordher
to bury them. At length things came to that pass, that
poor Miss Graham was at the last gasp for something to
drink ; she had ferreted out as well as she could a drop of
moisture here and there in the damp corners of the castle,
but now all that was gone : the fat cook had sucked himself to death, an' the little orphan boy died calmly away a
few hours afther him, lavin' the helpless lady with a tongue
swelled and furred, an' a mouth parched an' burned, for
want of drink. Still the blood of the Grahams was in her,
an' yield she would not to the villain that left her as she
was. Sich then was the transparency of her situation, whin,
happenin' to be on the battlements, to catch, if possible, a
little of the dew of heaven, she was surprised to see something flung up, that rolled down towards her feet : she
lifted it, an' on examinin' the contents, found it to be a stone
covered wid a piece of brown paper, inside of which was a
slip of white, containin' the words, 'Endure—relief is near
you.' But, poor young lady, of what retrospection could
these tidins be to one in her situation ?—she could hardly
see to read them ; her brain was dizzy, her mouth like a
cinder, her tongue swelled an' black, an' her breath felt as
hot as a furnace. She could barely braithe, an' was in the
very act of lyin' down undher the triumphant air of heaven
to die, when she heard the shrill voice of a young kid in the
castle yard, and immediently remembered that a brown
goat which her lover, a gentleman named Simpson, had,
when it was a kid, made her a present of, remained in the

castle about the stable durin' the whole siege. She instantly made her way slowly down stairs, got a bowl, and havin' milked the goat, she tuk a little of the milk, which I need not asseverate at once relieved her. By this means she recovered, an' findin' no further anticipation from druth, she resolved like a hairo to keep the Crumwellians out, an' to wait till either God or man might lend her a helpin' hand.

"Now, you must know that the miller's purty daughter had also a sweetheart, called *Suil Gair* Maguire, or sharp-eyed Maguire, an humble branch of the great Maguires of Enniskillen ; an' this same Suil Gair was servant an' foster brother to Simpson, the intended husband of Miss Graham. Simpson, who lived some miles off, on hearin' the condition of the castle, gathered together all the royalists far an' near ; and as Crummle was honestly hated by both Romans an' Prodestans, faith, you see, Maguire himself promised to send a few of his followers to the rescue. In the meantime Suil Gair dressed himself up like a fool or idiot, an' undher the purtection of the miller's daughter, who blarneyed Saveall in great style, was allowed to wandher about and joke wid the sogers ; but especially he took a fancy to Sandy, and challenged him to put one stone out of five in one of the port-holes of the castle, at a match of finger-stone. Sandy, who was nearly as famous at that as the musket, was rather relaxed when he saw that Suil Gair could at least put in every fifth stone, and that he himself could hardly put one in out of twenty. Well, at all events it was durin' their sport that fool Paddy, as they called him, contrived to fling the scrap of writin' I spoke of across the battlements at all chances ; for whin he undhertook to go to the castle, he gev up his life as lost ; but he didn't care for that, in case he was able to save either his foster brother or Miss Graham. But this is not at all indispensable, for it is well known that many a foster brother sacrificed his life the same way, and in cases of great danger, when the real brother would beg to decline the compliment.

" Things were now in a very connubial state entirely. Balgruntie heard that relief was comin' to the castle, an' what to do he did not know; there was little time to be lost, however, an' something must be done. He praiched flowery discoorses twice a day from the mill-hopper, an' sang psalms for grace to be directed in his righteous intentions; but as yet he derived no particular predilection from either. Sandy appeared to have got a more bountiful modelum of grace nor his captain, for he succeeded at last in bringin' the miller's daughter to sit undher the word at her father's hopper. Fool Paddy, as they called Maguire, had now become a great favourite wid the sogers, an' as he proved to be quite harmless and inoffensive, they let him run about the place widout opposition. The castle, to be sure, was still guarded, but Miss Graham kept her heart up in consequence of the note, for she hoped every day to get relief from her friends. Balgruntie, now seein' that the miller's daughter was becomin' more serious undher the taichin' of Saveall, formed a plan that he thought might enable him to penethrate the castle, an' bear off the lady an' the money. This was to strive wid very delicate meditation to prevail on the miller's daughter, through the renown that he thought Sandy had over her, to open a correspondency wid Miss Graham; for he knew that if one of the gates was unlocked, an' the unsuspectin' girl let in, the whole squadron would soon be in afther her. Now this plan was the more dangerous to Miss Graham, because the miller's daughter had intended to bring about the very same denouncement for a different purpose. Between her friends an' her enemies it was clear the poor lady had little chance; an' it was Balgruntie's intention, the moment he had sequestrated her an' the money, to make his escape, an' lave the castle to whosomever might choose to take it.

Things, however, were ordhered to take a different bereavement : the Hog of Cupar was to be trapped in the hydrostatics of his own hypocrisy, an' Saveall to be overmatched in his own premises. Well, the plot was mentioned to Sandy, who was promised a good sketch of the prog ; an' as it was jist the very thing he dreamt about night an' day, he snapped at it as a hungry dog would at a sheep's trotter. That night the miller's daughter—whose name I may as well say was Nannie Duffy, the purtiest girl an' the sweetest singer that ever was in the country—was to go to the castle an' tell Miss Graham that the sogers wor all gone, Crummle killed, an' his whole army massacrayed to atoms. This was a different plan from poor Nannie's, who now saw clearly what they were at. But never heed a woman for bein' witty when hard pushed.

" ' I don't like to do it,' sis she, ' for it looks like thrachery, espishilly as my father has left the neighbourhood, and I don't know where he is gone to ; an' you know thrachery's ondacent in either man or woman. Still, Sandy, it goes hard for me to refuse one that I—I—well, I wish I knew where my father is—I would like to know what he'd think of it.'

" ' Hut,' said Sandy, ' where's the use of such scruples in a good cause ?—when we get the money, we'll fly. It is principally for the sake of waining you an' her from the darkness of idolatry, that we do it. Indeed my conscience would not rest well if I let a soul an' body like yours remain a prey to Sathan, my darlin'.'

" ' Well,' said she, ' doesn't the captain exhort this evenin' ? '

" ' He does, my beloved, an' with a blessin' will expound a few verses from the song of Solomon.'

" ' It's betther then,' said she, ' to sit under the word, an' perhaps some light may be given to us.'

" This delighted Saveall's heart, who now looked upon

pretty Nannie as his own; indeed he was obliged to go
gradually and cautiously to work, for cruel though Nolly
Rednose was, Sandy knew that if any violent act of *that*
kind should raich him, the guilty party would sup sorrow.
Well, accordin' to this pious arrangement, Balgruntie assembled all his men, who were not on duty, about the
hopper, in which he stood as usual, an' had commenced a
powerful exhortation, the substratum of which was devoted
to Nannie; he dwelt upon the happiness of religious love;
said that scruples were often suggested by Satan, an' that
a heavenly duty was but terrestial when put in comparishment wid an earthly one.   He also made collusion to the
old Squire that was popped by Sandy; said it was often a
judgment for the wicked man to die in his sins; an' was
gettin' on wid great eloquence an' emulation, when a low
rumblin' noise was heard, an' Balgruntie, throwin' up his
clenched hands an' grindin' his teeth, shouted out, 'Hell
and d—n, I'll be ground to death!   The mill's going.
Murdher! Murdher! I'm gone!'

  " Faith, it was true enough—she had been wickedly set
a-goin' by some one; an' before they had time to stop her,
the Hog of Cupar had the feet and legs twisted off him
before their eyes—a fair illustration of his own doctrine,
that it is often a judgment for the wicked man to die in
his sins.   When the mill was stopped, he was pulled out,
but didn't live twenty minutes, in consequence of the loss
of blood.   Time was pressin', so they ran up a shell of a
coffin, and tumbled it into a pit that was hastily dug for it
on the mill-common.

  " This, however, by no manner of manes relieved poor
Nannie from her difficulty, for Saveall, now finding himself
first in command, determined not to lose a moment in
tolerating his plan upon the castle.

  " ' You see,' said he, ' that a way is opened for us that
we didn't expect; an' let us not close our eyes to the light

that has been given, lest it might be suddenly taken from
us again. In this instance I suspect that fool Paddy
has been made the chosen instrument ; for it appears upon
inquiry, that he too has disappeared. However, heaven's
will be done ! we will have the more to ourselves, my beloved—ehem ! It is now dark,' he proceeded, 'so I shall
go an' take my usual smoke at the mill window, an' in
about a quarther of an hour I'll be ready.'

"'But I'm all in a tremor after sich a frightful accident,'
replied Nannie : 'an' I want to get a few minutes' quiet
before we engage upon our undhertakin'.'

"This was very natural and Saveall accordingly took
his usual seat at a little windy in the gable of the mill, that
faced the miller's house ; an' from the way the bench was
fixed, he was obliged to sit with his face exactly towards
the same direction. There we leave him meditatin' upon
his own righteous approximations, till we folly *Suil Gair*
Maguire, or fool Paddy, as they called him, who practicated
all that was done.

"Maguire and Nannie, findin' that no time was to be
lost, gave all over as ruined, unless somethin' could be
acted on quickly. Suil Gair at once had thought of settin'
the mill a-goin', but kept the plan to himself, any farther
than tellin' her not to be surprised at anything she might
see. He then told her to steal him a gun, but if possible
to let it be Saveall's as he knew it could be depended on.
'But I hope you won't shed any blood if you can avoid it,'
said she ; 'that I don't like.' 'Tut,' replied Suil Gair,
makin' evasion to the question, ' it's good to have it about
me for my own defence.'

"He could often have shot either Balgruntie or Saveall
in daylight, but not without certain death to himself, as he
knew that escape was impossible. Besides, time was not
before so pressin' upon them, an' every day relief was expected. Now, however, that relief was so near—for

Simpson with a party of royalists an' Maguire's men must be within a couple of hours' journey—it would be too intrinsic entirely to see the castle plundhered, and the lady carried off by such a long-legged skybill as Saveall. Nannie, consequentially, at great risk, took an opportunity of slippin' his gun to Suil Gair, who was the best shot of the day in that or any other part of the country, and it was in consequence of this that he was called Suil Gair, or Sharp Eye. But, indeed, all the Maguires were famous shots; : n' I'm tould there's one of them now in Dublin that could hit a pigeon's egg, or a silver sixpence at the distance of a hundred yards.* Suil Gair did not merely raise the sluice when he set the mill a-goin', but he whipped it out altogether an' threw it into the dam, so that the possibility of saving the Hog of Cupar was irretrievable. He made off, however, an' threw himself among the tall ragweeds that grew upon the common, till it got dark, when Saveall, as was his custom, should take his evenin' smoke at the windy. Here he sat for some period, thinkin' over many ruminations, before he lit his cutty pipe, as he called it.

"' Now,' said he to himself, 'what is there to hindher me from takin' away, or rather from makin' sure of the grand lassie, instead of the miller's dochter? If I get intil the castle, it can be soon effected ; for if she has ony regard for her reputation, she will be quiet. I'm a braw handsome lad enough, a wee thought high in the check-bones, scaly in the skin, an' knock-kneed a trifle, but stout an' lathy, an' tough as a withy. But, again, what is to be done wi' Nannie? Hut, she's but a miller's dochter, an' may be disposed of if she gets troublesome. I know she's fond of me, but I dinna blame her for that. However, it wadna become me now to entertain scruples, seein' that the way is made so plain for me. But, save us! eh, sirs, that was

---

* The celebrated Brian Maguire, the first shot of his day, was at this time living in Dublin.

an awful death, an' very like a judgment on the Hog of
Cupar! It is often a judgment for the wicked to die in
their sins. Balgruntie wasna that'—— Whatever he intended to say further, cannot be analogized by man, for,
just as he had uttered the last word, which he did while
holding the candle to his pipe, the bullet of his own gun
entered between his eyes, and the next moment he was a
corpse.

"Suil Gair desarved the name he got, for truer did never
bullet go to the mark from Saveall's own aim than it did
from his. There is now little more to be superadded to my
story. Before daybreak the next mornin', Simpson came
to the relief of his intended wife; Crummle's party were
surprised, taken, an' cut to pieces; an' it so happened that
from that day to this the face of a soger belongin' to him
was never seen near the mill or castle of Aughentain, with
one exception only, and that was this: You all know
that the mill is often heard to go at night when nobody
sets her a-goin', an' that the most sevendable scrames of
torture come out of the hopper, an' that when any one has
the courage to look in, they're sure to see a man dressed
like a soger, with a white mealy face, in the act, so to say,
of havin' his legs ground off him. Many a guess was made
about who the spirit could be, but all to no purpose.
There, however, is the truth for yez; the spirit that shrieks
in the hopper is Balgruntie's ghost, an' he's to be ground
that way till the day of judgment.

"Be coorse, Simpson and Miss Graham were married
as war Nannie Duffy an' Suil Gair; an' if they all lived long
an' happy, I wish we may all live ten times longer an'
happier; an' so we will, but in a betther world than this,
plaise God."

"Well, but, Tom;" said Gordon, "how does that account
for my name, which you said you'd tell me?"

"Right," said Tom; "begad I was near forgettin' it.

Why you see, sich was their veneration for the goat that was the manes of savin' Miss Graham's life, that they changed the name of Simpson to Gordon, which signifies in Irish *gor dhun*, or a brown goat, that all their posterity might know the great obligations they lay undher to that reverend animal."

"An' do you mane to tell me." said Gordon, "that my name was never heard of until Oliver Crummle's time?"

"I do. Never in the wide an' subterraneous earth was sich a name known till afther the prognostication I tould you; an' it never would either, only for the goat, sure. I can prove it by the pathepathetics. Denny Mullin, will you give us another draw o' the pipe?"

Tom's authority in these matters was unquestionable, and, besides, there was no one present learned enough to contradict him, with any chance of success before such an audience. The argument was consequently, without further discussion, decided in his favour, and Gordon was silenced touching the origin and etymology of his own name.

BARNEY M'HAIGNEY,

The Irish Prophecy Man.

THE individual to whom the heading of this article is uniformly applied, stands, among the lower classes of his countrymen, in a different light and position from any of those characters that we have already described to our readers. The intercourse which *they* maintain with the people is one that simply involves the means of procuring subsistence for themselves by the exercise of their professional skill, and their powers of contributing to the lighter enjoyments and more harmless amusements of their fellow-countrymen. All the collateral influences they possess, as arising from the hold which the peculiar nature of this intercourse gives them, generally affect individuals only on those minor points of feeling that act upon the lighter phases of domestic life. They bring little to society beyond the mere accessories that are appended to the general modes of life and manners, and consequently, receive themselves as strong an impulse from those with whom they mingle, as they communicate to them in return.

Now, the Prophecy Man presents a character far different from all this. With the ordinary habits of life he has little sympathy. The amusements of the people are to him little else than vanity, if not something worse. He despises that class of men who live and think only for the present, without ever once performing their duties to posterity, by looking into those great events that lie in the womb of futurity. Domestic joys or distresses do not in the least affect him, because the man has not to do with feelings or emotions, but with principles. The speculations in which he indulges, and by which his whole life and conduct are regulated, place him far above the usual impulses of humanity. He cares not much who has been married or who has died, for his mind is, in point of time, communing with unborn generations upon affairs of high and solemn import. The past, indeed, is to him something—the future, everything; but the present, unless when marked by the prophetic symbols, little or nothing. The topics of his conversation are vast and mighty, being nothing less than the fate of kingdoms, the revolution of empires, the ruin or establishment of creeds, the fall of monarchies, or the rise and prostration of principalities and powers. How can a mind thus engaged descend to those petty subjects of ordinary life, which engage the common attention? How could a

man hard at work in evolving out of prophecy the sub-
jugation of some hostile state, care a farthing whether
Loghlin Roe's daughter was married to Gusty Given's son
or not?   The thing is impossible.   Like Fame, the head of
the Prophecy Man is always in the clouds, but so much
higher up as to be utterly above the reach of any intelligence
that does not affect the fate of nations.   There is an old
anecdote told of a very high and a very low man meeting.
"What news down there?" said the tall fellow   "Very
little," replied the other: "what kind of weather have you
above?"   Well, indeed, might the Prophecy Man ask what
news is there below, for his mind seldom leaves those aerial
heights from which it watches the fate of Europe, and the
shadowing forth of future changes.

The Prophecy Man—that is, he who solely devotes himself to an anxious observation of those political occurrences
which mark the signs of the times, as they bear upon the
future, the principal business of whose life it is to associate
them with his own prophetic theories—is now a rare character in Ireland.   He was, however, a very marked one.
The Senachie and other itinerant characters, had, when
compared with him, a very limited beat, indeed.   Instead
of being confined to a parish or a barony, the bounds of
the Prophecy Man's travels were those of the kingdom
itself; and, indeed, some of them have been known to make
excursions to the Highlands of Scotland, in order, if
possible, to pick up old prophecies, and to make themselves,
by cultivating an intimacy with the Scottish seers, capable
of getting a clearer insight into futurity, and surer rules for
developing the latent secrets of time.

One of the heaviest blows to the speculations of this
class was the downfall and death of Buonaparte—especially
the latter.   There are still living, however, those who can
get over this difficulty, and who will not hesitate to assure
you, with a look of much mystery, that the real " Bonyparty"

is alive and well, and will make his due appearance *when the time comes ;* he who surrendered himself to the English being but an accomplice of the true one.

The next fact is the failure of the old prophecy that a George the Fourth would never sit on the throne of England. His coronation and reign, however, puzzled our prophets sadly, and, indeed, sent adrift for ever the pretensions of this prophecy to truth.

But that which has nearly overturned the system, and routed the whole prophetic host, is the failure of the speculations so confidently put forward by Dr. Walmsey in his General History of the Christian Church, vulgarly called Pastorini's Prophecy, he having assumed the name Pastorini as an *incognito* or *nom de guerre.* The theory of Pastorini was, that Protestantism and all descriptions of heresy would disappear about the year eighteen hundred and twenty-five, an inference which he drew with considerable ingenuity and learning from Scriptural Prophecy, taken in connexion with past events, and which he argued with all the zeal and enthusiasm of a theorist naturally anxious to see the truth of his own prognostications verified. The failure of this, which was their great modern standard, has nearly demolished the political seers as a class, or compelled them to fall back upon the more antiquated revelations ascribed to St. Columkill, St. Bridget, and others.

Having thus given what we conceive to be such preliminary observations as are necessary to make both the subject and the person more easily understood, we shall proceed to give a short sketch of the only Prophecy Man we ever saw who deserved properly to be called so, in the full and unrestricted sense of the term. This individual's name was Barney M'Haigney ; but in what part of Ireland he was born I am not able to inform the reader. All I know is, that he was spoken of on every occasion as The Prophecy Man ; and that, although he could not himself

6

read, he carried about with him, in a variety of pockets, several old books and manuscripts that treated upon his favourite subject.

Barney was a tall man, by no means meanly dressed ; and it is unnecessary to say that he came not within the character or condition of a mendicant. On the contrary, he was considered as a person who must be received with respect, for the people knew perfectly well that it was not with every farmer in the neighbourhood he would condescend to sojourn. He had nothing of the ascetic and abstracted meagreness of the Prophet in his appearance. So far from that, he was inclined to corpulency ; but, like a certain class of fat men, his natural disposition was calm, but, at the same time, not unmixed with something of the pensive. His habits of thinking, as might be expected, were quiet and meditative ; his personal motions slow and regular ; and his transitions from one resting-place to another never of such length during a single day as to exceed ten miles. At this easy rate, however, he traversed the whole kingdom several times ; nor was there probably a local prophecy of any importance in the country with which he was not acquainted. He took much delight in the greater and lesser prophets of the Old Testament ; but his heart and soul lay, as he expressed it, "in the Revelations of St. John the Divine."

His usual practice was, when the family came home at night from their labour, to stretch himself upon two chairs, his head resting upon the hob, with a boss for a pillow, his eyes closed, as a proof that his mind was deeply engaged with the matter in hand. In this attitude he got some one to read the particular prophecy upon which he wished to descant ; and a most curious and amusing entertainment it generally was to hear the text, and his own singular and original commentaries upon it. That he must have been often hoaxed by wags and wits, was quite evident from the startling travesties of the text which had been put into his mouth, and which, having been once put there, his tenacious memory never forgot.

The fact of Barney's arrival in the neighbourhood soon went abroad, and the natural consequence was that the house in which he thought proper to reside for the time became crowded every night as soon as the hours of labour had passed, and the people got leisure to hear him. Having thus procured him an audience, it is full time that we should allow the fat old Prophet to speak for himself, and give us all an insight into futurity.

"Barney, ahagur," the good man his host would say, "here's a lot o' the neighbours come to hear a whirrangue from you on the Prophecies ; and, sure, if you can't give it to them, who is there to be found that can ?"

"Throth, Paddy Traynor, although I say it that should not say it, there's truth in that, at all evints. The same knowledge has cost me many a weary blisther an' sore heel in huntin' it up an' down, through mountain an' glen, in Ulsther, Munsther, Leinsther, an' Connaught, not forgettin' the Highlands of Scotland, where there's what they call the ' short prophecy,' or second sight, but wherein there's afther all but little of the Irish or long prophecy, that regards what's to befall the winged woman that flewn into the winderness. No, no ; their second sight isn't thrue prophecy at all. If a man goes out to fish, or steal a cow, an' that he happens to be drowned or shot, another man that has the second sight will see this in his mind about or afther the time it happens. Why, that's little. Many a time our own Irish drames are aiqual to it ; an', indeed I have it from a knowledgeable man, that the gift they boast of has four parents—an empty stomach, thin air, a weak head, an' strong whiskey—an' that a man must have all these, espeshilly the last, before he can have the second sight properly ; an' it's my own opinion. Now, I have a little book (indeed, I left

my books with a friend down at Errigle) that contains a
prophecy of the milk-white hind an' the bloody panther,
an' a forbodin' of the slaughter there's to be in the Valley
of the Black Pig, as foretould by Beal Derg, or the prophet
with the red mouth, who never was known to speak but
when he prophesied, or to prophesy but when he spoke."

" The Lord bless and keep us !—an' why was he called
the Man wid the Red Mouth, Barney ? "

" I'll tell you that. First bekase he always prophesied
about the slaughter an' fightin' that was to take place in the
time to come ; an' secondly, bekase, while he spoke, the red
blood always trickled out of his mouth, as a proof that what
he foretould was true."

" Glory be to God ! but that's wonderful all out. Well,
well ! "

" Ay, an' Beal Derg, or the Red Mouth is still livin'."

" Livin' ! why, is he a man of our own time ? "

" Our own time ! The Lord help you ! It's more than
a thousand years since he made the prophecy. The case
you see is this : he an' the ten thousand witnesses are lyin'
in an enchanted sleep, in one of the Montherlony mountains."

" An' how is that known, Barney ? "

" It's known. Every night at a certain hour one of the
witnesses—an' they're all sogers, by the way—must come
out to look for the sign that's to come."

" An' what is that, Barney ? "

" It's the fiery cross ; an' when he sees one on aich of the
four mountains of the north, he's to know that the same
sign's abroad in all the other parts of the kingdom. Beal
Derg an' his men are then to waken up, an' by their aid the
Valley of the Black Pig is to be set free for ever."

" An' what is the Black Pig, Barney ? "

" The Prosbytarian Church, that stretches from Enniskillen to Darry, an' back again from Darry to Enniskillen "

"Well, well, Barney ; but prophecy is a strange thing to be sure! Only think of men livin' a thousand years!"

"Every night one of Beal Derg's men must go to the mouth of the cave, which opens of itself, an' then look out for the sign that's expected. He walks up to the top of the mountain, an' turns to the four corners of the heavens to thry if he can see it ; an' when he finds that he cannot, he goes back to Beal Derg, who, afther the other touches him, starts up an' axes him, ' Is the time come ? ' He replies, ' No ; the *man is,* but the *hour* is *not* !' an' that instant they're both asleep again. Now, you see, while the soger is on the mountain top, the mouth of the cave is open, an' any one may go in that might happen to see it. One man, it appears, did, an' wishin' to know from curiosity whether the sogers were dead or livin', he touched one of them wid his hand, who started up, and axed him the same question, ' Is the time come ? ' Very fortunately he said ' *No ;* ' an' that minute the soger was as sound in his trance as before."

"An', Barney, what did the soger mane whin he said, ' The man is, but the hour is not'?"

"What did he mane? I'll tell you that. The man is Bonyparty, which manes, whin put into proper explanation, the *right side ;* that is, the true cause. Larned men have found *that* out."

" Barney, wasn't Columkill a great prophet ? "

" He was a great man entirely at prophecy, and so was St. Bridget. He prophesied, ' That the cock wid the purple comb is to have both his wings clipped by one of his own breed, before the struggle comes.' Before that time, too, we're to have the Black Militia, an' afther that it is time for every man to be prepared."

" An' Barney, who is the cock wid the purple comb ? "

" Why, the Orangemen, to be sure. Isn't purple their colour, the dirty thieves ? "

" An' the Black Militia, Barney, who are they ? "

" I have gone far an' near, through north an' through south, up an' down, by hill an' hollow, till my toes were corned, an' my heels in griskins, but could find no one able to resolve that, or bring it clear out of the prophecy.   They are to be sogers in Black, an' all their arms an' coutrements is to be the same colour ; an' farther than that is not known *as yet.*"

" It's a wondher *you* don't know it, Barney, for there's little about prophecy that you haven't at your finger ends."

" Three birds is to meet (Barney proceeded in a kind of recitative enthusiasm) upon the saes—two ravens an' a dove—the two ravens is to attack the dove until she's at the point of death ; but before they take her life, an aigle comes an tears the two ravens to pieces, and the dove recovers.

" There's to be two cries in the kingdom ; one of them is to rech from Giants' Causeway to the centre house of the town of Sligo ; the other is to rech from the Falls of Beleek to the Mill of Louth, which is to be turned three times with human blood ; but this is not to happen until a man with two thumbs an' six fingers upon his right hand happens to be the miller."

" Who's to give the sign of freedom to Ireland ? "

" The little boy wid the red coat that's born a dwarf, lives a giant, and dies a dwarf again !   He's lightest of foot, but leaves the heaviest foot-mark behind him.   An' it's he that's to give the sign of freedom to Ireland.*

" There's a period to come when Antichrist is to be upon the earth, attended by his two servants Gog and Magog."

" Who are they, Barney ? "

" They are the sons of *Hegog* an' *Shegog*, or in other words, of death an' Damnation, and cousin-jarmans to the

---

* This means fire.

Devil himself, which of coorse is the raison why he pro-
motes them."

"Lord save us! But I hope that won't be in our time,
Barney!"

"Antichrist is to come from the land of Crame o' Tarther
(Crim Tartary, according to Pastorini), which will account
for himself an' his army breathin' fire an' brimstone out of
their mouths, according to the glorious revelation of St.
John the Divine, an' the great prophecy of Pastorini, both
of which beautifully compromise on the subject.

"The prophet of the Black Stone is to come, who always
prophesies backwards, and foretells what has happened.
He is to be a mighty hunter, an' instead of ridin' to his fet-
locks *in* blood, he is to ride *upon* it, to the admiration of
his times. It's of him it is said 'that he is to be the only
prophet that ever went on horseback!'

"Then there's Bardolphus, who, as there was a prophet
wid the red mouth, is called 'the prophet wid the red nose.'
Ireland was, it appears from ancient books, undher wather
for many hundred years before her discovery; but bein'
allowed to become visible one day in every year, the en-
chantment was broken by a sword that was thrown upon
the earth, an' from that out she remained dry, an' became
inhabited. 'Woe, woe, woe,' says Bardolphus, 'the time
is to come when we'll have a second deluge, an' Ireland is
to be undher wather once more. A well is to open at Cork
that will cover the whole island from the Giant's Causeway
to Cape Clear. In them days St. Patrick will be despised,
an' will stand over the pleasant houses wid his pastoral
crook in his hand, crying out *Cead mille failtha* in vain!
Woe, woe, woe,' says Bardolphus, 'for in them days there
will be a great confusion of colours among the people,
there will be neither red noses nor pale cheeks, an' the
divine face of man, alas! will put forth blossoms no more.
The heart of the times will become changed; an' when they

rise up in the mornin', it will come to pass that there will
be no longer light heads or shaking hands among Irishmen!
Woe, woe, woe, men, women, and children will then die, an'
their only complaint, like all those who perished in flood
of ould, will be wather on the brain!—wather on the brain!
Woe, woe, woe,' says Bardolphus, ' for the changes that is to
come, an' the misfortunes that's to befall the many for the
noddification of the few! an' yet such things must be, for
I, in vertue of the red spirit that dwells in me, must prophecy them.   In those times men will be shod in liquid fire,
an' not be burned ; their breeches shall be made of fire, an'
will not burn them ; their bread shall be made of fire, an' it
will not burn them ; their meat shall be made of fire, an'
will not burn them ; an' why ?—Oh, woe, woe, wather shall
so prevail that the coolness of their bodies will keep them
safe ; yea, they shall even get fat, fair an' be full of health
an' strength, by wearing garments wrought out of liquid
fire, by eating liquid fire, an' all because they do not dhrink
liquid fire—an' this calamity shall come to pass,' says
Bardolphus, the prophet of the red-nose.

"Two widows shall be grinding at the Mill of Louth
(so saith the prophecy) ; one shall be taken, and the other
left."

Thus would Barney proceed, repeating such ludicrous
and heterogeneous mixtures of old traditionary prophecies
and spurious quotations from Scripture, as were concocted
for him by those who took delight in amusing themselves
and others at the expense of his inordinate love for prophecy.

"But, Barney, touchin' the Mill of Louth, of the two
widows grindin' there, whether will the one that is taken or
the one that's left be the best off ? "

"The prophecy doesn't say," replied Barney ; "an' that's
a matther that larned men are very much divided about.
My own opinion is, that the one that's taken will be the

best off for St. Bridget says, 'that betune wars an' pesti-
lences, an' famine, the men will be so scarce that several of
them will be torn to pieces by the women in their struggles
to see who will get them for husbands.' That time, they
say, is to come."

"But, Barney, isn't there many ould prophecies about
particular families in Ireland?"

"Ay, several: and I'll tell you one of them about a
family that's not far from us this minute. You all know
the hangin' wall of the ould church of Ballynasaggart, in
Errigle Keeran parish?"

"We do, to be sure, an' we know the prophecy too."

"Of coorse you do, bein' in the neighbourhood. Well
what is it in the manetime?"

"Why, that it's never to fall till it comes down upon and
takes the life of a M'Mahon."

"Right enough; but do you know the raison of
it?"

"We can't say that, Barney; but, however, we're at
home when you're here."

"Well, I'll tell you. St Keeran was, maybe, next to
Patrick himself, one of the greatest saints in Ireland, but
at any rate we may put him next to St. Columkill. Now,
you see when he was building the church of Ballynasaggart,
it came to pass that there arose a great famine in the land,
and the saint found it hard to feed the workmen where
there was no vittles. What to do he knew not, an' by
coorse he was at a sad amplush, no doubt of it. At length
sis he, 'Boys we're all hard set at present, an' widout food
bedad we can't work; but if you observe my directions,
we'll conthrive to have a bit o' mate in the manetime, an'
among ourselves it was seldom more wanted, for, to tell
you the thruth, I never thought my back an' belly would
become so well acquainted. For the last three days they
haven't been asundher, an' I find they are perfectly willing

to part as soon as possible, an' would be glad of anything that 'ud put betune them.'

"Now, the fact was, that, for drawin' timber an' stone, an' all the necessary matayrials for the church, they had but one bullock, an' him St. Keeran resolved to kill in the evenin', an' to give them a fog meal of him. He accordingly slaughtered him wid his own hands ; 'but,' sis he to the workmen, 'mind what I say, boys : if any one of you breaks a single bone, even the smallest, or injures the hide in the laste, you'll destroy all ; an' my sowl to glory but it'll be worse for you besides.'

"He thin tuk all the flesh off the bones, but not till he had biled them, of coorse ; afther which he sewed them up again in the skin, an' put thim in the shed wid a good wisp o' straw before them ; an' glory be to God, what do you think, but the next mornin' the bullock was alive, an' in as good condition as ever he was in during his life ! Betther fed workmen you couldn't see, an', bedad, the saint himself got so fat an' rosy that you'd scarcely know him to be the same man afther it. Now, this went on for some time : whenever they wanted mate, the bullock was killed, an' the bones an' skin kept safe as before. At last it happened that a long-sided fellow among them named M'Mahon, not satisfied wid his allowance of the mate, took a fancy to have a lick at the marrow, an' accordingly, in spite of all the saint said, he broke one of the legs, an' sucked the marrow out of it. But behold you !—the next day when they went to yoke the bullock, they found that he was useless, for the leg was broken an' he couldn't work. This, to be sure, was a sad misfortune to them all, but it couldn't be helped, an' they had to wait till betther times came ; for the truth is, that afther the marrow is broken, no power of man could make the leg as it was before until the cure is brought about by time. However, the saint was very much vexed, an' good right he had. 'Now M'Mahon,' said he to the guilty man, 'I ordher it an' prophesy that the church we're building will never fall till it falls upon the head of some one of your name, if it was to stand a thousand years. Mark my words, for they must come to pass.'

"An' sure enough you know as well as I do that it's all down long ago, wid the exception of a piece of the wall that's not standin' but hangin', widout any visible support in life, an' only propped up by the prophecy. It can't fall till a M'Mahon comes undher it; but although there's plenty of the name in the neighbourhood, ten of the strongest horses in the kingdom wouldn't drag one of 'em widin half a mile of it. There, now, is the prophecy that belongs to the hangin' wall of Ballynasaggart church."

"But, Barney, didn't you say something about the winged woman that flewn to the wilderness?"

"I did; that's a deep point, an' it's few that undherstands it. The baste wid seven heads an' ten horns is to come ; and whin he was to make his appearance, it was said to be time for thim that might be alive thin to go to their padareens."

"What does the seven heads an' ten horns mane, Barney?"

"Why, you see, as I am informed from good authority, the baste has come, an' it's clear from the *ten* horns that he could be no other than Harry the Eight, who was married to *five* wives, an' by all accounts they strengthened an' ornamented him sore agen his will. Now, set in case that aich of them—five times two is ten—hut! the thing's as clear as crystal. But I'll prove it betther. You see the woman wid the two wings is the church, an' she flew into the wilderness at the very time Harry the Eight wid his ten horns on him was in his greatest power."

" Bedad that's puttin' the explanations to it in great style."

" But the woman wid the wings is only to be in the wild-erness for a time, times, an' half a time, that's exactly three hundred an' fifty years, an' afther that there's to be no more Prodestans."

" Faith that's great ! "

" Sure Columkill prophesied that until H E M E I A M should come, the church would be in no danger, but that afther that she must be under a cloud for a time, times, an' half a time, jist in the same way."

"Well, but how do you explain that, Barney ? "

" An' St. Bridget prophesied that when D O C is upper-most, the church will be hard set in Ireland.   But, indeed, there's no end to the prophecies that there is concerning Ireland an' the church.   However, neighbours, do you know that I feel the heat o' the fire has made me rather drowsy, an' if you have no objection, I'll take a bit of a nap. There's great things near us, any how.   An' talkin' about D O C brings to my mind another ould prophecy, made up, they say, betune Columkill and St. Bridget ; an' it is this, that the triumph of the counthry will never be at hand till the D O C flourishes in Ireland."

Such were the speculations upon which the harmless mind of Barney M'Haigney ever dwelt.   From house to house, from parish to parish, and from province to province, did he thus trudge, never in a hurry, but always steady and constant in his motions.   He might be not inaptly termed the Old Mortality of traditionary prophecy, which he often chiselled anew, added to, and improved, in a manner that generally gratified himself and his hearers.   He was a harmless, kind man, and never known to stand in need of either clothes or money.   He paid little attention to the silent business of on-going life, and was consequently very nearly an abstraction.   He was always on the alert, how-ever, for the result of a battle ; and after having heard it, he would give no opinion whatsoever until he had first silently compared it with his own private theory in pro-phecy.   If it agreed with this, he immediately published it in connexion with his established text; but if it did not, he never opened his lips on the subject.

His class has nearly disappeared, and indeed it is so much the better, for the minds of the people were thus filled with antiquated nonsense that did them no good. Poor Barney, to his great mortification, lived to see with his own eyes the failure of his most favourite prophecies, but he was not to be disheartened even by this; though some might fail, all could not; and his stock was too varied and extensive not to furnish him with a sufficient number of others over which to cherish his imagination, and expatiate during the remainder of his inoffensive life.

FIN M'COUL,

The Knockmany Giant.

WHAT Irish man, woman, or child, has not heard of our renowned Hibernian Hercules, the great and glorious Fin M'Coul? Not one, from Cape Clear to the Giant's Causeway, nor from that back again to Cape Clear. And by the way, speaking of the Giant's Causeway brings me at once to the beginning of my story. Well, it so happened that Fin and his gigantic relatives were all working at the Causeway, in order to make a bridge, or what was still better, a good stout pad-road, across to Scotland; when Fin, who was very fond of his wife Oonagh, took it into his head that he would go home and see how the poor woman got on in his absence. To be sure, Fin was a true Irishman, and so the sorrow thing in life brought him back, only to see that she was snug and comfortable, and, above

all things, that she got her rest well at night ; for he knew
that the poor woman, when he was with her, used to be
subject to nightly qualms, and configurations, that kept
him very anxious, decent man, striving to keep her up to
the good spirits and health that she had when they were
first married. So, accordingly, he pulled up a fir tree, and,
after lopping off the roots and branches, made a walking-
stick of it, and set out on his way to Oonagh.

Oonagh, or rather Fin, lived at this time on the very tip-
top of Knockmany Hill, which faces a cousin of its own,
called Cullamore, that rises up, half-hill, half-mountain, on
the opposite side—east-east by south, as the sailors say,
when they wish to puzzle a landsman.

Now the truth is, for it must come out, that honest Fin's
affection for his wife, though cordial enough in itself, was by
no manner or means the real cause of his journey home.
There was at that time another giant named Cucullin—
some say he was Irish, and some say he was Scotch ; but
whether Scotch or Irish, sorrow doubt of it but he was a
targer. No other giant of the day could stand before him ;
and such was his strength, that, when well vexed, he could
give a stamp that shook the country about him. The fame
and name of him went far and near, and nothing in the
shape of a man, it was said, had any chance with him in a
fight. Whether the story is true or not, I cannot say, but
the report went that, by one blow of his fist, he flattened a
thunderbolt and kept it in his pocket in the shape of a pancake, to shew to his enemies when they were about to fight
him. Undoubtedly he had given every giant in Ireland a
considerable beating, barring Fin M'Coul himself ; and he
swore by the solemn contents of Moll Kelly's Primer, that
he would never rest, day or night, winter or summer, till he
would serve Fin with the same sauce, if he could catch
him. Fin, however, who no doubt was cock of the walk on
his own dunghill, had a strong disinclination to meet a

giant who could make a young earthquake, or flatten a
thunderbolt when he was angry; so he accordingly kept
dodging about from place to place, not much to his credit
as a Trojan to be sure, whenever he happened to get the
hard word that Cucullin was on the scent of him.   This,
then, was the marrow of the whole movement, although he
put it on his anxiety to see Oonagh, and I am not saying
but there was some truth in that too.   However, the short
and the long of it was, with reverence be it spoken, that he
heard Cucullin was coming to the Causeway to have a trial
of strength with him ; and he was naturally enough seized,
in consequence, with a very warm and sudden fit of affection for his wife, poor woman, who was delicate in her
health, and leading, besides, a very lonely uncomfortable
life of it (he assured them), in his absence.   He accordingly pulled up the fir-tree, as I said before, and having
snedded it into a walking-stick, set out on his affectionate
travels to see his darling Oonagh on the top of Knockmany,
by the way.

In truth, to state the suspicions of the country at the
time, the people wondered very much why it was that Fin
selected such a windy spot for his dwelling-house, and they
even went so far as to tell him as much.

"What can you mane, Mr. M'Coul," said they, "by
pitching your tent upon the top of Knockmany, where you
never are without a breeze, day or night, winter or summer,
and where you're often forced to take your nightcap without either going to bed or turning up your little finger ; ay,
an' where, besides, there's the sorrow's own want of water?"

"Why," said Fin, "ever since I was the height of a round
tower, I was known to be fond of having a good prospect of
my own ; and where the dickens, neighbours, could I find a
better spot for a good prospect than the top of Knockmany?
As for water, I am sinking a pump, and, plase goodness, as
soon as the Causeway's made I intend to finish it."

Now, this was more of Fin's philosophy, for the real state of the case was that he pitched on the top of Knockmany in order that he might be able to see Cucullin coming towards the house, and, of course, that he himself might go to look after his distant transactions in other parts of the country, rather than—but no matter—we do not wish to be too hard on Fin. All we have to say is, that if he wanted a spot from which to keep a sharp look-out—and, between ourselves, he did want it grievously—barring Slieve Croob, or Slieve Donard, o⁻ its own cousin, Cullamore, he could not find a neater or more convenient situation for it in the sweet and sagacious province of Ulster.

"God save all here!" said Fin, good-humouredly, on putting his honest face into his own door.

"Musha Fin, avick, an' you're welcome home to your own Oonagh, you darlin' bully." Here followed a smack that is said to have made the waters of the lake at the bottom of the hill curl, as it were, with kindness and sympathy.

"Faith," said Fin, "beautiful; an' how are you, Oonagh—and how did you sport your figure during my absence, my bilberry?"

"Never a merrier—as bouncing a grass widow as ever there was in sweet 'Tyrone among the bushes.'"

Fin gave a short good-humoured cough and laughed most heartily, to shew her how much he was delighted that she made herself happy in his absence.

"An' what brought you home so soon, Fin?" said she.

"Why, avourneen," said Fin, putting in his answer in the proper way, "never the thing but the purest of love and affection for yourself. Sure you know that's truth, any how, Oonagh."

Fin spent two or three happy days with Oonagh, and felt himself very comfortable considering the dread he had of Cucullin. This, however, grew upon him so much that his wife could not but perceive that something lay on his mind which he kept altogether to himself. Let a woman alone in the meantime, for ferreting or wheedling a secret out of her good man, when she wishes. Fin was a proof of this.

"It's this Cucullin," said he, "that's troubling me. When the fellow gets angry, and begins to stamp, he'll shake you a whole townland; and it's well known that he can stop a thunderbolt, for he always carries one about him in the shape of a pancake, to shew to any one that might mis-doubt it."

As he spoke, he clapped his thumb in his mouth, which he always did when he wanted to prophecy, or to know any thing that happened in his absence; and the wife, who knew what he did it for, said, very sweetly,

"Fin, darling, I hope you don't bite your thumb at me, dear?"

"No," said Fin; "but I bite my thumb, acushla," said he.

"Yes, jewel; but take care and don't draw blood," said she. "Ah, Fin! don't, my bully—don't."

"He's coming," said Fin; "I see him below Dungannon."

"Thank goodness, dear! an' who is it, avick? Glory be to God!"

"That baste Cucullin," replied Fin; "and how to manage I don't know. If I run away, I am disgraced; and I know that sooner or later I must meet him, for my thumb tells me so."

"When will he be here?" said she.

"To-morrow about two o'clock," replied Fin, with a groan.

"Well, my bully, don't be cast down," said Oonagh; "depend on me, and maybe I'll bring you better out of this scrape than ever you could bring yourself, by your rule o' thumb."

This quieted Fin's heart very much, for he knew that Oonagh was hand and glove with the fairies, and, indeed, to tell the truth, she was supposed to be a fairy herself. If she was, however, she must have been a kind-hearted one; for,

7

by all accounts, she never did any thing but good in the neighbourhood.

Now, it so happened that Oonagh had a sister named Granua, living opposite them, on the very top of Cullamore, which I have mentioned already, and this Granua was quite as powerful as herself. The beautiful valley that lies between them is not more than about three or four miles broad, so that of a summer's evening Granua and Oonagh were able to hold many an agreeable conversation across it, from the one hill-top to the other. Upon this occasion, Oonagh resolved to consult her sister as to what was best to be done in the difficulty that surrounded them.

"Granua," said she, "are you at home?"

"No," said the other; "I'm picking bilberries in Althad-hawan" (*Anglicé*, the Devil's Glen).

"Well," said Oonagh, "get up to the top of Cullamore, look about you, and tell us what you see."

"Very well," replied Granua, after a few minutes, "I am there now."

"What do you see?" asked the other.

"Goodness be about us!" exclaimed Granua, "I see the biggest giant that ever was known, coming up from Dungannon."

"Ay," said Oonagh, "there's our difficulty. That giant is the great Cucullin; and he's now coming up to leather Fin. What's to be done?"

"I'll call to him," she replied, "to come up to Cullamore, and refresh himself, and maybe that will give you and Fin time to think of some plan to get yourself out of the scrape. But," she proceeded, "I'm short of butter, having in the house only half a dozen firkins, and as I'm to have a few giants and giantesses to spend the evenin' with me, I'd feel thankful, Oonagh, if you'd throw me up fifteen or sixteen tubs, or the largest miscaun you have got, and you'll oblige me very much."

"I'll do that with a heart and a half," replied Oonagh; "and, indeed, Granua, I feel myself under great obligations to you for your kindness in keeping him off us, till we see what can be done; for what would become of us all if any thing happened Fin, poor man?"

She accordingly got the largest miscaun of butter she had—which might be about the weight of a couple dozen millstones, so that you may easily judge of its size—and calling up to her sister, "Granua," said she, "are you ready? I'm going to throw you up a miscaun, so be prepared to catch it."

"I will," said the other, "a good throw now, and take care it does not fall short."

Oonagh threw it; but in consequence of her anxiety about Fin and Cucullin, she forgot to say the charm that was to send it up, so that, instead of reaching Cullamore, as she expected, it fell about half way between the two hills, at the edge of the Broad Bog near Augher.

"My curse upon you!" she exclaimed; "you've disgraced me. I now change you into a grey stone. Lie there as a testimony of what has happened; and may evil betide the first living man that will ever attempt to remove or injure you!"

And, sure enough, there it lies to this day, with the mark of the four fingers and thumb imprinted in it, exactly as it came out of her hand.

"Never mind," said Granua; "I must only do the best I can with Cucullin. If all fail, I'll give him a cast of heather broth to keep the wind out of his stomach, or a panada of oak-bark to draw it in a bit; but, above all things, think of some plan to get Fin out of the scrape he's in, otherwise he's a lost man. You know you used to be sharp and ready-witted; and my opinion, Oonagh, is, that it will go hard with you, or you'll outdo Cucullin yet."

She then made a high smoke on the top of the hill, after

which she put her finger in her mouth, and gave three whistles, and by that Cucullin knew he was invited to Cullamore—for this was the way that the Irish long ago gave a sign to all strangers and travellers, to let them know they were welcome to come and take share of whatever was going.

In the meantime, Fin was very melancholy, and did not know what to do, or how to act at all. Cucullin was an ugly customer, no doubt, to meet with ; and, moreover, the idea of the confounded " cake," aforesaid, flattened the very heart within him. What chance could he have, strong and brave though he was, with a man who could, when put in a passion, walk the country into earthquakes and knock thunderbolts into pancakes ? The thing was impossible ; and Fin knew not on what hand to turn him. Right or left—backward or forward—where to go he could form no guess whatsoever.

" Oonagh," said he, " can you do nothing for me ? Where's all your invention ? Am I to be skivered like a rabbit before your eyes, and to have my name disgraced for ever in the sight of all my tribe, and me the best man among them ? How am I to fight this man-mountain—this huge cross between an earthquake and a thunderbolt ?—with a pancake in his pocket that was once——"

" Be easy, Fin," replied Oonagh ; " troth I am ashamed of you. Keep your toe in your pump, will you ? Talking of pancakes, maybe we'll give him as good as any he brings with him—thunderbolt or otherwise. If I don't treat him to as smart feeding as he's got this many a day, never trust Oonagh again. Leave him to me, and do just as I bid you."

This relieved Fin very much ; for, after all, he had great confidence in his wife, knowing, as he did, that she had got him out of many a quandary before. The present, however, was the greatest of all ; but still he began to get courage, and was able to eat his victuals as usual. Oonagh then drew the nine woollen threads of different colours, which she always did to find out the best way of succeeding in any thing of importance she went about. She then platted them into three plats with three colours in each, putting one to her right arm, one round her heart, and the third round her right ankle, for then she knew that nothing could fail with her that she undertook.

Having everything now prepared, she sent round to the neighbours and borrowed one-and-twenty iron griddles, which she took and kneaded into the hearts of one-and-twenty cakes of bread, and these she baked on the fire in the usual way, setting them aside in the cupboard according as they were done. She then put down a large pot of new milk, which she made into curds and whey, and gave Fin due instructions how to use the curds when Cucullin should come. Having done all this, she sat down quite contented, waiting for his arrival on the next day about two o'clock, that being the hour at which he was expected—for Fin knew as much by the sucking of his thumb. Now this was a curious property that Fin's thumb had; but, notwithstanding all the wisdom and logic he used to suck out of it, it never could have stood to him were it not for the wit of his wife. In this very thing, moreover, he was very much resembled by his great foe Cucullin; for it was well known that the huge strength he possessed all lay in the middle finger of his right hand, and that, if he happened by any mischance to lose it, he was no more, notwithstanding his bulk, than a common man.

At length the next day, he was seen coming across the valley, and Oonagh knew that it was time to commence operations. She immediately made the cradle, and desired Fin to lie down in it, and cover himself up with the clothes.

"You must pass for your own child," said she, "so just lie

there snug, and say nothing, but be guided by me." This, to
be sure, was wormwood to Fin—I mean going into the cradle
in such a cowardly manner—but he knew Oonagh well; and
finding that he had nothing else for it, with a very rueful
face he gathered himself into it, and lay snug as she had
desired him.

About two o'clock, as he had been expected, Cucullin
came in. "God save all here," said he; "is this where the
great Fin M'Coul lives?"

"Indeed it is is, honest man," replied Oonagh; "God save
you kindly—won't you be sitting?"

"Thank you, ma'am," says he, sitting down; "you're
Mrs. M'Coul, I suppose?"

"I am," said she; "and I have no reason, I hope, to be
ashamed of my husband."

"No," said the other; "he has the name of being the
strongest and bravest man in Ireland; but for all that,
there's a man not far from you that's very desirous of
taking a shake with him. Is he at home?"

"Why, then, no," she replied; "and if ever a man left
his house in a fury, he did. It appears that some one told
him of a big basthoon of a giant called Cucullin being down
at the Causeway to look for him, and so he set out there to
try if he could catch him. Troth, I hope, for the poor
giant's sake, he won't meet with him, for if he does, Fin
will make paste of him at once."

"Well," said the other, "I am Cucullin, and I have been
seeking him these twelvemonths, but he always kept clear
of me; and I will never rest night or day till I lay my
hands on him."

At this Oonagh set up a loud laugh, of great contempt,
by the way, and looked at him as if he was only a mere
handful of a man.

"Did you ever see Fin?" said she, changing her manner
all at once.

"How could I?" said he; "he always took care to keep his distance."

"I thought so," she replied; "I judged as much; and if you take my advice, you poor-looking creature, you'll pray night and day that you may never see him, for I tell you it will be a black day for you when you do. But, in the meantime, you perceive that the wind's on the door, and as Fin himself is from home, maybe you'd be civil enough to turn the house, for it's always what Fin does when he's here."

This was a startler even to Cucullin; but he got up, however, and after pulling the middle finger of his right hand until it cracked three times, he went outside, and getting his arms about the house, completely turned it as she had wished. When Fin saw this, he felt a certain description of moisture, which shall be nameless, oozing out through every pore of his skin; but Oonagh, depending upon her woman's wit, felt not a whit daunted.

"Arrah, then," said she, "as you are so civil maybe you'd do another obliging turn for us, as Fin's not here to do it himself. You see, after this long stretch of dry weather we've had, we feel very badly off for want of water. Now, Fin says there's a fine spring well somewhere under the rocks behind the hill here below, an' it was his intention to pull them asunder; but having heard of you, he left the place in such a fury, that he never thought of it. Now, if you try to find it, troth I'd feel it a kindness."

She then brought Cucullin down to see the place, which was then all one solid rock; and after looking at it for some time, he cracked his right middle finger nine times, and stooping down, tore a cleft about four hundred feet deep, and a quarter of a mile long, which has since been christened by the name of Lumford's Glen. This feat nearly threw Oonagh herself off her guard; but what won't a woman's sagacity and presence of mind accomplish?

"You'll now come in," said she, "and eat a bit of such

humble fare as we can give you. Fin, even although he and you are enemies, would scorn not to treat you kindly in his own house : and, indeed, if I didn't do it even in his absence, he would not be pleased with me."

She accordingly brought him in, and placing half a dozen of the cakes we spoke of before him, together with a can or two of butter, a side of boiled bacon, and a stack of cabbage, she desired him to help himself—for this, be it known, was long before the invention of potatoes. Cucullin, who, by the way, was a glutton as well as a hero, put one of the cakes in his mouth to take a huge whack out of it, when both Fin and Oonagh were stunned with a noise that resembled something between a growl and a yell. " Blood and fury!" he shouted; "how is this? Here are two of my teeth out! What kind of bread is this you gave me?"

"What's the matter?" said Oonagh coolly.

"Matter!" shouted the other again; "why, here are the two back teeth in my head gone!"

"Why," said she, " that's Fin's bread—the only bread he ever eats when at home ; but, indeed, I forgot to tell you that nobody can eat it but himself, and that child in the cradle there. I thought, however, that as you were reported to be rather a stout little fellow of your size, you might be able to manage it, and I did not wish to affront a man that thinks himself able to fight Fin. Here's another cake —maybe it's not so hard as that."

Cucullin at the moment was not only hungry but ravenous, so he accordingly made a fresh set at the second cake, and immediately another yell was heard twice as loud as the first. " Thunder and giblets!" he roared, "take your bread out of this, or I will not have a tooth in my head ; there's another pair of them gone!"

"Well, honest man," replied Oonagh, " if you're not able to eat the bread, say so quietly, and don't be wakening the child in the cradle here. There, now, he's awake upon me."

Fin now gave a skirl that startled the giant, as coming from such a youngster as he was represented to be. "Mother," said he, " I'm hungry—get me something to eat." Oonagh went over, and putting into his hand a cake *that had no griddle in it*, Fin, whose appetite in the meantime was sharpened by what he saw going forward, soon made it disappear. Cucullin was thunderstruck, and secretly thanked his stars that he had the good fortune to miss meeting Fin, for, as he said to himself, I'd have no chance with a man who could eat such bread as that, which even his son that's but in his cradle can munch before my eyes.

"I'd like to take a glimpse at the lad in the cradle," said he to Oonagh ; "for I can tell you that the infant who can manage that nutriment is no joke to look at, or to feed of a scarce summer."

"With all the veins of my heart," replied Oonagh. "Get up, acushla, and show this decent little man something that won't be unworthy of your father Fin M'Coul."

Fin, who was dressed for the occasion as much like a boy as possible, got up, and bringing Cucullin out—" Are you strong ?" said he.

"Thunder an' ounds!" exclaimed the other, "what a voice in so small a chap !"

"Are you strong ?" said Fin again ; "are you able to squeeze water out of that white stone ?" he asked, putting one into Cucullin's hand. The latter squeezed and squeezed the stone, but to no purpose : he might pull the rocks of Lumford's Glen asunder, and flatten a thunderbolt, but to squeeze water out of a white stone was beyond his strength. Fin eyed him with great contempt, as he kept straining and squeezing, and squeezing and straining, till he got black in the face with the efforts.

"Ah, you're a poor creature !" said Fin. "You a giant ! Give me the stone here, and when I'll shew what Fin's little son can do, you may then judge of what my daddy himself is."

Fin then took the stone, and slyly exchanging it for the curds, he squeezed the latter until the whey, as clear as water, oozed out in a little shower from his hand.

"I'll now go in," said he, "to my cradle; for I'd scorn to lose my time with any one that's not able to eat my daddy's bread, or squeeze water out of a stone. Bedad, you had better be off out of this before he comes back; for if he catches you, it's in flummery he'd have you in two minutes."

Cucullin, seeing what he had seen, was of the same opinion himself, his knees knocked together with the terror of Fin's return, and he accordingly hastened in to bid Oonagh farewell, and to assure her, that, from that day out, he never wished to hear of, much less to see, her husband. "I admit fairly that I'm not a match for him," said he, "strong as I am; tell him I will avoid him as I would the plague, and that I will make myself scarce in his part of the country while I live."

Fin, in the meantime, had gone into the cradle, where he lay very quietly, his heart in his mouth with delight that Cucullin was about to take his departure, without discovering the tricks that had been played off on him.

"It's well for you," said Oonagh, "that he doesn't happen to be here, for it's nothing but hawk's meat he'd make of you."

"I know that," says Cucullin; "divil a thing else he'd make of me; but before I go, will you let me feel what kind of teeth they are that can eat griddle-bread like *that?*"—and he pointed to it as he spoke.

"With all pleasure in life," said she, "only as they're far back in his head, you must put your finger a good way in."

Cucullin was surprised to find such a powerful set of grinders in one so young; but he was still much more so on finding, when he took his hand from Fin's mouth, that he had left the very finger upon which his whole strength depended, behind him. He gave one loud groan, and fell down at once with terror and weakness. This was all Fin wanted, who now knew that his most powerful and bitterest enemy was completely at his mercy. He instantly started out of the cradle, and in a few minutes the great Cucullin that was for such a length of time the terror of him and all his followers, lay a corpse before him. Thus did Fin, through the wit and invention of Oonagh, his wife, succeed in overcoming his enemy by stratagem, which he never could have done by force; and thus also is it proved that the women, if they bring us *into* many an unpleasant scrape, can sometimes succeed in getting us *out of* others that are as bad.

AROUND NED'S FIRESIDE;

OR,

The Story of the Squire.

SEATED in the clear-obscure of domestic light, which, after all, gives the heart a finer and more touching notion of enjoyment than the glitter of the theatre or the blaze of the saloon, might be found—first, Andy Morrow, the juryman of the quarter-sessions, sage and important in the consciousness of legal knowledge, and somewhat dictatorial withal in its application to such knotty points as arose out of the subjects of their nocturnal debates. Secondly, Bob Gott, who filled the foreign and military departments, and related the wonderful history of the ghost which appeared on the night after the battle of Bunker's Hill. To him succeeded Tom M'Roarkin, the little asthmatic anecdotarian of half the country, remarkable for chuckling at his own stories. Then came old Bill M'Kinny, poacher and horse-jockey; little, squeaking, thin-faced Alick M'Kinley, a facetious farmer of substance; and Shane Fadh, who handed down traditions and fairy-tales. Enthroned on one hob sat Pat Frayne, the schoolmaster, with the short arm, who read and explained the newspaper for "Ould Square Colwell," and was looked upon as premier to the aforesaid cabinet. Ned himself filled the opposite seat of honour.

One night, a little before the Christmas holidays, in the year 18—, the personages just described were seated around Ned's fire, some with their chirping pints of ale or porter, and others with their quantum of *Hugh Traynor*, or mountain dew, and all with good-humour and a strong tendency to happiness visible in their faces. The night was dark, close, and misty—so dark, indeed, that, as Nancy said, "you could hardly see your finger before you." Ned himself was full of fun, with a pint of porter beside him, and a pipe in his mouth, just in his glory for the night. Opposite to him was Pat Frayne, with an old newspaper on his knee, which he had just perused for the edification of his audience; beside him was Nancy, busily employed in knitting a pair of sheep's-grey stockings for Ned; the remaining personages formed a semicircular ring about the hearth. Behind, on the kitchen-table, sat Paddy Smith, the servant man, with three or four of the *gorsoons* of the village about him, engaged in a little under-plot of their own. On the other side, and a little removed from the light, sat Ned's two nieces, Biddy and Bessy Connolly, the former with Atty Johnston's mouth within whisper-reach of her ear, and the latter seated close to her professed admirer, Billy Fulton, her uncle's shopman. This group was completely abstracted from the entertainment which was going forward in the circle round the fire.

" I wondher," said Andy Morrow, " what makes Joe M'Crea throw down that fine ould castle of his in Aughentain ? "

" I'm tould," said M'Roarkin, " that he expects money ; for they say there's a lot of it buried somewhere about the same building."

" Jist as much as there's in my wig," replied Shane Fadh, " and there's ne'er a pocket to it yet. Why, bless your sowl, how could there be money in it, whin the last man of the Grameses that ow'd it—I mane of the ould stock, afore it went into Lord Mountjoy's hands—sould it out, ran through the money, and died begging afther. Did none of you ever hear of

'Ould John Grame,
' That *swally'd* the castle of Aughentain ! ' "

" That was long afore my time," said the poacher : " but I know that the rabbit-burrow between that and Jack Appleton's garden will soon be run out."

" *Your* time ! " responded Shane Fadh, with contempt ; " ay, and your father's afore you : *my* father doesn't remimber more nor seeing his funeral, and a merry one it was ; for my grandfather, and some of them that had a respect for the family and his forbarers, if they hadn't it for himself, made up as much money among them as berried him dacently, any how—ay, and gave him a rousin' wake into the bargain, with lashins of whiskey, stout beer, and ale ; for in them times—God be with them—every farmer brewed his own ale and beer ; more betoken, that one pint of it was worth a keg of this wash of yours, Ned."

" Wasn't it he that used to *appear ?* " inquired M'Roarkin.

" Sure enough he did, Tom."

" Lord save us," said Nancy, " what could trouble him, I dunna ? "

" Why," continued Shane Fadh, " some said one thing,

and some another ; but the upshot of it was this : when the last of the Grameses sould the estate, castle and all, it seems he didn't resave all the purchase money ; so, afther he had spint what he got, he applied to the purchaser for the re-mainder—him that the Mountjoy family bought it from ; but it seems he didn't draw up writings, or sell it according to law, so that the thief o' the world baffled him from day to day, and wouldn't give him a penny—bekase he knew, the blaggard, that the Square was then as poor as a church mouse, and hadn't money enough to thry it at law with him ; but the Square was always a simple asy-going man. One day he went to this fellow, riding on an ould garran, with a shoe loose—the only baste he had in the world—and axed him for God's sake, to give him some of what he owed him, if it were ever so little : ' for,' says he, ' I have not as much money betune me and death as will get a set of shoes for my horse.'

" ' Well,' says the nager, ' if you're not able to keep your horse shod, I would jist recommend you to sell him, and thin his shoes won't cost you anything,' says he.

" The old Square went away with tears in his eyes, for he loved the poor brute, bekase they wor the two last branches of the ould stock."

" Why," inquired M'Kinley, in his small squeaking voice, " was the horse related to the family ? "

" I didn't say he was related to the fam——Get out, you *shingaun !* " returned the old man, perceiving by the laugh that now went round the sly tendency of the question. " No, nor to *your* family either, for he had nothing of the ass in him—eh ? will you put that in your pocket, my little *skinadhre*—ha ! ha ! ha ! "

The laugh now turned against M'Kinley.

Shane Fadh proceeded : " The ould Square, as I was tellin' yees, cried to find himself an' the poor baste so dis-solute, but when he had gone a bit from the fellow, he comes

back to the vagabone. 'Now,' says he, 'mind my words—
if you happen to live afther me, you need never expect a
night's pace ; for I here make a serous an' solemn vow, that
as long as my property's in your possession, or in any of
your seed, breed, or ginerations, I'll never give over hauntin'
you an' them, till you'll rue to the back-bone your dis-
honesty an' chathery to me an this poor baste, that hasn't
a shoe to its foot.'

"'Well,' says the nager, 'I'll take chance of that, any
way.'"

"I'm tould, Shane," observed the poacher, "that the
Square was a fine man in his time, that wouldn't put up
with such thratement from anybody."

"Ay, but he was ould now," Shane replied, "and too
wakely to fight. A fine man, Bill !—he was the finest man,
'ceptin' ould Square Storey, that ever was in this counthry.
I hard my grandfather often say that he was six feet four,
and made in proportion—a handsome, black-a-vis'd man,
with great dark whiskers. Well ! he spint money like
sklates, and so he died miserable—but had a merry birrel,
as I said."

"But," inquired Nancy, "did he ever *appear* to the rogue
that chated him ? "

"Every night in the year, Nancy, exceptin' Sundays ;
and what was more, the horse along with him—for he used
to come ridin' at midnight upon the same garran ; and it
was no matther what place or company the other 'ud be in,
the ould Square would come regularly, and crave him for
what he owed him."

"So it appears that horses have sowls," observed M'Roarkin, philosophically, giving, at the same time, a cynical
chuckle at the sarcasm of his own conceit.

"Whether they have sowls or bodies," replied the narrator,
"what I'm tellin' you is the thruth ; every night in the year
the ould chap would come for what was indue him ; and as

the two went along, the noise of the loose shoe upon the
horse would be hard rattlin', and seen knockin' the fire out
of the stones, by the neighbours and the thief that chated
him, even before the Square would appear, at all at
all."

"Oh, wurrah!" exclaimed Nancy, shuddering with terror,
" I wouldn't take anything, and be out now on the Drum-
furrar road, and nobody with me but myself."

"I think if you wor," said M'Kinley, "the light weights
and short measures would be coming acrass your conscience."

"No, in throth, Alick, wouldn't they ; but maybe if *you*
wor, the promise you broke to Sally Mitchell might trouble
you a bit : at any rate, I've a prayer, and if I only repated
it *wanst*, I mightn't be afeared of all the divils in hell."

"Throth, but it's worth havin', Nancy : where did you get
it ?" asked M'Kinley.

" Hould your wicked tongue, you thief of a heretic," said
Nancy, laughing, "when will *you* larn anything that's good ?
I got it from one that wouldn't have it if it *wasn't* good—
Darby M'Murt, the pilgrim, since you must know."

"Whisht !" said Frayne : "upon my word, I blieve the
ould Square's comin' to pay us a visit ; does any of yees
hear a horse trottin' with a shoe loose ? "

"I sartinly hear it," observed Andy Morrow.

"And I," said Ned, himself.

There was now a general pause, and in the silence a horse,
proceeding from the moors in the direction of the house,
was distinctly heard ; and nothing could be less problematical than that one of his shoes was loose.

"Boys, take care of yourselves," said Shane Fadh ; "if
the Square comes, he won't be a pleasant customer—he was
a terrible fellow in his day : I'll hould goold to silver that
he'll have the smell of brimstone about him."

" Nancy, where's your prayer *now ?*" said M'Kinley with
a grin.   " I think you had better out with it, and thry if it

keeps this ould brimstone Square on the wrong side of the house."

"Behave yourself, Alick; it's a shame for you to be sich a hardened crathur: upon my sannies, I blieve you're afeard of neither God nor the divil—the Lord purtect and guard us from the dirty baste!"

"You mane particklarly them that uses short measures and light weights," rejoined M'Kinley.

There was another pause, for the horseman was within a few perches of the cross-roads. At this moment an unusual gust of wind, accompanied by torrents of rain, burst against the house with a violence that made its ribs creak; and the stranger's horse, the shoe still clanking, was distinctly heard to turn in from the road to Ned's door, where it stopped, and the next moment a loud knocking intimated the horse-man's intention to enter. The company now looked at each other, as if uncertain what to do. Nancy herself grew pale, and, in the agitation of the moment, forgot to think of her protecting prayer. Biddy and Bessy Connolly started from the *settle* on which they had been sitting with their sweethearts, and sprung beside their uncle on the hob. The stranger was still knocking with great violence, yet there was no disposition among the company to admit him, notwithstanding the severity of the night—blowing, as it really did, a perfect hurricane. At length a sheet of light-ning flashed through the house, followed by an amazing loud clap of thunder; while, with a sudden push from with-out, the door gave way, and in stalked a personage whose statue was at least six feet four, with dark eyes and com-plexion, and coal-black whiskers of an enormous size, the very image of the Squire they had been describing. He was dressed in a long black surtout, which made him appear even taller than he actually was, had a pair of heavy boots upon him, and carried a tremendous whip, large enough to fell an ox. He was in a rage on entering; and the heavy, dark, close-knit brows, from beneath which a pair of eyes, equally black, shot actual fire, and the Turk-like whiskers, which curled themselves up, as it were, in sympathy with his fury, joined to his towering height, gave him altogether, when we consider the frame of mind in which he found the company, an appalling and almost supernatural appearance.

"Confound you, for a knot of lazy scoundrels," exclaimed the stranger. "Why do you sit here so calmly, while any being craves admittance on such a night as this? Here, you lubber in the corner, with the pipe in your mouth, come and put up this horse of mine until the night settles."

"May the blessed Mother purtect us!" exclaimed Nancy, in a whisper to Andy Morrow, "if I blieve he's a right thing!—would it be the ould Square? Did you ever set your eyes upon sich a——"

"Will you bestir yourself, you boor, and not keep my horse and saddle out under such a torrent?" he cried, "otherwise I must only bring him into the house, and then you may say for once that you've had the devil under your roof."

"Paddy Smith, you lazy spalpeen," said Nancy, winking at Ned to have nothing to do with the horse, "why don't you fly and put up the gintleman's horse? And you, Atty, avourneen, jist go out with him, and hould the candle while he's doin' it: be quick now, and I'll give you glasses apiece when you come in."

"Let them put him up quickly; but I say, you Caliban," added the stranger, addressing Smith, "don't be rash about him, except you can bear fire and brimstone; get him, at all events, a good feed of oats. Poor Satan!" he continued, patting the horse's head, which was now within the door, "you have had a hard night of it, my poor Satan, as well as myself. That's my dark spirit—my brave chuck, that fears neither man nor devil."

This language was by no means calculated to allay the

suspicions of those who were present, particularly of Nancy and her two nieces. Ned sat in astonishment, with the pipe in his hand, which he had, in the surprise of the moment, taken from his mouth, his eyes fixed upon the stranger, and his mouth open. The latter noticed him, and, stretching over the heads of the circle, tapped him on the shoulder with his whip.

"I have a few words to say to you, sir," he said.

"To me, your honour!" exclaimed Ned, without stirring, however.

"Yes," replied the other, "but you seem to be fastened to your seat : come this way."

"By all manner of manes, sir," said Ned, starting up, and going over to the dresser, against which the stranger stood

When the latter had got him there, he very coolly walked up, and secured Ned's comfortable seat on the hob, at the same time observing :

"You hadn't the manners to ask me to sit down ; but I always make it a point of conscience to take care of myself, landlord."

There was not a man about the fire who did not stand up, as if struck with a sudden recollection, and offer him a seat.

"No," said he, "thank you, my good fellows, I am very well as it is : I suppose, mistress, you are the landlady," addressing Nancy ; "if you be, I'll thank you to bring me a gill of your best whisky—your *best*, mind. Let it be as strong as an evil spirit let loose, and as hot as fire ; for it can't be a jot too ardent such a night as this, for a being that rides the devil."

Nancy started up instinctively, exclaiming, "Indeed, plase your honour's reverence, I am the landlady, as you say, sir, sure enough ; but, the Lawk save and guard us ! won't a gallon of raw whisky be too much for one man to drink ?"

"A gallon! I only said a gill, my good hostess; bring me a gill;—but I forget—I believe you have no such measure in this country; bring me a pint, then."

Nancy now went into the bar, whither she gave Ned a wink to follow her; and truly was glad of an opportunity of escaping from the presence of the visitor. When there, she ejaculated,

"May the holy Mother keep and guard us, Ned, but I'm afeard that's no Christian crathur, at all at all! Arrah, Ned, aroon, would he be that ould Square Grame, that Shane Fadh maybe, angered, by spakin' of him?"

"Troth," said Ned, "myself doesn't know what he is; he bates any mortal *I* ever seen."

"Well, hould, agra! I have it: we'll see whether he'll drink this or not, any how."

"Why, what's that you're doin'?" asked Ned.

"Jist," replied Nancy, "mixin' the smallest taste in the world of holy wather with the whisky, and if he drinks *that*, you know he can be nothing that's bad."

Nancy, however, did not perceive that the trepidation of her hand was such as to incapacitate her from making nice distinctions in the admixture. She now brought the spirits to the stranger, who no sooner took a mouthful of it than he immediately stopped it on its passage, and, fixing his eyes earnestly on Nancy, squirted it into the fire, and the next moment the whisky was in a blaze that seemed likely to set the chimney in flames.

"Why, my *honest* hostess," he exclaimed, "do you give this to me for whisky? Confound me, but two-thirds of it is water; and I have no notion to pay for water when I want spirits: have the goodness to exchange this, and get me some better stuff, if you have it."

He again put the jug to his mouth, and having taken a little, swallowed it: "Why, I tell you, woman, you must have made some mistake; one-half of it is water."

Now, Nancy, from the moment he refused to swallow the liquor, had been lock-jawed; the fact was she thought that the devil himself, or old Squire Graham, had got under her roof; and she stood behind Ned, who was nearly as terrified as herself, with her hands raised, her tongue clinging to the roof of her mouth, and the perspiration falling from her pale face in large drops. But as soon as she saw him swallow a portion of that liquid, which she deemed beyond the deglutition of ghost or devil, she instantly revived—her tongue resumed its accustomed office—her courage, as well as her good-humour, returned, and she went up to him with great confidence, saying:

" Why, then, your reverence's honour, maybe I did make a bit of a mistake, sir," taking up the jug, and tasting its contents. " Hut! bad scran to me, but I did, beggin' your honour's pardon; how-an-diver, I'll soon rightify that, your reverence."

So saying, she went and brought him a pint of the stoutest the house afforded. The stranger drank a glass of it, and then ordered hot water and sugar, adding:

" My honest friends here about the fire will have no objection to help me with this; but, on second consideration, you had better get us another quart, that, as the night is cold, we may have a jorum at this pleasant fire that will do our hearts good; and this pretty girl here," addressing Biddy, who really deserved the epithet, " will sit beside me, and give us a song."

It was surprising what an effect the punch, even in perspective, had upon the visual organs of the company; second sight was rather its precursor than its attendant; for, with intuitive penetration, they now discovered various good qualities in his ghostship that had hitherto been beyond their ken; and those very personal properties which before struck them dumb with terror already called forth their applause.

"What a fine man he is!" one would whisper, loud enough, however, to be heard by the object of his panegyric.

" He is, indeed, and a rale gintleman," another would respond, in the same key.

"Hut! he's none of your proud, stingy, upsthart *bodaghs* —none of your beggarly half-sirs," a third would remark; " he's the dacent thing entirely—you see he hasn't his heart in a thrifle."

When the punch was made, and the kitchen-table placed endwise towards the fire, the stranger, finding himself very comfortable, inquired if he could be accommodated with a bed and supper, to which Nancy replied in the affirmative.

Shane Fadh now took courage to repeat the story of old Squire Graham and his horse with the loose shoe, informing the stranger, at the same time, of the singular likeness which he bore to the subject of the story, both in face and size, and dwelling upon the remarkable coincidence in the time and manner of his approach.

"Tut, man!" said the stranger, " a far more extraordinary adventure happened to one of my father's tenants, which, if none of you have any objection, I will relate."

There was a buzz of approbation at this; and they all thanked his honour, expressing the strongest desire to hear his story. He was just proceeding to gratify them, when another rap came to the door, and, before any of the inmates had time to open it, Father Neddy Deleery and his curate made their appearance, having been on their way home from a conference held in the town of M——, eighteen miles from the scene of our present story.

" There, Pether," said Father Ned, as he entered, " hook my bridle along with your own, as your hand is in.—God save all here! Paddy Smith, ma bouchal, put these horses in the stable, till we dry ourselves a bit—Father Pether and I."

"Musha, but you're both welcome," said Nancy, wishing to wipe out the effects of the last tift with Father Neddy, by the assistance of the stranger's punch : " will ye bounce, ye spalpeens, and let them to the fire. Father Neddy, you're dhreepin' with the rain ; and, Father Pether, avourneen, you're wet to the skin, too."

"Troth, and he is, Nancy, and a little bit farther, if you knew but all—four tumblers, Ned—deuce a *spudh** less. Mr. Morrow, how do you do, sir ?—And—eh ?—Who's this we've got in the corner? A gintleman, boys, if cloth can make one ! Mr. Morrow, introduce me."

"Indeed, Father Ned, I haven't the pleasure of knowin' the gintleman myself."

"Well, no matter—come up, Pether. Sir, I have the honour of introducing you to my curate and coadjuthor, the Reverend Pether M'Clatchaghan, and to myself, his excellent friend, but spiritual superior, the Reverend Ned—hem !—the Reverend *Edward* Deleery, Roman Catholic rector of this highly respectable and extensive parish ; and I have further the pleasure," he continued, taking up Andy Morrow's punch, " of drinking your very good health, sir."

"And I have the honour," returned the stranger, rising up, and driving his head among the flitches of bacon that hung in the chimney, " of introducing you and the Rev. M'—M'—M'—"

"—Clatchaghan, sir," subjoined Father Ned.

"Peter M'Illclatchaghan, to Mr. Longinus Polysyllabus Alexandrinus."

"My word, sir, but it's a good and appropriate name, sure enough," said Father Ned, surveying his enormous length : " success to me, but you're an Alexandrine from head to foot—*non solum Longinus, sed Alexandrinus.*"

"You're wrong, sir, in the Latin," said Father Peter.

" Prove it, Pether—prove it."

* Drop—the least quantity.

"It should be *non tantum*, sir."

"By what rule, Pether?"

"Why, sir, there's a phrase in Corderius's Colloquies that I could condimn you from, if I had the book."

"Pether, you think you're a scholar, and to do you justice, you're cute enough sometimes; but, Pether, you didn't travel for it, as I did—nor were you obliged to leap out of a college windy in Paris, at the time of the French Revolution, for your larning, as I was: not you, man, you ate the king's mutton comfortably at home in Maynooth, instead of travelling for it, like your betters."

"I'll appale to this gintleman," said Father Peter, turning to the stranger. "Are you a classical scholar, sir—that is, do you understand Latin?"

"What kind?" demanded the stranger, dryly.

"If you have read Corderius's Colloquies, it will do," said Father Peter.

"No, sir," replied the other, "but I have read his commentator, *Bardolphus*, who wrote a treatise upon the *Ogalvus* of the ancients."

"Well, sir, if you did, it's probable that you may be able to understand our dispute, so—"

"Pether, I'm afeard you've gotten into the wrong box; for I say he's no chicken that read *Bardolphus*, I can tell you that; I had my own trouble with him: but, at any rate, will you take your punch, man alive, and don't bother us with your Latin."

"I beg your pardon, Father Ned: I insist that I'm right; and I'll convince you that you're wrong, if God spares me to see Corderius to-morrow."

"Very well then, Pether, if you're to decide it to-morrow, let us have no more of it to-night."

During this conversation between the two reverend worthies, the group around the fire were utterly astonished at the erudition displayed in this learned dispute.

"Well, to be sure, larnin's a great thing entirely," said M'Roarkin, aside, to Shane Fadh.

"Ah, Tom, there's nothing like it: well, any way, it's wondherful what *they* know!"

"Indeed it is, Shane—and in so short a time, to! Sure it's not more nor five or six years since Father Pether there used to be digging praties on the one ridge with myself— by the same token, an excellent *spadesman* he was—and now he knows more nor all the Protestant parsons in the Diocy."

"Why, how could *they* know anything, when they don't belong to the thrue church?" said Shane.

"Thrue for you, Shane," replied M'Roarkin; "I dis-remimbered that clincher."

This discourse ran parallel with the dispute between the two priests, but in so low a tone as not to reach the ear of the *classical* champions, who would have ill brooked this eulogium upon Father Peter's agricultural talent.

"Don't bother us, Pether, with your arguing, to-night," said Father Neddy, "it's enough for you to be seven days in the week at your disputation.—Sir, I drink to our better acquaintance."

"With all my heart, sir," replied the stranger.

"Father Ned," said Nancy, "the gintleman was going to tell us a sthrange story, sir, and maybe your reverence would wish to hear it, Docthor."

"Certainly, Nancy, we'll be very happy to hear any story the gintleman may plase to tell us; but, Nancy, achora, before he begins, what if you'd just fry a slice or two of that glorious flitch, hanging over his head, in the corner?— that, and about six eggs, Nancy, and you'll have the priest's blessing, *gratis*."

"Why, Father Ned, it's too fresh, entirely—sure it's not a week hanging yet."

"Sorra matter, Nancy dheelish, we'll take with all that— just try your hand at a slice of it. I rode eighteen miles,

and took four tumblers since I dined, and I feel a craving,
Nancy, a *whacuum* in my stomach, that's rather troublesome."

"To be sure, Father Ned, you must get a slice, with all
the veins of my heart ; but I thought maybe you wouldn't
like it *so fresh :* but what on earth will we do for eggs, for
there's not an egg undher the roof with me."

"Biddy, a hagur," said Father Ned, "just slip out to
Molshey Johnston, and tell her to send me six eggs for a
rasher, by the same token that I heard two or three hens
cackling in the byre, as I was going to Conference this
morning."

"Well, Docthor," said Pat Frayne, when Biddy had been
gone some time, on which embassy she delayed longer than
the priest's judgment, influenced by the cravings of his
stomach, calculated to be necessary—"Well, Docthor, I
often pity you for fasting so long; I'm sure, I dunna how
you can stand it at all, at all."

"Troth, and you may well wonder, Pat ; but we have
that to support us, that you, or anyone like you, know
nothing about—*inward* support, Pat—inward support."

"Only for that, Father Ned," said Shane Fadh, "I suppose you could never get through with it."

"Very right, Shane—very right : only for it, we never
could do.—What the dickens is keeping this girl with the
eggs?—why, she might be at Mr. Morrow's, here, since.
By the way, Mr. Morrow, you must come over to our
church ; you're a good neighbour, and a worthy fellow, and
it's a thousand pities you should be damned."

"Why, Docthor," said Andy, "do you really believe I'll
be damned?"

"Ah, Mr. Morrow, don't ask me that question—out of
the pale, you know—out of the pale."

"Then you think, sir, there's no chance for me, at all,"
said Andy, smiling.

"Not the laste, Andy; you must go this way," said Father Ned, striking the floor with the butt end of his whip, "to the lower regions; and, upon my knowledge, to tell you the truth, I'm sorry for it, for you're a worthy fellow."

"Ah, Docthor," said Ned, "it's a great thing entirely to be born in the true church—one's always sure, then."

"Ay, ay; you may say that, Ned," returned the priest; "come or go what will, a man's always safe at the long run, except he dies without his clargy.—Shane, hand me the jug, if you please.—Where did you get this stuff, Nancy?—faith, it's excellent."

"You forget, Father Ned, that that's a sacret.—But here's Biddy with the eggs, and now you'll have your rasher in no time."

During this conversation, Father Peter, turning to Alick M'Kinley, said, "Alick, isn't your eldest son at the Latin?"

"He is, sir," said Alick.

"How long is he at it, Alick?"

"About six months, sir."

"And do you know what book he's reading?"

"Not a one of myself knows," said Alick, "but I know he has a great batch of them."

"You couldn't tell me if he has got a Cordery?"

"He has, sir," said Alick, "a jacket and trousers of it.'

"Of what?" said the curate, looking at him with surprise.

"Of corduroy," said the other.

"Oh, I mean a book!" said Father Peter.

"Consumin' to the know I know what's the name of one of them," replied Alick.

"I wish to heavens I had one, till I'd confute that man!" said Father Peter, looking with a most mortified visage into the fire.

When the two clergymen had discussed the rashers and

eggs, and while the happy group were making themselves
intimately acquainted with a fresh jug of punch, as it circu-
lated round the table :

"Now, sir," said Father Ned to the stranger, "we'll hear
your story with the greatest satisfaction possible ; but I
think you might charge your tumbler before you set to it."

When the stranger had complied with this last hint :
"Well, gentlemen," said he, "as I am rather fatigued, will
you excuse me for the position I am about to occupy
which is simply to stretch myself along the hob here, with
my head upon this straw hassock ; and if you have no objection to that, I will relate the story."

To this, of course, a general assent was given.   When he
was stretched completely at his ease—

"Well, upon my veracity," observed Father Peter, "the
gentleman's supernaturally long."

"Yes, Pether," replied Father Neddy, "but observe his
position—*Polysyllaba cuncta supina*, as Prosody says.—
Arrah, salvation to me, but you're dull, man, afther all !—
but we're interrupting the gentleman.   Sir, go on, if you
plase, with your story."

"Give me a few minutes," said he, "until I recollect the
particulars."

He accordingly continued quiescent for two or three
minutes more, apparently arranging the materials of his
intended narration, and then commenced to gratify the
eager expectations of his auditory—by emitting those nasal
enunciations which are the usual accompaniments of sleep !

"Why, bad luck to the morsel of 'im but's asleep," said
Ned ; "Lord pardon me for swearin' in your reverence's
presence."

"That's certainly the language of a sleeping man," replied
Father Neddy ; "but there might have been a little more
respect than all that snoring comes to.   Your health,
boys ! "

The stranger had now wound up his nasal organ to a high pitch, after which he commenced again with somewhat of a lower and finer tone.

"He's beginning a new paragraph," observed Father Peter, with a smile at the joke.

"Not at all," said Father Neddy, "he's turning the tune; don't you perceive he's snoring, 'God save the King,' in the key of *bass relievo.*"

"I'm no judge of instrumental music, as you are," said the curate, "but I think it's liker the ' Dead March of Saul ' than 'God save the King;' however, if you be right, the gentleman certainly snores in a truly loyal strain."

"That," said little M'Roarkin, "is liker the swine's melody, or the Bedfordshire hornpipe—he—he—he !"

"The poor gintleman's tired," observed Nancy, "after a hard day's thravelling."

"I daresay he is," said Father Ned, in the sincere hospitality of his country; "at all events take care of him, Nancy, he's a stranger, and get the best supper you can for him—he appears to be a truly respectable and well-bred man."

"I think," said M'Kinley, with a comical grin, "you might know that by his high-flown manner of sleeping—he snores very politely, and like a gintleman, all out."

"Well done, Alick," said the priest, laughing; "go home, boys, it's near bedtime; Paddy, ma bouchal, are the horses ready ?"

"They'll be at the door in a jiffey, your reverence," said Paddy, going out.

THE IRISH STUDENT;

OR,

How the Protestant Church was Invented by Luther and the Devil.

YOUNG Denis O'Shaughnessy was old Denis's son; and old Denis, like many great men before him, was the son of his father and mother in particular, and of a long line of respectable ancestors in general. He was, moreover, a great historian, a perplexing controversialist, deeply read in Dr. Gallagher and Pastorini, and equally profound in the history of Harry the eighth, and Luther's partnership with the devil, at that particular period when they invented the Protestant Church between them, and gave the Popeship of it to Her Holiness, Queen Elizabeth.

When young Denis had reached the age of sixteen or seventeen, he was looked upon by his father and his family, as well as by all their relations in general, as a prodigy. It was amusing to witness the delight with which the worthy man would call upon his son to exhibit his talents, a call to which the son instantly attended. This was usually done by commencing a mock controversy for the gratification of some neighbour to whom the father was anxious to prove the great talents of his son. When old Denis got the young *sogarth* fairly in motion, he gently drew himself out of the dispute, but continued a running comment upon the son's erudition, pointed out his good things, and occasionally resumed the posture of a controversialist, to reinspirit the boy if he appeared to flag.

" Dinny, abouchal, will you come up till Phadrick Murray hears you arguin' Scripther wid myself, Dinny. Now, Phadrick, listen, but keep your tongue sayin' nothin'; jist lave us to ourselves. Come up, Dinny, till you have a hate at arguin' wid myself."

"Fadher, I condimnate you at once—I condimnate you as being a most ungrammatical ould man, an' not fit to argue wid anyone that knows Murray's English Grammar, an' more espaciously the three concords of Lilly's Latin one; that is the cognation between the nominative case and the verb, the consanguinity between the substantive and the adjective, and the blood relationship that irritates between the relative and the antecedent."

"I tould you, Phadrick! There's the boy that can rattle off the high English, and the larned Latin, jist as if he was born wid an English Dictionary in one cheek, a Latin Neksuggawn in the other, an' Doctor Gallagher's Irish Sarmons nately on the top of his tongue between the two."

"Fadher, but that unfortunately I am afflicted wid modesty, I'd blush *crocus* for your ignorance, as Virgil asserts in his Bucolics, *ut Virgilius ait in Bucolicis;* and as Horatius, a book that I'm well acquainted wid, says in another place, '*Huc pertinent verba,*' says he, '*commodandi, comparandi, dandi, promittendi, solvendi imperandi nuntiandi, fidendi, obsequendi, minandi, irascendi, et iis contraria.*'"

"That's a good boy, Dinny; but why would you blush for *my* ignorance, avourneen? Take care of yourself now, an' spake deep, for I'll out argue you at the heel o' the hunt, cute as you are."

"Why do I blush for your ignorance, is it? why, thin I'm sure I have sound rasons for it: only think of the gross persivarance wid which you call that larned work, the Lexicon in Greek, a Necksuggan. Fadher, never attimpt to argue or display your ignorance wid me again. But, moreover, I can probate you to be an ungrammatical man, from your own *modus* of argument."

"Go on, avourneen. Phadrick!"

"I'm listenin'. The sorra's no match for his cuteness, an' one's puzzled to think where he can get it all."

" Why, you don't know at all what I could do by larnin'.
It would be no throuble to me to divide myself into two
halves, an' argue the one agin the other."

" You would, in throth, Dinny."

" Ay, father, or cut myself acrass, an' dispute my head,
maybe, agin my heels."

" Throth would you ! "

" Or practise logic wid my right hand, and bate that agin
wid my left."

" The sarra lie in it."

" Or read the Greek Tistament wid my right eye, an'
thranslate it at the same time wid my left, according to the
Greek an' English sides of my face, wid my tongue
constrein' into Irish, unknownst to both o' them."

" Why, Dennis, he must have a head like a bell to be
able to get into things."

" Throth an' he has that, an' 'ill make a noise in
conthroversy yet, if he lives. Now, Dinny, let us have a
hate at histhory."

" A hate at histhory ?—wid all my heart ; but before we
begin, I tell you that I'll confound you precipitately ; for
you see, if you bate me in the English, I'll scarify you wid
Latin, and give you a bang or two of Greek into the
bargain. Och ! I wish you'd hear the sackin' I gave Tom
Reilly the other day ; rubbed him down, as the masther
says, wid a Greek towel, an' whenever I complimented him
with the loan of a cut on the head, I always gave him a
plaster of Latin to heal it ; but the sorra worse healin'
flesh in the world than Tom's is for the Latin, so I bruised
a few Greek roots and laid them to his *caput* so nate that
you'd laugh to see him. Well, is it histhory we are to
begin wid ? If it is, come on—advance. I'm ready for you
—in protection—wid my guards up."

" Ha, ha, ha ! Well, if he isn't the drollest crathur, an'
so cute ! But now for the *histhory*. Can you prove to me,

upon a clear foundation, the differ atween black an' white, or prove that Phadrick Murray here, long life to him, is n ass? Now, Phadrick, listen, for you must decide betune us.'

"Orra, have you no other larnin' than that to argue upon? Sure if you call upon me to decide, I must give it agin Dinny. Why, my judgment won't be worth a haporth if he makes an ass of me!"

"What matter how you decide, man alive, if he proves you to be one; sure that's all we want. Never heed shakin' your head—listen an' it will be well worth your while. Why, man, you'll know more nor you ever knew or suspected before, when he proves you to be an ass."

"In the first place, fadher, you're ungrammatical in one word; instead of sayin' 'prove,' always say probate or probe; the word is descinded, that is, the ancisthor of it is *probo*, a deep Greek word—*probo, probas, prob-ass*—that is to say, I'm to *probe* Phadrick here to be an *ass*. Now, do you see how pat I brought that in? That's the way, Phadrick, I chastise my fadher with the languages."

"In thorth it is; go an, avick. Phadrick!"

"I'm listenin'."

"Phadrick, do you know the differ atween black an' white?"

"Atween black an' white? Hut, gorsoon, to be sure I do."

"Well, an' what might it be, Phadrick, my larned Athiop? What might it be, I negotiate?"

"Why, thin, the differ atween them is this, Dinny, that black is—let me see—why—that black is *not* red—nor yallow—nor brown—nor green—nor purple—nor cutbeard —nor a heather colour—nor a grogram——"

"Nor a white?"

"Surely, Dinny, not a white, abouchal; don't think to come over me that way."

"But I want to know what colour it *is*, most larned sager."

"All rasonable, Dinny. Why, thin, black is—let me see—but, death alive!—it's—a—a—why, it's black, an' that's all I can say about it ; yes, faix, I can—black is the colour of Father Curtis's coat."

"An' what colour is that, Phadrick ? "

"Why, it's black to be sure."

"Well, now, what colour is white, Phadrick ? "

"Why, it's a snow-colour ; for all the world the colour of snow."

"White is ? "

"Ay, is it."

"The dear help your head, Phadrick, if that's all you know about snow. In England, man, snow is an Oxford grey, an' in Scotland a pepper an' salt, an' sometimes a cutbeard, when they get a hard winther. I found that much in the Greek, anyway, Phadrick. Thry agin, you imigrant, I'll give you another chance—what colour is white ? "

"Why, thin, it's—white—an' nothin' else. The sorra one but you'd puzzle a saint wid your long-headed screwtations from books."

"So, Phadrick, your preamble is that white is white, and black is black."

"Asy, avick. I said, sure enough, that white is white ; but the black I deny—I said it was the colour of Father Curtis's black coat."

"Oh, you barbarian of the world, how I scorn your pro-fundity an' emotions ! You're a disgrace to the human sex by your superciliousness of knowledge, an' your various quotations of ignorance. *Ignorantia*, Phadrick, is your date an' superscription. Now, stretch out your ears, till I probate, or probe to you the differ atween black an' white."

"Phadrick ! !" said the father.

"I'm listenin'."

"Now, Phadrick, here's the griddle, an' here's a clane plate. Do you see them here beside one another?"

"I'm lookin' at them."

"Now shut your eyes."

"Is that *your* way, Denis, of judgin' colours?"

"Shut your eyes, I say, till I give you *ocular* demonstration of the differ atween these two respectable colours."

"Well, they're shut."

"An' keep them so. Now, what differ do you *see* atween them?"

"The sorra taste, man alive; I never *seen* anything in my whole life so clearly of a colour as they are both this minute."

"Don't you see now, Phadrick, that there's not the smallest taste o' differ in them, an' that's accordin' to Euclid."

"Sure enough, Phadrick, that's the point settled. There's no discrimination at all atween black an' white. They're both of the same colour—so long as you keep your eyes shut."

"But if a man happens to open his eyes, Dinny?"

"He has no *right* to open them, Phadrick, if he wants to prove the truth of a thing. I should have said *probe*—but it does not significate."

"The heavens mark you to grace, Dinny. You did that in brave style. Phadrick, ahagur, he'll make the darlin' of an arguer when he gets the robes an him."

"I don't deny that; he'll be aquil to the best o' thim: still, Denis, I'd rather, whin I want to pronounce upon colours, that he'd let me keep my eyes open."

"Ay, but he did it out o' the books, man alive; and there's no goin' beyant thim. Sure he could prove it out o' the Divinity, if you went to that. An' what is still more, he could, by shuttin' your eyes, in the same way prove black to be white, an' white black, jist as asy."

"Surely myself doesn't doubt it. I suppose, by shutting my eyes, the same lad could prove anything to me."

" But, Dinny, avourneen, you didn't prove Phadrick to be
an ass yit.   Will you do that by histhory, too, Dinny, or
by the norrations of Illocution ? "

" Father, I'm surprised at your gross imperception.
Why, man, if you were not a *rara avis* of somnolency, a
man of most frolicsome determinations, you'd be able to see
that I've proved Phadrick to be an ass already."

" Throth, I deny that you did ; there wasn't a word about
my bein' an ass in the last discoorse.   It was all upon the
differ atween black an' white."

" Oh, how I scorn your gravity, man !   *Ignorantia*, as I
said, is your date an' superscription : an' when you die you
ought to go an' engage a stone-cutter to carve you a head-
stone, an' make him write on it, *Hic jacet Ignorantius
Redivivus.*   An' the translation of that is, accordin'
Publius Virgilius Maro—'Here lies a quadruped who
didn't know the differ atween black an' white.'"

" But, Dinny, won't you give us the histhory of how the
Protestant Church was invinted by the divil an' Luther,
backed by Harry the Aighth, while he was a Protestant ?
Give it to Phadrick, Dinny, till he hears it."

" Yes, my worthy *paterfamilias*, it shall be done ; but
upon the hypothesis of your taciturnity.   *Experientia docet*
—which is, on bein' rendered into vernacularity, ' You are
too much addicted to intherruption, an' throw the darkness
of your intellect over the splendour of my narrations.' "

" But afore you go on, Dinny, will you thranslate *doshet*
for Phadrick ? "

" Fadher, I'll tolerate incongruity in no man.   If you
must become jocular, why go an' larn Latin an' Greek to
substantiate your jocularity.   Become erudite for yourself,
an' tell the story to your friends ; but I vow to Demos-
thenes, if you provoke me I'll unsluice the floodgates of my
classicality, an' bear you off like a sthraw on the surface of
my larned indignation."

" Well, I won't, Dinny ; I won't, avick. I'll say nothin'
barrin' listen. Phadrick, isn't that the larnin' ? "

" Bedad, it couldn't be bate."

" Well ! is it the history of the confab atween Luther
an' the invintor o' the long-tailed heresy I'm to give you ? "

" But why was it long-tailed, Dinny ? Tell that to
Phadrick."

" Fadher, I tould you before that I'll not tolerate incongruity in any man who is ignorant of the classics. Was it
not that Phadrick Murray's ignorance protects you, I'd take
the liberty of lettin' you contemplate your own im-
penetrability to admonition. I call the Protestant heresy
long-tailed for three reasons : first—*id est—primo*——"

" Phadrick ! ! ! "

" I'm list'nin' ! "

"*Primo*—Because it was not short. *Secundo*—Because
the dragon that invinted it in the Revelations had a tail
that reached over the third part of heaven. *Tertio*—Because the divil, who was joint partner wid the dragon, never
goes widout a switcher ; so that it is from the purest of
logic, I call it the long-tailed heresy. Are you now
satisfied ? "

" Throth, we are, avick. Isn't that the larnin',
Phadrick ? "

" Bedad, he's as ould as Killileagh bog, all but one bank."

" Well ! *Quid multis ?* Luther was sittin' one evenin'
in his *studium* or study, afther havin' secured a profound
dinner ; one foot was upon the hob, an' the other in the
most convanient place, of coorse. One elbow was placed
upon a round black table, near a decanther of wine an' a
bottle of Ennishowen whisky. I will not purtind to say
which he was most in the habit of drinkin', lest I might
glide into veracity. Ovid says, in his metamorphoses, that
tradition is in favour of the whisky. His words are—
'*Lutherus semper potavit merum Ennishonum*,' which has

puzzled the commentators very much. St. Augustin, who
was a good judge, thinks that ' merum Ennishonum ' means
the ' pure native,' which, he says, is jolly drink. Paul the
Hermit, an' St. Anthony, on the other hand, say that
' merum Ennishonum ' is incorrect ; for that had he stuck,
as they did, to ' merum Ennishonum,' he would never have
left the Church. Others read ' clarum Ennishonum ;' however, it does not significate. There he sat, as I have
chalked him out for you, in a state of relaxation, frolicsome
an' solitary, wid his countenance placid an' bloomin', his
rosy, semidemi-quaver dewlap dependin' from his chin, just
ripe for meditation an' a tumbler.

" ' Now, Luther, you sinner,' says he, lookin' over at his
own shadow upon the wall beyant—' Luther,' says he, ' here
you sit, wid a good coat to your back, good shoes to your
feet, good Connemara stockins to your legs, and excellent
linen undher your penitential hair-cloth shirt. What more
do you want, you knave, you ? ' says he, continuin' to hould
a logical controversy wid himself. ' I say, you born
desaver,' says he, ' what is it you would be at ? Maybe
it's a fat mithre you'd be smellin' afther? But I doubt,'
says he, ' that an ecclesiastical union between your
head an' a mithre was never intinded to be *in rerum
natura.*'"

" Phadrick ! ! ! "

" I'm list'nin' ! "

" ' What would you be at then ? ' says he, carryin' on the
controversy ; ' haven't you enough o' the world ? Haven't
you ase an' indepindence, an' susceptibility, an' tergiversation, not to mintion that a fast dinner wid you would make
a faste for a layman ! Go off wid you,' says he to a fly
that was leadin' a party of pleasure towards his nose, ' go
'long wid you, you sinner, an' don't be timptin' me ! The
fact or *factum* is, Luther,' says he——"

" Dinny, thranslate whack'dem for Phadrick."

"Fadher, you're incorrigible. Why, *factum's* a fact, an' so is what I'm relatin'. 'The fact or *factum* is, Luther,' says he, 'that you are anxious to thranslate some honest man's daughter into an *uxor* for yourself. You are,' says he, 'you born sconce; an' you're puzzlin' your *pineal gland* how to effectuate the *vinculum matrimonii*.' He was thinkin', too, at the time, of a small taste of a vow—*votum* it is in the larned languages—that he had to dispose of at first cost, because the shabby intintion was in him. But no matther: it was all the same to honest Luther in the Greek.

"'Hould up your anterior countenance,' says he, 'an' look yourself straight in the face widout blushin', if you can.'"

"What's the manin' of antlerian countenance,' Dinny?"

"It significs, fadher, that part of the human *caput* upon which the faces of most single-faced gintlemen are to be found."

"An' where do thim that have two faces keep the second, Dinny?"

"Did you never hear of the *facies Hypocritica*, an' the *facies atra*? The *facies Hypocritica* is worn over the *facies atra*, like a mask on a blackamoor. The former, fadher, is for the world in general, an' the latter for private use, when the wearer happens to practise a trifle in the reflectin' style. These belong to the double-faced gintlemen. There is a third, called the *facies candida*, which every fool an' knave can look through; but it's not worth washin'. I wouldn't give three sthraws for the *faices candida*. No, no; commend me to the other two."

"Sure they say, Dinny, two heads is betther than one; an' so, of coorse, is two faces."

"Right, fadher. *Saltem recte dixisti.* I'll practise wid both myself, plase the fates."

"Throth, you will, avick."

"'Well,' the Reformer proceeded, 'Luther, how are we to manage?　You're health! in the meantime,' says he, puttin' the dilution to his lips.　'Our best plan, at all evints, is to dhrink upon it.　It's a hard subject, an' requires to be softened by the moisture, so as to make it tractable.　The fact is,' he went on, 'that you're gettin' frolicsome on my hands—you are, you sinner; and have a tendency to make some honest man's daughter flesh of your flesh, an' bone of your bone, by effectin' the *vinculum.*　Isn't that the case, Luther?'

"'Faith, I bleeve so,' said he to himself; 'but I'd give a thrifle to know in what manner I could accomplish the union.　However, the fact cannot be denied that I'm runnin' fast into *uxoriety,* an' will marry, if the whole Christian world should become champions of abnegation.　There's nothin' like a plural life,' says Luther.　'I'll not only live in my own person, but by proxy, as the bishops an' cardinals go to heaven.'

"In this manner was Luther debatin' the subject wid himself, assisted by the dilution, when a grave-looking man, in the garbage of a monk, walked into him.　He had all the appearance of a steady, sober ecclesiastic; his countenance was what they call a slate-colour—'*vulius slate-colorius,*' as Jugurtha says when giving an account of the transaction to Cornelius Agrippa, the centurion.

"'*Salve Lutherum,*' says the *peregrinus;* which is, 'Good-morrow, Luther.'

"'*Tu sis salvus quoque,*' says Luther, back to him; which is, 'Good-morrow, an' good luck.'"

"Phadrick!!"

"I'm list'nin'."

"'Won't you take a sate, brother,' says Luther, 'an' be sated.'

"'Thank you kindly, brother,' replied the other.　They called each other brothers, because the stranger w⟨ ⟩dressed, as I said, in the garbage o' a monk, the vagrant. 'Thank you kindly,' says he ; 'an' if you'll allow me, I'll also take a tumbler of Ennishowen,' says he, 'bein' a little warm an' thirsty afther my walk.'

"'You're as welcome as the flowers o' May,' says Luther, 'to the best in my house. Katty, get another tumbler an' more hot wather, an' place a chair over there on the opposite side o' the table. I'm sorry, brother,' says he, 'that I haven't somethin' betther to offer you ; but the thruth is, this bein' a fast day wid me, I had only a cut o' salmon, an' two or three other things, more in the shape of a colla-tion than a dinner—not but that I came undher the excep-tion, an' might have ate meat ; for, indeed, I wasn't to say too well to-day. However, I always think it right to observe the rules o' the Church, an' to practise maccrosity an' timperance. Here's to our betther acquaint-ance !'

"'Thank you kindly, an' here's ditto,' says the other. 'I'm much of your way o' thinkin' myself,' says he, 'an' think it both clerical an' churchmanlike to mortify myself upon turbot, salmon, or any other miserable substitute for a dinner that smacks of penance : though, indeed, like yourself, I wasn't to say well to-day, bein' rather feverish, an' might have practised the exception too.'

"'In that case, then,' said Luther, 'I'll ordher down a couple of fat pullets an' a ham for supper. You know we're commanded to observe hospitality towards God's saints ; but in case you have a scruple about the exception, why I'll absolve you, an' you'll absolve me, so that, after all, it won't signify. The thing's as long as it's short,' says Luther. 'Shud orth !' says he, puttin' the dilution to his lips agin.

"'Here's to your best wishes !' says the other 'Yes, Luther,' says he, with a sigh of devotion : 'there's nothin' like humility an' carnation in a religious ministher. We

have weighty duties to perform, an' we ought to see that
the practise of self-denial is properly theorized in our own
persons, an' its theory reduced to practicality by the hardened laity, who would ate an' dhrink like ourselves, an' en-
croach upon our other privileges widout remorse, as if they
had a right to them. They would ate like bastes, an' dhrink
like fishes, Luther, if we allowed them,' says he. ' Here's to
you ! '

"' They would, the vulgarians,' says Luther. ' Katty,
more hot wather ; an', Katty, asthore, put down two of the
fattest of them crammed pullets, an' a ham, an' have them
ready for supper, an' fetch another bottle of Ennishowen ;
afther which, Katty, we'll give you a dispensation for absence
until supper time. Well but, my worthy,' says Luther,
  what's your opinion of clerical affairs in general ? Don't
you think they're in a bad state ? '

"' Not at all,' says the other. ' I think they're just as
they ought to be.'

"' I doubt that,' says Luther. ' The infarior clergy laid
under great restrictions, in quensequence of their poverty.
Look at the cardinals, an' bishops, an' rich abbots ! Why,
they've a monoply of all that the world's good for.'

"' Thrue,' said the *peregrinus*."

" Phadrick ! ! ! "

" I'm list'nin' ! "

"' Thrue,' says the *peregrinus*, ' an' my wish is to see that
broken down.'

"' An' so is mine,' says Luther. ' They won't allow us
infarior clargy to take wives to ourselves, though they're
not ashamed to carry comforters about their necks in the
open face of day. A poor clerical now can't afford to be
licentious, for want o' money.'

"' Thrue ; an' I would wish to see it made chape,' says
the other, ' if it was only to vex the wealthy.'

"' You know as well as I do,' says Luther, ' that profligacy at present is at an extravagant price. The rich can afford to buy themselves dispensations for a month's or three month's licentiousness, or from a year's to seven years' indulgence, or seven hundred years' for that matther, if they lay down the cash ; but wid us it's different : we can't afford to purchase the right to sin an' threspass, yet we won't be allowed to marry. Now, I'm determined to rescue the people an' the dhrudgin' clargy from this tyranny.'

" ' Then you'd wish to see the clargy married, an' dispensations taken away ? '

" ' To be sure I would ; an' an interesting sight it ud be, to see the rogues, every man wid a legal doxy undher his arm. I tell you, the *vinculum* must be effected.'

" ' I have no objection to the *vinculum*,' replied the *advena*, ' for it's all the same thing in the end. How do you think it could be brought about ? '

" Luther, who was meditatin' upon the subject in the time, didn't hear him.

" ' I'll hould you a gallon of Roscrea to a gallon of Ennishowen,' says the strange monk, ' that I could put you on a plan of havin' them married in scores—ay, in dhroves.'

" ' If you do,' says Luther, ' I'll say you're a cleverer man than I am.'

"'Do you know much about England?' says the sthranger.

" ' A thrifle,' says Luther.

" ' Well,' says the other, ' there's Harry the Aighth goin' to put away his wife, an' to take another in her place. Now's your time,' says he, ' strike while the iron's hot. He's at loggerheads wid the Pope an' the Church in gineral, an' will defend the right o' marrying to the last day of his life. Broach the subject now, Luther, an' he's the boy will support it.'

" ' Give me your hand,' says Luther : ' eh, St. Pether ! but your palm's burnin'.'

"'Not at all,' says the other, 'I'm naturally hot; besides, as I said a while ago, I'm a thrifle faverish. Will you take my hint?'

"'Would a cat take new milk?' says Luther.

"'Well then,' says the other, 'I'll give you some advice.'"

"But, Dinny," said the father, "wasn't all the two thieves said about the Church lies?"

"Every word of it a lie—as gross as Luther himself. There was no such thing as tyranny, or persecution, or overgrown wealth in the Church then, at all. No man ud be punished for not thinkin' or spakin' accordin' as the Church commanded. The clargy were as mild as lambs, an' didn't lord it over or trample upon the people, good or bad. If a washerwoman was to summon a bishop for his quarther's washin', he'd attend like any other man, an' pay down the money, if he had it, or if he hadn't, he'd give it to her at half a crown a week; so that Luther, the dirty vagrant, had no grounds for makin' such a schism in the Church as he did."

"Phadrick, there's the knowledge!"

"Bedad, it bangs!"

"The *advena* thin instructed Luther at a great rate, tellin' him how he'd get on wid his heresy, an' many other things o' that nature. Luther, however, began to feel unasy where he sat. He first put one finger to his nosthril, afther that his thumb to the other, lookin' arnestly at the monk all the time.

"'I beg your pardon,' says he, 'but maybe you'd take the other side o' the room; I think you'd find yourself more comfortable in it. There's a blast o' wind from your side,' says he, 'that's not pleasant, somehow.'

"'Oh, that ud be too much throuble,' says the other: 'I'm very well where I am.'

"'No throuble in life, to me,' says Luther, 'but the conthrary. I find that I'm no sich theologian as you are;

an' I think it but right that you should keep me at as respectful a distance as possible. I'll thank you to take the other side o' the room, I say; or indeed, for that matther, if you sat on the outside for some time, it ud be as well. A thrifle o' fresh air ud sarve us both.'

" ' Why, you're too delicate entirely,' said the stranger.

" ' Don't stand on ceremony wid me,' says Luther; ' you may go out like shot, an' I'll never say ill you did it. St. Pether, what's this at all ! '

" He then looked at the monk, an' saw a grim sneer upon his face : his eyes, too, began to blaze, an' a circle o' fire played round his head. Another peep undher the tabie showed Luther the cloven foot, an' a long tail coiled round the chair. Luther, however, was a hardened sinner that there was no puttin' fear into ; so he instantly whipped up the poker that had been stickin' between the bars, an of coorse, red hot ; an' the monk, seein' him about to commence the attack, took the liberty of rethratin' in double-quick time.

" ' Ha ! ' exclaimed Luther, ' there you go, you common vagabone ; but a sweet perfume do you lave behind you ! '

" Now, Phadrick, that's the way the Protestant Church was invinted by the devil an' Martin Luther. Harry the Aighth, an' his daughther Elizabeth, who was then Queen o' Scotland, both came in an' supported him aftherwards."

" Well, by the livin', Dinny, I dunna where you get all this deep readin' ! "

" Sure he gets it all in the Dixonary."

" Bedad, that Dixonary must be a fine book entirely, to thim that can undherstand it."

" But, Dinny, will you tell Phadrick the Case of Con-science atween Barny Branagan's two goats an' Parra Ghastha's mare ? "

" Fadher, if you were a grammarian I'd castigate your incompatibility as it desarves—I'd lay the scourge o' syntax upon you, as no man ever got it since the invintion o' the nine parts o' speech. By what rule of logic can you say that aither Barny Branagan's goats or Parra Ghastha's mare had a conscience? I tell you it wasn't they had the conscience, but the divine who decided the difficulty. Phadrick, lie down till I illusthrate."

"How is that, Dinny? I can hear you sittin'."

"Lie down, you reptile, or I shall decline the narration altogether."

"Arra, lie down, Phadrick; sure he only wants to show you the rason o' the thing."

"Well, well; I'm down. Now, Dinny, don't let your feet be too larned, if you plase."

"Silence!—taceto! you reptile. Now, Phadrick, here, on this side o' you, lies Barny Branagan's field; an' there, on that side, lies a field of Parra Ghastha's: you're the ditch o' mud betuxt them."

"The ditch o' mud! Faix, that's dacent!"

"Now here, on Barny Branagan's side, feeds Parra Ghastha's mare; an' there, on Parra Ghastha's side, feed Barny Branagan's goats. Do you comprehend? Do you insinuate?"

"I do—I do. Death alive! there's no use in punchin' my sides wid your feet that way."

"Well, get up now an' set your ears."

"Now listen to him, Phadrick!"

"It was one night in winter, when all nature shone in the nocturnal beauty of tenebrosity: the sun had set about three hours before; an', accordin' to the best logicians, there was a dearth of light. It's the general opinion of philosophers—that is, of the soundest o' them—that when the sun is down, the moon an' stars are usually up; an' so they were on the night that I'm narratin' about. The moon was, wid great respect to her character, night-walkin' in the sky; and the stars vegetated in celestial genuflexion around her. Nature, Phadrick, was in great state; the earth was undher our feet, an' the sky above us. The frost, too, was hard, Phadrick, the air keen, an' the grass tendher. All things were enrobed wid verisimilitude an' scrupulosity. In this manner was the terraqueous part of our system, when Parra Ghastha's mare, after havin' taken a could collation on Barny Branagan's grass, was returnin' to her master's side o' the merin; an' Barny Branagan's goats, havin' tasted the sweets of Parra Ghastha's cabbages, were on their way acrass the said merin to their own side. Now it so happened that they met exactly at a narrow gap in the ditch behind Rosha Halpin's house. The goats, bein' coupled together, got one on each side of the rift, wid the rope that coupled them extended acrass it. The mare stood in the middle of it, so that the goats were in the way of the mare, an' the mare in the way of the goats. In the meantime they surveyed one another wid great composure, but had neither of them the politeness to stir, until Rosha Halpin came suddenly out, an' emptied a vessel of untransparent wather into the ditch. The mare, who must have been an animal endowed wid great sensibility of soul, stooped her head suddenly at the noise; an' the goats, who were equally sentimental, gave a start from nervishness. The mare, on raisin' her head came in contact wid the cord that united the goats; an' the goats, havin' lost their commandin' position, came in contact wid the neck o' the mare. *Quid multis?* They pulled an' she pulled, an' she pulled an' they pulled, until at length the mare was compelled to practice the virtue of resignation in the ditch, wid the goats about her neck. She died by suspinsion; but the mettlesome ould crathur, wid a love of justice that did her honour, hanged the goats in requittal; for they departed this vale of tears on the mountain-side along wid her, so that they had the satisfaction of dyin' a social death together. Now, Phadrick, you quadruped, the case of conscience is, whether Parra Ghastha has a right to make restitution to Barny Branagan for the loss of his goats, or Barny Branagan to Parra Ghastha for the loss of his mare?"

"Bedad, that's a puzzler!"

"Isn't it, Phadrick? But wait till you hear how he'll clear it up! Do it for Phadrick, Dinny."

"Yis, Phadrick, I'll illusthrate your intellects by divinity. You see, Phadrick, you're to suppose me to be in the chair, as Confessor. Very well—or *valde*, in the larned languages —Parra Ghastha comes to confess to me, an' tells me that Barny Branagan wants to be paid for his goats. I tell him it's a disputed point, an' that the price o' the *goats* must go to the Church. On the other hand, Barny Branagan tells me that Parra Ghastha wishes to be paid for his mare. I say, again, it's a disputed point, an' that the price o' the *mare* must go to the Church—the amount of the proceeds to be applied in prayer towards the benefit of the parties in the first instance, an' of the faithful in general aftherwards."

"Phadrick!!!"

"Oh, that I may never, but he bates the globe!"

Denny's character is a very common one in the remote parts of Ireland, where knowledge is novelty, and where the slightest tinge of learning is looked upon with such reverence and admiration as can be properly understood only by those who have an opportunity of witnessing it. Indeed, few circumstances prove the great moral influence which the Irish priesthood possess over the common people more forcibly than the extraordinary respect paid by the latter to such as are designed for the "mission." The moment the determination is made, an incipient sanctity begins, as it were, to consecrate the young priest, and a high opinion of his learning and talents to be entertained, no matter how dull he may be, so far as honest nature is concerned.

END OF FIRST SERIES.

AMUSING IRISH TALES.

SECOND SERIES.

MICKEY M'ROREY,

The Country Fiddler.

IN my native parish there were four or five fiddlers—all good in their way; but the Paganini of the district was the far-famed Mickey M'Rorey. Where Mickey properly lived, I never could actually discover, and for the best reason in the world,—he was not at home once in twelve months. As Colley Cibber says in the play, he was "a kind of a here-and-thereian—a stranger nowhere." This, however, mattered little; for though perpetually shifting day after day from place to place, yet it somehow happened that nobody ever was at a loss where to find him. The truth is, he never felt disposed to travel *incog.*, because he knew that his interest must suffer by doing so; the consequence was, that wherever he went, a little nucleus of local fame always attended him, which rendered it an easy matter to find his whereabouts.

Mickey was blind from his infancy, and, as usual, owed to the small-pox the loss of his sight. He was about the middle size, of rather a slender make, and possessed an intelligent countenance, on which beamed that singular expression of inward serenity so peculiar to the blind. His temper was sweet and even, but capable of rising through the buoyancy of his own humour to a high pitch of exhilaration and enjoyment. The dress he wore, as far as I can remember, was always the same in colour and fabric —to wit, a brown coat, a sober-tinted cotton waistcoat, gray stockings, and black corduroys. Poor Mickey! I

think I see him before me, his head erect, as the heads of
all blind men are, the fiddle-case under his left arm, and
his hazel staff held out like a feeler, exploring with
experimental pokes the nature of the ground before him
even although some happy urchin leads him onward with
an exulting eye ; an honour of which he will boast to his
companions for many a mortal month to come.

The first time I ever heard Mickey play was also the first
I ever heard a fiddle. Well and distinctly do I remember
the occasion. The season was summer—but summer *was*
summer then—and a new house belonging to Frank Thomas
had been finished, and was just ready to receive him and
his family. The floors of Irish houses in the country,
generally consist at first of wet clay, and when this is
sufficiently well smoothed and hardened, a dance is known
to be an excellent thing to bind and prevent them from
cracking. On this occasion the evening had been appointed,
and the day was nearly half advanced, but no appearance
of the fiddler. The state of excitement in which I found
myself, could not be described. The name of Mickey
M'Rorey had been ringing in my ears for God knows how
long, but I had never seen him, or even heard his fiddle.
Every two minutes I was on the top of a little eminence
looking out for him, my eyes straining out of their sockets,
and my head dizzy with the prophetic expectation of
rapture and delight. Human patience, however, could
bear this painful suspense no longer, and I privately
resolved to find Mickey, or perish. I accordingly proceeded across the hills, a distance of about three miles, to a
place called Kilnahushogue, where I found him waiting for
a guide. At this time I could not have been more than
seven years of age ; and how I wrought out my way over
the lonely hills, or through what mysterious instinct I was
led to him, and that by a path, too, over which I had never
travelled before, must be left unrevealed until it shall please

that Power that guides the bee to its home, and the bird for thousands of miles through the air, to disclose the principle upon which it is accomplished.

On our return home I could see the young persons of both sexes flying out to the little eminence I spoke of, looking eagerly towards the spot we travelled from, and immediately scampering in again, clapping their hands and shouting with delight. Instantly the whole village was out, young and old, standing for a moment to satisfy themselves that the intelligence was correct; after which, about a dozen of the youngsters sprang forward, with the speed of so many antelopes, to meet us, whilst the elders returned with a soberer, but not less satisfied, manner into the houses. Then commenced the usual battle, as to whom should be honoured by permission to carry the fiddle-case. Oh! that fiddle-case! For seven long years it was an honour exclusively allowed to myself, whenever Mickey attended a dance anywhere near us; and never was the Lord Chancellor's mace—to which, by the way, with great respect for his Lordship, it bore a considerable resemblance —carried with a prouder heart or a more exulting eye. But so it is—

"These little things are great to *little men*."

"Blood alive, Mickey, you're welcome!"   "How is every bone of you, Mickey? Bedad we gev you up."   "No, we didn't give you up, Mickey; never heed him; sure we knew very well you'd not desart the Towny boys,—whoo!—Fol de rol lol!"   "Ah, Mickey, won't you sing 'There was a wee devil came over the wall?'"   "To be sure he will, but wait till he comes home and gets his dinner first. Is it off an empty stomach you'd have him to sing?"   "Mickey, give me the fiddle-case, won't you Mickey?"   "No, to *me*, Mickey."   "Never heed them, Mickey: you promised it to me at the dance in Carntaul."

"Aisy, boys, aisy.   The truth is, none of yez can get the fiddle-case.   Shibby, my fiddle, hasn't been well for the last day or two, and can't bear to be carried by any one barrin' myself."

"Blood alive ! sick is it, Mickey ?—an' what ails her ? "

"Why, some o' the doctors says there's a frog in her, an' others that she has got the cholic ; but I'm goin' to give her a dose of balgriffauns when I get up to the house above. Ould Harry Connolly says she's with-fiddle ; an' if that's true, boys, maybe some o' yez won't be in luck.   I'll be able to spare a young fiddle or two among yez."

Many a tiny hand was clapped, and many an eye was lit up with the hope of getting a young fiddle; for gospel itself was never looked upon to be more true than this assertion of Mickey's.   And no wonder.   The fact is, he used to amuse himself by making small fiddles of deal and horse-hair, which he carried about with him, as presents for such youngsters as he took a fancy to.   This he made a serious business of, and carried it on with an importance becoming the intimation just given.   Indeed, I remember the time when I watched one of them, which I was so happy as to receive from him, day and night, with the hope of being able to report that it was growing larger ; for my firm belief was, that in due time it would reach the usual size.

As we went along, Mickey, with his usual tact, got out of us all the information respecting the several courtships of the neighbourhood that had reached us, and as much, too, of the village gossip and scandal as we knew.

Nothing can exceed the overflowing kindness and affection with which the Irish fiddler is received on the occasion of a dance or merry-making ; and to do him justice he loses no opportunity of exaggerating his own importance. From habit, and his position among the people, his wit and power of repartee are necessarily cultivated and sharpened.

Not one of his jokes ever fails—a circumstance which improves his humour mightily ; for nothing on earth sustains it so much as knowing that, whether good or bad, it will be laughed at. Mickey, by the way, was a bachelor, and though blind, was able, as he himself used to say, to see through his ears better than another could through the eyes. He knew every voice at once, and every boy and girl in the parish by name, the moment he heard them speak.

On reaching the house he is bound for, he either partakes of, or at least is offered, refreshment, after which comes the ecstatic moment to the youngsters : but all this is done by due and solemn preparation. First he calls for a pair of scissors, with which he pares or seems to pare his nails, then asks for a piece of rosin, and in an instant half a dozen boys are off at a break-neck pace, to the next shoe-maker's, to procure it; whilst in the mean time he deliberately pulls a piece out of his pocket and rosins his bow. But, heavens! what a ceremony the opening of that fiddle-case is! The manipulation of the blind man as he runs his hand down to the key-hole—the turning of the key—the taking out of the fiddle—the twang twang—and then the first ecstatic sound, as the bow is drawn across the strings ; then comes a screwing, then a delicious saw or two ; again another screwing—twang twang—and away he goes with the favourite tune of the good woman, for such is the etiquette upon these occasions. The house is immediately thronged with the neighbours, and a preliminary dance is taken, in which the old folks, with good-humoured violence, are literally dragged out, and forced to join. Then come the congratulations—"Ah, Jack, you could do it wanst," says Mickey, "an' can still, you have a kick in you yet." "Why, Mickey, I seen dancin' in my time," the old man will reply, his brow relaxed by a remnant of his former pride, and the hilarity of the moment, "but you see

the breath isn't what it used to be wid me, when I could
dance the *Baltchorum Jig* on the bottom of a ten gallon
cask. But I think a glass o' whiskey will do us no harm
after that. Heighho!—well, well—I'm sure I thought *my*
dancin' days wor over."

"Bedad an' you wor matched any how," rejoined the
fiddler. "Molshy carried as light a heel as ever you did :
sorra woman of her years ever I seen could cut the buckle
wid her. You would know the tune on her feet still."

"Ah, Mickey, the truth is," the good woman would say,
"we have no sich dancin' now as there was in my days.
Thry that glass."

"But as good fiddlers, Molshy, eh ? Here's to you both,
and long may ye live to shake the toe ! Whoo ! bedad
that's great stuff. Come now sit down, Jack, till I give you
your ould favourite, '*Cannie Soogah.*'"

These were happy moments and happy times, which
might well be looked upon as picturing the simple manners
of country life with very little of moral shadow to obscure
the cheerfulness which lit up the Irish heart and hearth
into humble happiness. Mickey, with his usual good
nature, never forgot the younger portion of his audience.
After entertaining the old and full-grown, he would call for
a key, one end of which he placed in his mouth, in order to
make the fiddle sing for the children their favourite song,
beginning with

"Oh grand-mamma, will you squeeze my wig ?

This he did in such a manner, through the medium of the
key, that the words seemed to be spoken by the instrument, and not by himself. After this was over, he would
sing us, to his own accompaniment, another favourite,
"There was a wee devil looked over the wall," which
generally closed that portion of the entertainment, so
kindly designed for *us*.

Upon those moments I have often witnessed marks of deep and pious feeling, occasioned by some memory of the absent or the dead, that were as beautiful as they were affecting. If, for instance, a favourite son or daughter happened to be removed by death, the father or mother, remembering the air which was loved best by the departed, would pause a moment, and with a voice full of sorrow, say, " Mickey, there is *one tune* that I would like to hear ; I love to think of it, and to hear it ; I do, for the sake of them that's gone—my darlin' son that's lyin' low : it was he that loved it. His ear is closed against it now ; but for *his* sake —ay, for your sake avourneen machree—we will hear it once more."

Mickey always played such tunes in his best style, and amidst a silence that was only broken by sobs, suppressed moanings, and the other tokens of profound sorrow. These gushes, however, of natural feeling soon passed away. In a few minutes the smiles returned, the mirth broke out again, and the lively dance went on, as if their hearts had been incapable of such affection for the dead—affection at once so deep and tender, But many a time the light of cheerfulness plays along the stream of Irish feeling, when cherished sorrow lies removed from the human eye far down from the surface.

These preliminary amusements being now over, Mickey is conducted to the dance house, where he is carefully installed in the best chair, and immediately the dancing commences. It is not my purpose to describe an Irish dance here, having done it more than once elsewhere. It is enough to say that Mickey is now in his glory ; and proud may the young man be who fills the honourable post of his companion, and sits next him. He is a living store-house of intelligence, a travelling directory for the parish— the lover's text book—the young woman's best companion ; for where is the courtship going on of which he is not cognizant? where is there a marriage on the tapis, with the particulars of which he is not acquainted? He is an authority whom nobody would think of questioning. It is now, too, that he scatters his jokes about; and so correct and well trained is his ear, that he can frequently name the young man who dances, by the peculiarity of his step.

"Ah ha! Paddy Brien, you're there? Sure I'd know the sound of your smoothin'-irons any where. Is it thrue, Paddy, that you wor sint for down to Errigle Keerogue, to kill the clocks for Dan M'Mahon? But, nabuklish! Paddy, what'll you have?"

"Is that Grace Reilly on the flure? Faix, avourneen, you can do it; devil o' your likes I *see* any where. I'll lay Shibby to a penny trump that you could dance your own namesake—the *Caleen dhas dhun*, the bonny brown girl— upon a spider's cobweb, without brakin' it. Don't be in a hurry, Grace dear, to tie the knot; *I'll* wait for you."

Several times in the course of the night a plate is brought round, and a collection made for the fiddler: this was the moment when Mickey used to let the jokes fly in every direction. The timid he shamed into liberality, the vain he praised, and the niggardly he assailed by open hardy satire; all managed, however, with such an under-current of good humour that no one could take offence. No joke ever told better than that of the broken string. Whenever this happened at night, Mickey would call out to some soft fellow, "Blood alive, Ned Martin, will you bring me a candle? I've broken a string." The unthinking young man, forgetting that he was blind, would take the candle in a hurry, and fetch it to him.

"Faix, Ned, I knew you wor jist fit for't; houldin' a candle to a dark man! Isn't he a beauty, boys?—look at him, girls—as 'cute as a pancake."

It is unnecessary to say, that the mirth on such occasions was convulsive. Another similar joke was also played off by him against such as he knew to be ungenerous at the collection.

"Paddy Smith, I want a word wid you. I'm goin' across the counthry as far as Ned Donnelly's, and I want you to help me along the road, as the night is dark."

"To be sure, Mickey. I'll bring you over as snug as if you wor on a clean plate, man alive!"

"Thank you, Paddy; throth you've the dacency in you; an' kind father for you, Paddy. Maybe I'll do as much for you some other time."

Mickey never spoke of this until the trick was played off, after which, he published it to the whole parish; and Paddy of course was made the standing jest for being so silly as to think that night or day had any difference to a man who could not see.

Thus passed the life of Mickey M'Rorey, and thus pass the lives of most of his class, serenely and happily. As the sailor to his ship, the sportsman to his gun, so is the fiddler attached to his fiddle. His hopes and pleasures, though limited, are full. His heart is necessarily light, for he comes in contact with the best and brightest side of life and nature; and the consequence is, that their mild and mellow lights are reflected on and from himself. I am ignorant whether poor Mickey is dead or not; but I dare say he forgets the boy to whose young spirit he communicated so much delight, and who often danced with a buoyant and careless heart to the pleasant notes of his fiddle. Mickey M'Rorey, farewell! Whether living or dead, peace be with you.

ROSE MOAN,

The Country Mid-Wife.

THE village of Ballycomaisy was as pleasant a little place as one might wish to see of a summer day. To be sure, like all other Irish villages, it was remarkable for a super-fluity of "pigs, praties, and childre," which being the stock in trade of the Irish cabin, it is to be presumed that very few villages either in Ireland or elsewhere could go on properly without them. It consisted principally of one long street, which you entered from the north-west side by one of those old-fashioned bridges, the arches of which were much more akin to the Gothic than the Roman. Most of the houses were of mud, a few of stone, one or two of which had the honour of being slated on the front side of the roof, and rustically thatched on the back, where ostentation was not necessary. There were two or three shops, a liberal sprinkling of public houses, a chapel a little out of the town, and an old dilapidated market-house near the centre. A few little bye-streets projected in a lateral direction from the main one, which was terminated on the side opposite to the north-west by a pound, through which, as usual, ran a shallow stream, that was gathered into a little gutter as it crossed the road. A crazy antiquated mill, all covered and cobwebbed with grey mealy dust, stood about two hundred yards out of the town, to which two straggling rows of houses, that looked like an abortive street, led you. This mill was surrounded by a green common, which was again hemmed in by a fine river, that ran round in a curving line from under the hunchbacked arch of the bridge we mentioned at the beginning. Now, a little behind, or rather above this mill, on the skirt of the aforesaid common, stood a rather neat-looking, whitish cabin, with about half a rood of garden behind it. It was but small, and consisted merely of a sleeping-room and kitchen. On one side of the door was a window opening on hinges ; and on the outside, to the right as you entered the house, there was placed a large stone, about four feet high, backed by a sloping mound of earth, so graduated as to allow a person to ascend the stone, without any difficulty. In this cabin lived Rose Moan, the midwife ; and we need scarcely inform our readers that the stone in question was her mounting-stone, by which she was enabled to place herself on a pillion or crupper, as the case happened, when called out upon her usual avocation.

Rose was what might be called a *flahoolagh*, or portly woman, with a good-humoured set of Milesian features ; that is to say, a pair of red, broad cheeks, a well-set nose allowing for the disposition to turn up, and two black twinkling eyes, with a mellow expression that betokened good nature, and a peculiar description of knowing *professional* humour that is never to be met with in any *but* a midwife. Rose was dressed in a red flannel petticoat, a warm cotton sack or wrapper, which pinned easily over a large bust, and a comfortable woollen shawl. She always wore a long-bordered morning cap, over which, while travelling, she pinned a second shawl of Scotch plaid ; and to protect her from the cold night air, she enfolded her precious person in a deep blue cloak of the true indigo tint. On her head, over cloak and shawl and morning cap, was fixed a black "splush hat" with the leaf strapped down by her ears on each side, so that in point of fact she cared little how it blew, and never once dreamed that such a process as that of Raper or Mackintosh was necessary to keep the liege subjects of these realms warm and water-proof, nor that two systems should exist in Ireland so strongly antithetical to each other as those of Raper and Father Mathew.

Having thus given a brief sketch of her local habitation and personal appearance, we shall transfer our readers to the house of a young new-married farmer named Keho, who lived in a distant part of the parish. Keho was a comfortable fellow, full of good nature and credulity; but his wife happened to be one of the sharpest, meanest, most suspicious, and miserable devils that ever was raised in good-humoured Ireland. Her voice was as sharp and her heart as cold as an icicle; and as for her tongue, it was incessant and interminable. Were it not that her husband, who, though good-natured, was fiery and resolute when provoked, exercised a firm and salutary control over her, she would have starved both him and her servants into perfect skeletons. And what was still worse, with a temper that was vindictive and tyrannical, she affected to be religious, and upon those who did not know her, actually attempted to pass herself off as a saint.

One night, about ten or twelve months after his marriage, honest Corney Keho came out to the barn where slept his two farm servants, named Phil Hannigan and Barney Casey. He had been sitting by himself, composing his mind for a calm night's sleep, or probably for a curtain lecture, by taking a contemplative whiff of the pipe, when the servant wench, with a certain air of hurry, importance and authority, entered the kitchen and informed him that Rose Moan must immediately be sent for.

"The misthress isn't well, masther, an' the sooner she's sint for the betther. So mind my words, sir, if you plaise, an' pack aff either Phil or Barny for Rose Moan, an' I hope I wont have to ax it again—ahem!"

Dandy Keho—for so Corney was called as being remarkable for slovenliness—started up hastily, and having taken the pipe out of his mouth, was about to place it on the hob; but reflecting that the whiff could not much retard him in the delivery of his orders, he sallied out to the barn, and knocked,

" Who's there ? "

" Lave that, wid you, unless you wish to be shotted."
This was followed by a loud laugh from within.

" Boys, get up wid all haste : it's the misthress. Phil,
saddle Hollowback and fly—(puff)—fly in a jiffy for Rose
Moan ; an' do you, Barny, clap a black sugaun—(puff)—an
Sobersides, an' be aff for the misthress's mother—(puff)."

Both were dressing themselves before he had concluded,
and in a very few minutes were off in different directions,
each according to the orders he had received. With Barny
we have nothing to do, unless to say that he lost little time
in bringing Mrs. Keho's mother to her aid ; but as Phil is
gone for a much more important character, we beg our
readers to return with us to the cabin of Rose Moan, who
is now fast asleep—for it is twelve o'clock of a beautiful
moonlight night, in the pleasant month of August. Tap-
tap. " Is Mrs. Moan at home ? " In about half a minute
her warm good-looking face, enveloped in flannel, is protruded from the window.

" Who's that, *in God's name ?* " The words in italics were
added, lest the message should be one from the fairies.

" I'm Dandy Keho's servants—one of them at any rate—
an' my misthress has got a stitch in her side—ha ! ha !
ha ! "

" Aisy, avick—so she's *down* thin—aisy—I'll be wid you
like a bow out of an arrow. Put your horse over to ' the
stone,' an' have him ready. The Lord bring her over her
difficulties, any way, amin, a chierna ! "

She then pulled in her head, and in about three or four
minutes sallied out dressed as we have described her ; and
having placed herself on the crupper, coolly put her right
arm round Phil's body, and desired him to ride on with all
possible haste.

" Push an, avouchal, push an—time's precious at all times,
but on business like this, every minute is worth a life. But

there's always one comfort, that God is marciful. Push forrid avick."

"Never fear, Mrs. Moan. If it's in Hollowback, bedad I'm the babe that will take it out of him. Come, ould Hackball, trot out—you don't know the message you're an, nor who you're carryin'."

"Isn't your misthress—manin' the Dandy's wife—a daughter of ould Fitzy Finnegan's, the schrew of Glendhu ? "

"Faith, you may say that, Rose, as we all know to our cost. Be me song, she does have us sometimes that you might see through us ; an' only for the masther——but, dang it, no matter—she's down now, poor woman, an' it's not jist the time to be rakin' up her failins."

"It is not, an' God mark you to grace for sayin' so. At a time like this we must forget everything, only to do the best we can for our fellow-creatures. What are you looking at, avick ? "

Now, this question naturally arose from the fact that honest Phil had been, during their short conversation, peering keenly on each side of him, as if he expected an apparition to rise from every furze-bush on the common. The truth is, he was almost proverbial for his terror of ghosts, and fairies, and all supernatural visitants whatever ; but upon this occasion his fears rose to a painful height, in consequence of the popular belief, that, when a midwife is sent for, the Good People throw every possible obstruction in her way, either by laming the horse, if she rides, or by disqualifying the guide from performing his duty as such. Phil, however, felt ashamed to avow his fears on these points, but still could not help unconsciously turning the conversation to the very topic he thought to have avoided.

"What war you lookin' at, avick ? "

"Why, bedad, there appeared something there beyant, like a man, only it was darker. But be this and be that—

hem, ehem !—if I could get my hands on him, whatsomever he "——

" Hushth, boy, hould your tongue ; you don't know but it's the very word you war goin' to say might do us harm."

" —Whatsomever he is, that I'd give him a lift on Hollowback, if he happened to be any poor fellow that stood in need of it. Oh ! the sorra word I was goin' to say against any thing or any body."

" You're right, dear. If you knew as much as I could tell you—push an—you'd have a dhrop o' sweat at the ind of every hair on your head."

" Be me song, I'm tould you know a power o' quare things, Mrs. Moan ; an' if all that's said is thruc, you sartinly do."

Now, had Mrs. Moan and her heroic guide passed through the village of Ballycomaisy, the latter would not have felt his fears so strong upon him. The road, however, along which they were now going, was a grass-grown *bohreen*, that led them from behind her cabin through a waste and lonely part of the country ; and as it was a saving of better than two miles in point of distance, Mrs. Moan would not hear of their proceeding by any other direction. The tenor of her conversation, however, was fast bringing Phil to the state she so graphically and pithily described.

" What's your name ? " she asked.

" Phil Hannigan, a son of fat Phil's of Balnasaggart, an' a cousin to Paddy, who lost a finger in the Gansy (Guernsey) wars."

" I know. Well, Phil, in throth the hairs 'ud stand like stalks o' barley, upon your head, if you heard all I could mintion."

Phil instinctively put his hand up and pressed down his hat, as if it had been disposed to fly from off his head.

" Hem ! ahem ! Why, I'm tould it's wondherful. But is it thruc, Mrs. Moan, that you have been brought *on busi-*

ness to some o' the "—here Phil looked about him
cautiously, and lowered his voice to a whisper—"to some
o' the fairy women?"

"Hushth, man alive—what the sorra timpted you to call
them anything but the Good People? This day's Thursday—God stand betune us an' harm. No, Phil, I name
nobody. But there was a woman, a midwife—mind, avick,
that I don't say *who* she was—may be I know why too, an'
may be it would be as much as my life is worth "——

"Aisy, Mrs. Moan! God presarve us! what is that tall
thing there to the right?"—and he commenced the Lord's
Prayer in Irish, as fast as he could get out the words.

"Why, don't you see, boy, it's a fir-tree?"

"Ay, faix, an' so it is; bedad I thought it was gettin'
taller an' taller. Ay,—hut! it *is* only a tree."

"Well, dear, there was a woman, an' she was called away
one night by a little gentleman dressed in green. I'll tell
you the story some time—only this, that havin' done her
duty, an' tuck no payment, she was called out the same
night to a neighbour's wife, an' a purtier boy you couldn't
see than she left behind her. But it seems she happened
to touch one of his eyes wid a hand that had a taste of
their panado an it; an' as the child grew up, every one
wondhered to hear him speak of the multitudes o' thim
that he seen in all directions. Well, my dear, he kept never
sayin' anything to them, until one day, when he was in the
fair of Ballycomaisy, that he saw them whippin' away meal
an' cotton an' butther, an' everything that they thought
serviceable to them; so you see he could hould in no
longer, an' says he, to a little fellow that was very active
an' thievish among them, 'Why duv you take what doesn't
belong to you?' says he. The little fellow looked up at
him "——

"God be about us, Rose, what is that white thing goin
along the ditch to the left of us?"

"It's a sheep, don't you see? Faix, I believe you're cowardly at night."

"Ay, faix, an' so it is, but it looked very quare, somehow."

"—'An', says he, 'how do you know that?' 'Because I see you all,' says the other. 'An' which eye do you see us all wid?' says he again. 'Why, wid the left,' says the boy. Wid that, he gave a short whiff of a blast up into the eye, an' from that day not a stime the poor boy was never able to see wid it. No, Phil, I didn't say it was *myself*—I named *nobody*."

"An', Mrs. Moan, is it thrue that you can put the dughaughs upon them that trate their wives badly?"

"Whist, Phil. When you marry, keep your timper—that's all. You knew long Ned Donnelly?"

"Ay, bedad, sure enough; there was quare things said about "——

"Push an, avick, push an; for who knows how some of us is wanted? You have a good masther, I believe, Phil? It's poison the same Ned would give me if he could. Push an' dear."

Phil felt that he had got his answer. The abrupt mystery of her manner and her curt allusions left him little, indeed, to guess at. In this way did the conversation continue, Phil feloniously filching, as he thought, from her own lips, a corroboration of the various knowledge and extraordinary powers which she was believed to possess, and she ingeniously feeding his credulity, merely by enigmatical hints and masked allusions; for, although she took care to affirm nothing directly or personally of herself, yet did she contrive to answer him in such a manner as to confirm every report that had gone abroad of the strange purposes she could effect.

"Phil, wasn't there an uncle o' yours up in the Mountain Bar that didn't live happily for some time wid his wife?"

11

"I believe so, Rose; but it was before my time, or any way when I was only a young shaver."

"An' did you ever hear how the reconcilement came betune them?"

"No, bedad," replied Phil, "I never did; an' that's no wondher, for it was a thing they never liked to spake of."

"Troth, it's thrue for you, boy. Well, I brought about ——Push an', dear, push an'.——They're as happy a couple now as breaks bread, any way, and that's all they wanted."

"I'd wager a thirteen it was you did that, Rose."

"Hut, gorsoon, hould your tongue. Sure they're happy, now, I say, whosomever did it. I named nobody, nor I take no pride to myself, Phil, out o' sich things. Some people's gifted above others, an' that's all. But, Phil?"

"Well, ma'am?"

"How does the Dandy an' his scald of a wife agree? for, throth I'm tould she's nothing else."

"Faix, but middlin' itself. As I tould you, she often has us as empty as a paper lanthern, wid the devil a thing but the light of a good conscience inside of us. If we *pray* ourselves begorra she'll take care we'll have the *fastin'* at first cost; so that you see, ma'am, we hould a devout situation undher her."

"An' so that's the way wid you?"

"Ay, the downright thruth, an' no mistake. Why, the stirabout she makes would run nine miles along a dale boord, an' scald a man at the far end of it."

"Throth, Phil, I never like to go next or near sich women, or sich places; but for the sake o' the innocent we must forget the guilty. So, push an, avick, push an. Who knows but it's life an' death wid us? Have you ne'er a spur on?"

"The devil a spur I tuck time to wait for."

"Well, afther all, it's not right to let a messenger come for a woman like me, widout what is called the Midwife's

Spur—a spur in the head—for it has long been said that one in the head is worth two in the heel, an' so indeed it is, —on business like this, any way."

"Mrs. Moan, do you know the Moriartys of Ballaghmore, ma'am?"

"Which o' them, honey?"

"Mick o' the Esker Beg."

"To be sure I do. A well-favoured dacent family they are, an' full o' the world too, the Lord spare it to them."

"Bedad, they are, ma'am, a well-favoured* family. Well, ma'am, isn't odd, but somehow there's neither man, woman, nor child in the parish but gives you the good word above all the women in it; but as for a midwife, why, I heard my aunt say that if ever mother an' child owended their lives to another, she did her's and the babby's to you."

The reader may here perceive that Phil's flattery must have had some peculiar design in it, in connexion with the Moriartys, and such indeed was the fact. But we had better allow him to explain matters himself.

"Well, honey, sure that was but my duty; but God be praised for all; for everything depends on the Man above. She should call in one o' these new-fangled women that take out their Dispatches from the Lying-in-College in Dublin below; for you see, Phil, there is sich a place there —an' it stans to raison that there should be a Fondlin' Hospital beside it, which there is too, they say; but, honey, what are these poor ignorant creatures but *new lights*, every one o' them, that a dacent woman's life isn't safe wid?"

"To be sure, Mrs. Moan, an' every one knows they're not to be put in comparishment wid a woman like you, that knows sich a power. But how does it happen, ma'am, that the Moriartys does be spakin' but middlin' of you?'

"Of me, avick?"

"Ay, faix; I'm tould they spread the mouth at you

* This term in Ireland means "handsome"—"good-looking."

sometimes, espishily whin the people does be talkin' about all the quare things you can do."

"Well, well, dear, let them have their laugh—they may laugh that win, you know. Still, one doesn't like to be provoked—no indeed."

"Faix, an' Mick Moriarty has a purty daughter, Mrs. Moan, an' a purty penny he can give her, by all accounts. The nerra one o' myself but 'ud be glad to put my commedher on her, if I knew how. I hope you find your-self aisy on your sate, ma'am?"

"I do, honey. Let them talk, Phil: let them talk; it may come their turn yet—only I didn't expect it from *them*. You! hut, avick, what chance would *you* have with Mick Moriarty's daughter?"

"Ay, every chance an' sartinty too, if some one that I know an' that every one that knows her respects, would only give me a lift. There's no use in comin' about the bush, Mrs. Moan—bedad it's yourself I mane. You could do it. An' whisper, betune you and me, it would be only sarvin' them right, in regard of the way they spake of you —sayin', indeed, an' galivantin' to the world that you know no more than another woman, an' that ould Pol Doolin of Ballymagowan knows oceans more than you do." ·

This was, perhaps, as artful a plot as could be laid for engaging the assistance of Mrs. Moan, in Phil's design upon Moriarty's daughter. He knew full well that she would not, unless strongly influenced, lend herself to anything of the kind between two persons whose circumstances in life differed so widely as those of a respectable farmer's daughter with a good portion, and a penniless labouring boy. With great adroitness, therefore, he contrived to excite her prejudices against them by the most successful arguments he could possibly use, namely, a contempt for her imputed knowledge, and praise of her rival. Still, she was in the habit of acting coolly, and, less from impulse than from a shrewd knowledge of the best way to sustain her own reputation, without undertaking too much.

"Well, honey, an' so you wish me to assist you? Maybe I could do it, an' maybe—But push an, dear, move him an —we'll think of it, an' spake more about it some other time. I must think of what's afore me now—so move, move, acushla—push an."

Much conversation of the same nature took place between them, in which each bore a somewhat characteristic part; for to say truth, Phil was as knowing a "boy" as you might wish to become acquainted with. In Rose, however, he had a woman of no ordinary shrewdness to encounter; and the consequence was, that each, after a little more chat, began to understand the other a little too well to render the topic of the Moriartys, to which Phil again reverted, so interesting as it had been. Rose soon saw that Phil was only a *plasthey*, or sweetener, and only "soothered" her for his own purposes; and Phil perceived that Rose understood his tactics too well to render any further tampering with her vanity either safe or successful.

At length they arrived at Dandy Keho's house, and in a moment the Dandy himself took her in his arms, and placing her gently on the ground, shook hands with and cordially welcomed her. It is very singular, but no less true, that the moment a midwife enters the house of her patient she always uses the plural number, whether speaking in her own person or in that of the former.

"You're welcome, Rose, an' I'm proud an' happy to see you here, an' it'll make poor Bridget strong, an' give her courage, to know you're near her."

"How are we, Dandy? how are we, avick?"

"Oh, bedad, middlin', wishin' very much for you of coorse, as I hear "——

"Well, honey, go away now. I have some words to say

afore I go in, that'll sarve us, maybe—a charm it is that
has great vartue in it."

The Dandy then withdrew to the barn, where the male
portion of the family were staying until the *ultimatum*
should be known. A good bottle of potteen, however, was
circulating among them, for every one knows that occasions
of this nature usually generate a festive and hospitable
spirit.

Rose now went round the house in the direction from
east to west, stopping for a short time at each of the
windows, which she marked with the sign of a cross five
times ; that is to say, once at each corner, and once in the
middle. At each corner also of the house she signed the
cross, and repeated the following words or charm :—

> The four Evangels and the four Divines,
> God bless the moon and us when it shines.
> New moon, * true moon, God bless me,
> God bless this house an' this family.
> Matthew, Mark, Luke, and John,
> God bless the bed that she lies on.
> God bless the manger where Christ was born,
> An' lave joy an' comfort here in the morn.
> St. Bridget an' St. Patrick, an' the holy spouse,
> Keep the fairies for ever far from this house. Amen.
> Glora yea, Glora yea, Glora yea yeelish,
> Glora n'ahir, Glora n'vac, Glora n' spirid neev. Amen.

These are the veritable words of the charm, which she
uttered in the manner and with the forms aforesaid. Having concluded them, she then entered into the house, where
we leave her for a time with our best wishes.

In the barn, the company were very merry, Dandy himself being as pleasant as any of them, unless when his
brow became shaded by the very natural anxiety for the
welfare of his wife and child, which from time to time

* If it did not happen to be new moon, the words were "good moon," &c.

returned upon him. Stories were told, songs sung, and jokes passed, all full of good nature and not a little fun, some of it at the expense of the Dandy himself, who laughed at and took it all in good part. An occasional *bulletin* came out through a servant maid, that matters were just in the same way ; a piece of intelligence which damped Keho's mirth considerably. At length he himself was sent for by the midwife, who wished to speak with him at the door.

" I hope there's nothing like danger, Rose ? "

" Not at all honey ; but the truth is, we want a seventh son who isn't left-handed."

" A seventh son ! Why, what do you want him for ? "

" Why, dear, just to give her three shakes in his arms— it never fails."

" Bedad, an' that's fortunate ; for there's Mickey M'Sorley of the Broad Bog's a seventh son, an' he's not two gunshots from this."

" Well, aroon, hurry off one or two o' the boys for him, and tell Phil, if he makes haste, that I'll have a word to say to him afore I go." This intimation to Phil put feathers to his heels ; for from the moment that he and Barney started, he did not once cease to go at the top of his speed. It followed as a matter of course, that honest Mickey M'Sorley dressed himself and was back at Keho's house before the family believed it possible the parties could have been there. This ceremony of getting a seventh son to shake the sick woman, in cases where difficulty or danger may be appre- hended, is one which frequently occurs in remote parts of the country. To be sure, it is only a form, the man merely taking her in his arms, and moving her gently three times. The writer of this, when young, saw it performed with his own eyes, as the saying is ; but in his case the man was not a seventh son, for no such person could be procured. When this difficulty arises, any man who has the character of being lucky, provided he is not married to a red-haired wife, may be called in to give the three shakes. In other and more dangerous cases, Rose would send out persons to gather half a dozen heads of blasted barley; and having stripped them of the black fine powder with which they were covered, she would administer it in a little new milk, and this was always attended by the best effects. It is somewhat surprising that the whole Faculty should have adopted this singular medicine in cases of similar difficulty, for, in truth, it is that which is now administered under the more scientific name of *Ergot of Rye*.

In the case before us, the seventh son sustained his reputation for good luck. In about three quarters of an hour Dandy was called in "to kiss a strange young gintleman that wanted to see him." This was an agreeable ceremony to Dandy, as it always is, to catch the first glimpse of one's own first born. On entering, he found Rose sitting beside the bed in all the pomp of authority and pride of success, bearing the infant in her arms, and dandling it up and down, more from habit than any necessity that then existed for doing so.

"Well," said she, "here we are, all safe and sound, God willin'; an' if you're not the father of as purty a young man as ever I laid eyes on, I'm not here. Corny Keho, come an' kiss your son, I say."

Corny advanced, somewhat puzzled whether to laugh or to cry, and taking the child up, with a smile, he kissed it five times—for that is the mystic number—and as he placed it once more in Rose's arms there was a solitary tear on its cheek.

"Arra, go and kiss your wife, man alive, an' tell her to have a good heart, and to be as kind to all her fellow-creatures as God has been to her this night. It isn't upon this world the heart ought to be fixed, for we see how small a thing an' how short a time can take us out of it."

"Oh, bedad," said Dandy who had now recovered the touch of feeling excited by the child, "it would be too bad if I'd grudge her a smack." He accordingly stooped, and kissed her; but in truth to confess, he did it with a very cool and business-like air. "I know," he proceeded, "that she'll have a heart like a jyant, now that the son is come."

"To be sure she will, an' she must; or if not, *I'll* play the sorra, and break things. Well, well, let her get strength a bit first, an' rest and quiet; an' in the meantime get the groanin'-malt ready, until every one in the house drinks the health of the stranger. My sowl to happiness, but he's a born beauty. The nerra Keho of you all ever was the aiquals of what he'll be yet, plaise God. Throth, Corny, he has daddy's nose upon him, any how. Ay, you may laugh; but, faix, it's true. You may take with him, you may own to him any where. Arra, look at that! My sowl to happiness, if one egg's liker another! Eh, my poesy! Where was it, alanna? Ay, you're there, my duck o' diamonds! Throth, you'll be the flower o' the flock, so you will. An' now, Mrs. Keho, honey, we'll lave you to yourself awhile, till we thrate these poor cratures of sarvints; the likes o' them oughtn't to be overlooked; an', indeed, they did feel a great dale itself, poor things, about you; an' moreover, they'll be longin' of coorse to see the darlin' here."

Mrs. Keho's mother and Rose superintended the birth-treat between them. It is unnecessary to say that the young men and girls had their own sly fun upon the occasion; and now that Dandy's apprehension of danger was over, he joined in their mirth with as much glee as any of them. This being over, they all retired to rest; and honest Mickey M'Sorley went home very *hearty*, in consequence of Dandy's grateful sense of the aid he had rendered his wife. The next morning, Rose, after dressing the infant and performing all the usual duties that one expected from her, took her leave in these words:—

"Now, Mrs. Keho, God bless you an' yours, an' take care of yourself. I'll see you again on Sunday next, when it's to be christened. Until then, throw out no dirty wather before sunrise or after sunset; an' when Father Molly is goin' to christen it, let Corny tell him not to forget to christen it *against the fairies*, an' thin it'll be safe. Good-bye, ma'am, an' look you to her, Mrs. Finnegan," said she, addressing her patient's mother, "an' *banaght lath* till I see all again."

CORNEY KEHO'S BABY;

OR,

The Irish Christening.

ON Sunday morning, Rose paid an early visit to her patient, for, as it was the day of young Dandy's christening, her presence was considered indispensable. There is, besides, something in the appearance and bearing of a midwife upon those occasions which diffuses a spirit of lightheartedness not only through the immediate family, but also through all who may happen to participate in the ceremony, or partake of the good cheer. In many instances it is known that the very presence of a medical attendant communicates such a cheerful confidence to his patient, as, independently of any prescription, is felt to be a manifest relief. So it is with the midwife; with this difference, that she exercises a greater and more comical latitude of consolation than the doctor, although it must be admitted that she generally falls wofully short of that conventional dress with which we cover nudity of expression. No doubt many of her very choicest stock jokes, to carry on the metaphor, are a little too *fashionably* dressed to pass current out of the sphere in which they are used; but be this as it may, they are so traditional in character, and so humorous in conception, that we never knew the veriest prude to feel offended, or the morosest temperament to maintain its sourness, at their recital. Not that she is at all gross or un-womanly in any thing she may say, but there is generally in her apothegms a passing touch of fancy—a quick but terse vivacity of insinuation, at once so full of fun and sprightliness, and that truth which all know but few like to acknowledge, that we defy any one not irretrievably gone in some incurable melancholy to resist her humour. The moment she was seen approaching the house, every one in it felt an immediate elevation of spirits, with the exception of Mrs. Keho herself, who knew that wherever Rose had had the arrangement of the bill of fare, there was sure to be what the Irish call "full an' plinty"—"lashins an' lavins" —a fact which made her groan in spirit at the bare contemplation of such waste and extravagance. She was indeed a woman of a very un-Irish heart—so sharp in her temper and so penurious in soul, that one would imagine her veins were filled with vinegar instead of blood.

"*Banaght Dhea in shoh*" (the blessing of God be here), Rose exclaimed on entering.

"*Banaght Dhea agus Murra ghuid*" (the blessing of God and the Virgin on you), replied Corny, "an' you're welcome, Rose, ahagur."

"I know that, Corny. Well, how are we?—how is my son?"

"Begarra, thrivin' like a pair o' throopers."

"Thank God for it! Hav'n't we a good right to be grateful to him any way? An' is my little man to be christened to-day?"

"Indeed he is—the gossips will be here presently, an' so will *her* mother. But, Rose, dear, will you take the ordherin' of the aitin' an' dhrinkin' part of it?—you're betther up to these things than we are, an' so you ought of

coorse. Let there be no want of anything; an' if there's
an overplush, sorra may care; there'll be poor mouths
enough about the door for whatever's left. So, you see,
keep never mindin' any hint *she* may give you—you know
she's a little o' the closest; but no matther. Let there, as
I said, be enough an' to spare."

"Throth, there spoke your father's son, Corny: all the
ould dacency's not dead yet, any how. Well, I'll do my
best. But she's not fit to be up, you know, an' of coorse,
can't disturb us." The expression of her eye could not be
misunderstood as she uttered this. "I see," said Corny—
"devil a betther, if you manage that, all's right.'

"An' now I must go in, till I see how she an' my son's
gettin an: that's always my first start ; bekase you know,
Corny, honey, that *their* health goes afore every thing."

Having thus undertaken the task required of her, she
passed into the bed-room of Mrs. Keho, whom she found
determined to be up, in order, as she said, " to be at the
head of her own table."

"Well, alanna, if you must, you must : but in the name
of goodness I wash my hands out of the business tectotally.
Dshk, dshk, dshk ! Oh, wurra ! to think of a woman in your
state risin' to sit at her own table ! That I may never, if
I'll see it, or be about the place at all. If you take your
life by your own wilfulness, why, God forgive you ; but it
mustn't be while I'm here. Howandiver, since you're bent
on it, why, give me the child, an' afore I go, any how, I
may as well dress it, poor thing ! The heavens pity it—my
little man—eh ?—where was it ?—cheep—that's it, a ducky ;
stretch away. Aye stretchin' an thrivin' an, my son ! O,
thin, wurra, Mrs. Keho, but it's you that ought to ax God's
pardon for goin' to do what might lave that darlin' o' the
world an orphan, may be. Arra be the vestments, if I can
have patience wid you. May God pity you, my child. If
any thing happened your mother, what 'ud become of you,

and what ud' become of your poor father this day ? Dshk dshk, dshk !"   These latter sounds, exclamations of surprise and regret, were produced by striking the tongue against that part of the inner gum which covers the roots of the upper teeth.

"Indeed, Rose," replied her patient, in her sharp, shrill, quick voice, " I'm able enough to get up ; if I don't, we'll be harrished. Corny's a fool, an' it'll be only rap an' rive wid every one in the place."

" Wait, ma'am, if you plaise.—Where's his little barrow ? Ay, I have it.—Wait, ma'am, if you plaise, till I get the child dressed, an' I'll soon take myself out o' this. Heaven presarve us ! I have seen the like o' this afore—ay, have I —where it was as clear as crystal *that there was somethin' over them*—ay, over them that took their own way as you're doin'."

"But if I don't get up "—

" Oh, by all manes, ma'am—by all manes. I suppose you have a laise of your life, that's all. It's what I wish I could get."

" An' must I stay here in bed all day, an' be able to rise, an' sich wilful waste as will go an too ? "

" Remember you're warned. This is your first babby, God bless it an' spare you both. But, Mrs. Keho, does it stand to raison that you're as good a judge of these things as a woman like me, that it's my business ? I ax you that, ma'am."

This poser in fact settled the question, not only by the reasonable force of the conclusion to be derived from it, but by the cool authoritative manner in which it was put.

" Well," said the other, " in that case, I suppose, I must give in. You ought to know best."

" Thank you kindly, ma'am ; have you found it out at last ? No, but you ought to put your two hands undher my feet for previntin' you from doin' what you intinded.

That I may never sup sorrow, but it was as much as your life was worth. Compose yourself; I'll see that there's no waste, and that's enough. Here, hould my son—why, thin, isn't he the beauty o' the world, now that he has got his little dress upon him?—till I pin up this apron across the windy; the light's too strong for you. There now: the light's apt to give one a head-ache when it comes in full bint upon the eyes that way. Come alanna, come an now, till I shew you to your father an' them all. Wurra, thin, Mrs. Keho, darlin','' (this was said in a low confidential whisper, and in a low wheedling tone which baffles all description), " wurra, thin, Mrs. Keho, darlin', but it's he that's the proud man, the proud Corny, this day. Rise your head a little—aisy—there now, that'll do—one kiss to my son, now, before he laives his mammy, he says, for a weeny while, till he pays his little respects to his daddy an' to all his friends, he says, an' thin he'll come back to mammy agin—to his own little bottle, he says."

Young Corny soon went the rounds of the whole family, from his father down to the little herd-boy who followed and took care of the cattle. Many were the jokes which passed between the youngsters on this occasion—jokes which have been registered by such personages as Rose, almost in every family in the kingdom, for centuries, and with which most of the Irish people are too intimately and thoroughly acquainted to render it necessary for us to repeat them here.

Rose now addressed herself to the task of preparing breakfast, which, in honour of the happy event, was nothing less than "tay, white bread, and Boxty," with a glass of potheen to sharpen the appetite. As Boxty, however, is a description of bread not generally known to our readers, we shall give them a sketch of the manner in which this Irish luxury is made. A basket of the best potatoes is got, which are washed and peeled raw; then is procured a tin

grater, on which they are grated : the water is then shired
off them, and the macerated mass is put into a clean sheet,
or table-cloth, or bolster-cover. This is caught at each end
by two strong men, who twist it in opposite directions, until
the contortions drive up the substance into the middle of
the sheet, &c. ; this of course expels the water also ; but
lest the twisting should be insufficient for that purpose, it
is placed, like a cheese-cake, under a heavy weight, until it
is properly dried. They then knead it into cakes, and bake
it on a pan or griddle ; and when eaten with butter, we can
assure our readers, that it is quite delicious.

The hour was now about nine o'clock, and the company
asked to the christening began to assemble. The gossips,
or sponsors, were four in number ; two of them wealthy
friends of the family, that had never been married, and the
two others a simple country pair, who were anxious to
follow in the matrimonial steps of Corny and his wife. The
rest were, as usual, neighbours, relatives, and *cleaveens*, to
the amount of sixteen or eighteen persons, men, women,
and children, all dressed in their best apparel, and disposed
to mirth and friendship. Along with the rest was Bob
M'Cann, the fool, who, by the way, could smell out a good
dinner with as keen a nostril as the wisest man in the
parish could boast of, and who on such occasions carried
turf and water in quantities that indicated the supernatural
strength of a Scotch brownie rather than that of a human
being. Bob's qualities, however, were well proportioned to
each other, for, truth to say, his appetite was equal to his
strength, and his cunning to either.

Corny and Mrs. Moan were in great spirits, and indeed
we might predicate as much for all who were present. Not
a soul entered the house who was not brought up by Corny
to an out-shot room, as a private mark of his friendship,
and treated to an underhand glass of as good potheen " as
ever went down the red lane," to use a phrase common

among the people. Nothing upon an occasion naturally pleasant gives conversation a more cheerful impulse than this; and the consequence was, that in a short time the scene was animated and mirthful to an unusual degree.

Breakfast at length commenced in due form. Two bottles of whisky were placed upon the table, and the first thing done was to administer another glass to each guest.

"Come, neighbours," said Corny, "we must drink the good woman's health before we ate, especially as it's the first time, any how."

"To be sure they will, achora, an' why not? An' if it's the first time, Corny, it won't be the last, plaise goodness! Musha! you're welcome, Mrs. M'Cann! and jist in time too"—this she said, addressing his mother-in-law, who then entered. "Look at this swaddy, Mrs. M'Cann; my soul to happiness, but he's fit to be the son of a lord. Eh, a pet? Where was my darlin'? Corny, let me dip my finger in the whisky till I rub his gums wid it. That's my bully! Oh, the heavens love it: see how it puts the little mouth about lookin' for it agin. Throth you'll have the spunk in you yet, acushla, an' it's a credit to the Kehos you'll be, if you're spared, as you will, plaise the heavens!"

"Well, Corny," said one of the gossips, "here's a speedy uprise an' a sudden recovery to the good woman, an' the little sthranger's health, an' God bless the baker that gives thirteen to the dozen, any how."

"Ay, ay, Paddy Rafferty, you'll have your joke any way; an' throth you're welcome to it, Paddy; if you weren't, it isn't standin' for young Corny you'd be to-day."

"Thrue enough," said Rose, "an' by the dickens, Paddy isn't the boy to be long undher an obligation to any one. Eh, Paddy, did I help you there, avick? Aisy, childre; you'll smother my son if you crush about him that way." This was addressed to some of the youngsters, who were pressing round to look at and touch the infant.

"It won't be my fault if I do, Rose," said Paddy, slyly eyeing Peggy Betagh, then betrothed to him, who sat opposite, her dark eyes flashing with repressed humour and affection. Deafness, however, is sometimes a very convenient malady to young ladies, for Peggy immediately commenced a series of playful attentions to the unconscious infant, which were just sufficient to excuse her from noticing this allusion to their marriage. Rose looked at her, then nodded comically to Paddy, shutting both her eyes, by way of a wink, adding aloud, "Throth you'll be the happy boy, Paddy; an' woe betide you if you aren't the sweetest end of a honeycomb to her. Take care an' don't bring me upon you. Well, Peggy, never mind, alanna; who has a betther right to his joke than the dacent boy that's—aisy, childre: saints above! but ye'll smother the child, so you will. Where did I get him, Dinney? sure I brought him as a present to Mrs. Keho; I never come but I bring a purty little babby along wid me—nor the dacent boy, dear, that's soon to be your lovin' husband? Arra, take your glass, acushla; the sorra harm it'll do you."

"Bedad, I'm afeard, Mrs. Moan. What if it 'ud get into my head, an' me's to stand for my little godson? No, bad scran to me if I could—faix, a glass 'ud be too many for me."

"It's not more than half filled, dear; but there's sense in what the girl says, so don't press it an her."

In the brief space allotted to us we could not possibly give anything like a full and correct picture of the happiness and hilarity that prevailed at the breakfast in question. When it was over, they all prepared to go to the parish chapel, which was distant at least a couple of miles, the midwife staying at home to see that all the necessary preparations were made for dinner. As they were departing, Rose took Dandy aside, and addressed him thus:

"Now, Dandy, when you see the priest, tell him that it
is your wish, above all things, that he should christen it
against the fairies.   If you say that, it's enough.   An'
Peggy, achora, come here.   You're not carryin' that child
right, alanna ; but you'll know betther yet, plaise goodness.
No, avilish, don't keep its little head so closely covered wid
your cloak ; the day's a burnin' day, glory be to God, an'
the Lord guard my child ; sure the laist thing in the world,
where there's too much hait, 'ud smother my darlin'.
Keep its head out farther, and jist shade its little face
that way from the sun.   Och, will I ever forget the Sunday
whin poor Molly M'Guigan wint to take Patt Feasthalagh's
child from undher her cloak to be christened, the poor
infant was a corpse ; an' only that the Lord put it into my
head to have it privately christened, the father and mother's
heart would break.   Glory be to God ! Mrs. Duggan, if
the child gets cross, dear, or misses anything, act the
mother by him, the little man.   Eh, alanna ! where was it?
Where was my duck o' diamonds—my little Con Roe ?
My own sweety little ace o' hearts—eh, alanna !   Well,
God keep it till I see it again, the jewel."

Well, the child was baptised by the name of his father,
and the persons assembled, after their return from chapel,
lounged about Corny's house, or took little strolls in the
neighbourhood, until the hour of dinner.   This of course
was much more convivial, and ten times more vociferous,
than the breakfast, cheerful as that meal was.   At dinner
they had a dish, which we believe is, like the Boxty,
peculiarly Irish in its composition : we mean what is called
sthilk.   This consists of potatoes and beans, pounded up
together in such a manner that the beans are not broken,
and on this account the potatoes are well champed before
the beans are put into them.   This is dished in a large
bowl, and a hole made in the middle of it, into which a
miscaun of butter is thrust, and then covered up until it is

melted.   After this every one takes a spoon and digs away with his utmost vigour, dipping every morsel into the well of butter in the middle, before he puts it into his mouth. Indeed, from the strong competition which goes forward and the rapid motion of each right hand, no spectator could be mistaken in ascribing the motive of their proceedings to the principle of the old proverb, devil take the hindmost. *Sthilk* differs from another dish made of potatoes in much the same way, called *colcannon*.   If there were beans, for instance, in *colcannon*, it would be *sthilk*.   This practice of many persons eating out of the same dish, though Irish, and not cleanly, is of very old antiquity.   Christ himself mentions it at the last supper.   Let us hope, however, that like the old custom which once prevailed in Ireland, of several persons drinking at meals out of the same mether, the usage we speak of will soon be replaced by one of more cleanliness and individual comfort.

After dinner the whisky began to go round, for in these days punch was a luxury almost unknown to the class we are writing of.   In fact, nobody there knew how to make it but the midwife, who wisely kept the secret to herself, aware that if the whisky were presented to them in such a palatable shape they would not know when to stop, and she herself might fall short of the snug bottle that is usually kept as a treat for those visits which she continues to pay during the convalescence of her patients.

"Come, Rose," said Corny, who was beginning to soften fast, " it's your turn now to thry a glass of what never seen wather."   " I'll take the glass, Dandy—'deed will I—but the thruth is, I never dhrink it *hard*.   No, but I'll jist take a dhrop o' hot wather an' a grain o' sugar, an' scald it ; that an' as much carraway seeds as will lie upon a sixpence does me good : for, God help me, the stomach isn't at all sthrong wid me, in regard o' being up so much at night, an' deprived of my nathural rest."

"Rose," said one of them, "is it thrue that you war called out one night, an' brought blindfoulded to some grand lady belongin' to the quality?"

"Wait, avick, till I make a dhrop o' *wan-grace** for the misthress, poor thing; an', Corny, I'll jist throuble you for about a thimbleful o' spirits to take the smell o' the wather off it. The poor crature, she's a little weak still, an' indeed it's wondherful how she stood it out; but, my dear, God's good to his own, an' fits the back to the burden, praise be to his name!"

She then proceeded to scald the drop of spirits for her-self, or, in other words, to mix a good tumbler of ladies' punch, making it, as the phrase goes, hot, strong, and sweet —not forgetting the carraways, to give it a flavour. This being accomplished, she made the wan-grace for Mrs. Keho, still throwing in a word now and then to sustain her part in the conversation, which was now rising fast into mirth, laughter, and clamour.

"Well, but, Rose, about the lady of quality, will you tell us that?"

"Oh, many a thing happened me as well worth tellin', if you go to that; but I'll tell it to you, childre, for sure the curiosity's nathural to yez. Why, I was one night at home an' asleep, an' I hears a horse's fut gallopin' for the bare life up to the door. I immediately put my head out, an' the horseman says, 'Are you Mrs. Moan?'"

"That's the name that's an me, your honour,' sis myself.

"'Dress yourself, thin,' sis he, 'for you're sadly wanted; dress yourself, and mount behind me, for there's not a moment to be lost.' At the same time I forgot to say that his hat was tied about his face in sich a way that I couldn't catch a glimpse of it. Well, my dear, we didn't let the grass grow undher our feet for about a mile or so. 'Now,'

---

* A wan-grace is a kind of small gruel or meal-tea sweetened with sugar.

sis he, 'you must allow yourself to be blindfoulded, an' it's uscless to oppose it, for it must be done. There's the character, maybe the life of a great lady at stake; so be quiet till I cover your eyes, or,' sis he, lettin' out a great oath, 'it'll be worse for you. I'm a desperate man;' an' sure enough I could feel the heart of him beatin' undher his ribs, as if it would burst in pieces. Well, my dears, what could I do in the hands of a man that was strong and desperate? So, sis I, 'Cover my eyes an' welcome; only, for the lady's sake, make no delay.' Wid that he dashed his spurs into the poor horse, an' he foamin' an' smokin' like a lime-kiln already. Any way, in about half an hour I found myself in a grand bed-room; an' jist as I was put into the door, he whispers me to bring the child to him in the next room, as soon as it would be born. Well, sure I did so, after lavin' the mother in a fair way. But what 'ud you have of it?—the first thing I see, lyin' an the table, was a purse of money an' a case of pistols. Whin I looked at him, I thought the devil, Lord guard us! was in his face, he looked so black and terrible about the brows. 'Now, my good woman,' sis he, 'so far you've acted well, but there's more to be done yet. Take your choice of these two,' sis he, 'this purse, or the contents of one of these pistols, as your reward. You must murdher the child on the spot.' 'In the name of God an' his Mother, be you man or devil, I defy you,' sis I; 'an innocent blood'll never be shed by these hands.' 'I'll give you ten minutes,' sis he, 'to put an end to that brat there;' an' wid that he cocked one o' the pistols. My dears, I had nothin' for it but to say *in* to myself a *pather* an' *ave* as fast as I could, for I thought it was all over wid me. However, glory be to God, the prayers gave me great strinth, an' I spoke stoutly, 'Whin the king of Jerusalem,' sis I,—' an' he was a greater man than ever you'll be—whin the king of Jerusalem ordhered the midwives of Aigyp to put Moses to death, they wouldn't

do it, an' God presarved them in spite of him, king though
he was,' says I ; 'an' from that day to this it was never
known that a midwife took away the life of the babe she
aided into the world—no, an' I'm not goin' to be the first
that'll do it.' ' The time is out,' sis he, puttin' the pistol to
my ear, ' but I'll give you a minute more.' ' Let me go to
my knees first,' sis I ; ' an' now may God have mercy on
my sowl, for, bad as I am, I'm willing to die sooner than
commit murdher an the innocent.' He gave a start as I
spoke, and threw the pistol down. ' Ay,' sis he, ' an the
innocent—an the innocent—that is thrue. But you are an
extraordinary woman : you have saved the child's life, and
previnted me from committing two great crimes, for it was
my intintion to murder you afther you had murdhered it.'
I thin, by his ordhers, brought the poor child to its mother,
and whin I kem back to the room, ' Take that purse,' says
he, ' an' keep it as a reward for your honesty.' ' Wid the
help o' God,' says I, ' a penny of it'll never come into my
company, so it's no use to ax me.' ' Well,' sis he, 'afore you
lave this, you must swear not to mintion to a livin' sowl
what has happened this night, for a year and a day.' It
didn't signify to me whether I mintioned it or not, so bein'
jack-indifferent about it, I tuck the oath and kept it. He
thin bound my eyes agin, hoisted me up behind him, an' in
a short time left me at home. Indeed, I wasn't the betther
o' the start it tuck out o' me for as good as six weeks afther."

The company now began to grow musical ; several songs
were sung ; and when the evening got farther advanced a
neighbouring fiddler was sent for, and the little party had a
dance in the barn, to which they adjourned lest the noise
might disturb Mrs. Keho, had they held it in the dwelling-
house. Before this occurred, however, "the midwife's glass"
went the round of the gossips, each of whom drank her
health and dropped some silver, at the same time, into the
bottom of it. It was then returned to her, and with a

smiling face she gave the following toast :—" Health to the parent stock! So long as it thrives, there will always be branches. Corny Keho, long life an' good health to you an' yours! May your son live to see himself as happy as his father! Youngsters, here's that you may follow a good example. The company's health in general I wish ; an' Paddy Rafferty, that you may never have a blind child but you'll have a lame one to lead it! ha! ha! ha! What's the world without a joke? I must see the good woman an' my little son afore I go ; but as I won't follow yez to the barn, I'll bid yez good-night, neighbours, an' the blessing of Rose Moan be among yez."

BARNEY BRADY'S GOOSE;

or,

Mysterious Doings at Slathbeg.

BARNEY BRADY was a good-natured, placid man, and never lost his temper, unless, as he said himself, when he got "privication ;" he was also strict in attending his duty ; a fact which Mrs., or rather, as she was called, Ailey Brady, candidly and justly admitted, and to which the priest himself bore ample testimony. Barney, however, had the misfortune to be married at a time when a mystery was abroad among women. Mysteries, resembling the Elusinian in nothing but the exclusion of men, were then prevalent among the matrons in all parts of the country. Of the nature of these secret rites it would be premature now to speak ; in time the secret will be revealed ; suffice it to say, that the mysteries were full of alarm to the husbands, and held by them to be a grievous offence against their welfare and authority. The domestic manners of my beloved

countrywomen were certainly in a state of awful and
deplorable transition at the time, and many a worthy
husband's head ached at a state of things which no vigilance
on his part could alter or repress.   Many a secret consultation was held among the good men of the respective villages
throughout the country at large, as to the best mode of
checking this disastrous epidemic, which came home to
their very beds and bosoms, and many a groan was vainly
uttered from hearts that grew heavy in proportion as the
evil, which they felt but could not see, spread about through
all directions of the kingdom.

Nay to such a height did this terrible business rise, that
the aggrieved parties had notions of petitioning the king to
keep their wives virtuous ; but this, upon second consideration, was given up, inasmuch as the king himself, with
reverence be it spoken, was at the bottom of the evil, and
what was still worse, even the queen was not ashamed to
corrupt their wives by her example.   How then could
things be in a healthy state when the very villany of which
the good broken-hearted men complained, descended from
the court to the people ?   A warning this to all future
sovereigns not without good forethought, and much virtuous
consideration, to set a bad precedent to their subjects.
What then could the worthy husbands do, unless to put
their hands dolorously to their heads and bear their griev-
ances in silence ; which, however, the reader perceives they
did not.   After mutually, but with great caution, disclosing
their injuries, they certainly condoled with each other ;
they planned means of redress, sought out the best modes
of detection, and having entered into a general confederacy
against their respective wives, each man solemnly promised
to become a spy and informer in his own family.   To come
to this resolution was as much as they could do under such
unhappy circumstances, and of course they did it.

Their wives, on the other hand, were anything but idle.

They also sat in secret council upon their own affairs, and discussed their condition with an anxiety and circumspection which set the vigilance of their husbands at complete defiance. And it may be observed here, just to show the untractable obstinancy of women when bent on gratifying their own wills, that not one of them ever returned home to her husband from these closed-door meetings, without having committed the very act of which she was suspected. Not that these cautious good women were, after all, so successful in every instance as to escape detection. Some occasional discoveries were actually made in consequence of the systematic *espionage* of their husbands, and one or two of them were actually caught, as the law term has it, *with the maner,* that is, in the very act of offence. Now, contumacy is ever impudent and outrageous, and disposed to carry everything with a high hand, or at all events, with a loud tongue. This, the husbands of those who had been detected soon felt; for, no sooner had they proclaimed their wrongs to their fellow sufferers than they were branded by their wives with the vile and trying epithet of "*stag*," and intrepidly charged home with letting themselves sink to the mean spirited office of informers against the wives of their bosoms.

Some of the good men now took fire, and demanded an explanation ; others looked at their wives with amazement, and stopped short, as if irresolute how to act ; and other some shrugged their shoulders, took a silent and meditative blast of the pipe upon the hob, and said no more about it. So far, then, there was no great victory either on the one side or the other. Now, the state of human society is never so bad, even in the most depraved times, but that there are always to be found in it many persons uncorrupted by the prevailing contamination ; and it was supposed to be so here. Barney Brady as yet hoped in heaven that Ailey had escaped the contagion, which operated upon her sex so secretly, yet so surely. For some time past he had held her under strict *surveillance* ; but with such judgment that she did not even dream of being suspected. In this manner did matters proceed between them—Barney slily on the alert, and Ailey on a shrewd look-out for means and opportunity; when one Friday he proposed to visit his aunt Madge, up in Carrickmore, on the next Saturday evening, and accordingly informed Ailey that he would not return until the Monday following. To this Ailey could offer no possible objection ; but, on the contrary, highly applauded him for showing such a mark of respect and affection for his aunt, who, by the way, had been very kind to them both since their marriage. "It's only right," said she, "and yonr duty besides to go an' see her, for betwixt you an' me, Barney, she has been the best feather in our wing. There's thim Finnigans, the dirty low pack, sure, bekase indeed they're the same relations to her that we are, they'd kiss the dirt of her feet, if they thought they cud bone a penny by it, an' they're lavin' no stone unturned to get the soft side of her, hopin', the dirty squad o' *cabogues*, to cum in for what she has, an' to cut us out from her. So go to her, Barney ; an' if you don't palaver her, the sorra one o' you's worth a pound o' goat's wool."

Barney, having then got on a clean shirt and his holiday frieze coat, took his shilellah in hand, and set out to visit his aunt Madge Brady, up among the hills of Carrickmore, as a most attached and disinterested nephew, who, as the song says, "loved her for herself alone." He had not gone many yards from the door, however, when he returned.

"Madge," said he, "I'm jist goin' to mintion to you afore I set out, that I'd as soon you'd keep away from the Maguigans ; I mane the women of them. Both their husbands tould me not a month o' Sundays agone, that they suspect them to be not safe. So you see you can learn nothing that's good from them. God's thruth is, I'm afeard that they're tarred wid the same stick that has marked the women o' the whole neighbourhood. So now, that you know this, I hope you'll keep your distance from them."

"Arra, what business, Barney, could I have wid them? The sorra eye I layed on one o' them this fortnight back. I have my own business on these two childre, the crathurs, to take care of."

"That's a darlin', Madge, give us a smack; an' now *banaght lath* till Monday, please goodness. Kiss me, childhre. Hadn't you betther tie a bit of flannin about poor Barney's neck, till that cough laves him?"

"Don't yon see it dhryin' there on the stool, before the fire?"

"That's right. Now, you'll mind my words, Ailey."

"Arra, bad scran be from me, but you'd—so you would, arra——"

She spoke this with an indignant abruptness; but the reader will please to observe, that she made no promise whatsoever.

"I'm off, I'm off. I know you won't. God bless yez all!"

And so Barney went to see his aunt Madge, up in Carrickmore.

"Well! it is a sad thing to be a mere chronicler of truth, which, indeed, every man who delineates human nature must be; because unhappily for him who lives in the world of human nature, there is no fiction at hand. It is only those who live out of it that can make fiction available to their purposes. This has been forced from us, not by Barney, however, but by his wife.

He had scarcely been half an hour gone, when Ailey threw a bonnet on her head, a blue cloak about her shoulders, and after having "made a play" for the children, to keep them quiet, and given them a slice of griddle bread each, she locked the door, rolled the big stone upon the hole that was under it, which the pig had grubbed away, in order to work himself a passage into the house, and immediately proceeded to visit the two tainted wives of the Maguigans! The act was—but it is not for us to characterize it; the consequence of it will speak for themselves. The two brothers to whom they were united in wedlock, lived next door to each other, or, what is called, under the same roof; and she, consequently, found both their good women at home. Two or three "slips" of both sexes, who had been amusing themselves in the elder brother's house, where the conference resulting from her visit was about to be held, were immediately desired to play abroad, "an' not be gamestherin' an' rampadghin' through the house that way, makin' a ruction, that people can't hear their own ears wid yez; go along, an' take the sthreets on your head, and stretch your limbs, ye pack o' young thieves, yez!"

The moment they bounded away, Ailey's face assumed an air of considerable importance—a circumstance which the others instantly noticed; for nothing is so observant of symptoms that indicate its own discovery as a consciousness of error.

"Ailey," said one of them, alarmed, "you've heard something? What is it? Are we found out, clane?"

"If you're not found out," replied Ailey, in the same low, guarded tone, "you're strongly suspected; but the devil may care for that. Barney is away up to his ould aunt Madge Brady's, at Carrickmore above, an' won't be back till Monday; so that the coast's clear till then, any way. All you have to do is to slip up about dusk, for there'll be nobody but ourselves, an' I'll put the childhre to bed, not that they dare tell *him* any thing they'd see."

"So, thin, we are suspicted?" said the other with much chagrin.

"It's truth. Dick an' Harry confessed it to Barney; an' he tould me."

"Troth, an' we'll outdo them, if they wor ten times as sharp," replied Mrs. Dick Maguigan, or Betty, as she was called. "Indeed, I knew myself that he was for a good while past peepin' and pokin' about, as if he expected to find a leprechaun or a mare's nest; an' faith sure enough, he was wanst widin' an ace of catchin' us; but, as luck would have it, he didn't search undher the bed."

"And I suppose that Barney's backin' them in all this," observed Mrs. Harry Maguigan, or, as we shall call her, Bid.

"Throth, you may swear that," replied his faithful wife; "an' warned me strongly afore he went to the aunt's to hould away from yez both, for he said ye wor tainted, tarred with the same stick that has marked all the rotten sheep in the country."

The three audacious conspirators, instead of expressing either regret or repentance at the conduct which had justified the well-founded suspicions of their husbands, burst out, on the contrary, into one united and harmonious chorus of laughter, which lasted at least five minutes!

"Well," said Ailey, hastily getting up and throwing the cloak about her, "I can't stop a jiffey, for there's no one at home but the childhre that I locked in; and I'm always unaisy when I lave the crathurs that way, for fraid they might go too near the fire, or that that sarra of a pig 'ud work the stone from undher the door an' get in. So as the coast's clear, you'll both slip up about dusk."

This they promised; and accordingly, when darkness had completely set in, the door of Barney Brady's house was closed, and bolted inside with all possible security; and this was necessary, for truly a surprise would have been an awful, though perhaps a just, winding up of their iniquities. What peculiar mysteries or rites took place there, on that night, it is not our province, good reader, to disclose; but of this you may rest assured, that each ful-

filled the old and excellent adage, " that stolen enjoyments
are the sweetest." With what feelings Betty and Bid
Maguigan faced their husbands, they themselves best know ;
but that each was received with suspicion, and severely
cross-examined upon the cause of their absence, we can inform the reader.

But what did that avail ? The delinquents on their way
home, had fabricated a story—and they are never good that
possess a facility at fabricating stories,—to which both
were determined to adhere with most inflexible pertinacity.
" They had jist ran up to see little Madge Brady, for Ailey
had been down to tell them that she was afeard it was
takin' the mazles ; but it was nothin' but a small *rash* that
came out upon its breast, the crathur, though Bid (her
sister-in-law), thought it was the hives ; an' indeed, after
all, she didn't know herself but it was. But God send it
safe over whatsomever it was, poor thing ! Amin, this
night ! "

Now, who would think ?—but no matter; there is still
worse to come ! The reader will not believe our word, when
we assure him that these two women, Betty and Bid
Maguigan, did not scruple, though loaded with the just
suspicions of their husbands, to kneel down and say their
prayers on that very night before they went to bed.

The next day being Sunday, and their husbands having
more leisure, it is scarcely necessary to say that the two
good men kept a sharp eye upon their spouses, who found
themselves dodged in every motion. Several times they
attempted a stolen visit to Ailey Brady's, but were detected
just in the act of putting on their cloaks and bonnets. In
fact, they were so completely hampered, that they resolved,
at length, to brazen it out, having lost temper considerably
by seeing that all their designs were fairly contravened, and
that whatever must be done as to reaching the scene of their
transgression must be done with honest, open defiance.

They once more, therefore, had recourse to the cloaks and bonnets, and were in the very act of setting out, when their husbands, who sat smoking each a pipe, after having coolly eyed them for some time, calmly inquired—

"Where are yez bound for, good women?"

"Up to Ailey Brady's, to see the child, poor thing! Deed, it's a burnin' shame that we didn't call sooner, espishilly as Barney's not at home wid her. She may want something, an' has no one to send out for it."

"Well," said Dick, addressing his own wife Betty, "grantin' all that, isn't one o' ye enough to go?"

"Plenty," replied his sister-in-law Bid; "but I've some notion of goin' up as far as my mother's, while Betty's sittin' wid Ailey Brady."

"By the tarlin' sweep!" exclaimed Harry taking the pipe hastily out of his mouth, and casting a keen and indignant glance at the last speaker,—"yez are enough to bate down the patience of a saint. How can you look us in the face, ye schamers o' the devil? Goin' to see Ailey Brady's child, indeed! Why, I was up wid Ailey Brady this very mornin', an' there's not a blast o' wind wrong wid either of her childhre, not as much as a hair turned on them! What have yez to say now? An' yet ye came both home last night wid a lie in your mouths; that 'Ailey Brady's child was gettin' the mazles,' says one; 'it has a *rash*,' says the other; 'but sure God send it safe over whatsomever it has, poor thing!' Be the mortal man I won't bear this. There now, to show yez I won't."

As he spoke the last word he took the pipe out of his mouth and shivered it to atoms against the opposite wall. His brother seeing this energetic display, resolved not to be outdone in the vigour of his indignation.

"Yes, be me sowl, nor I aither," he exclaimed hurling his dudeen in an opposite direction, and immediately kicking the stool on which he sat to the lower end of the kitchen.

" That's to shew yez that ye won't have your tongues in
your cheeks at uz," he added; "an' be this an' be that, for
three straws I would not lave a thraneen's worth on the
dhresser but I'd smash to smithereens. An' I'll tell yez
what it is," he proceeded, raising his voice to its highest
pitch, and stamping furiously on the hearth, "I'll tell yez
what it is, yez must put an end to this work, wanst for all.
Our substance isn't to go this way. We'll have no collogin,
among yez; no huggermuggerin' between you an' the other
black sheep o' the neighbourhood. Don't think but we
know what's goin' on, an' what brought you both up to
Ailey Brady's last night. Too well we know it; an' now
I tell yez again that yez must avoid that woman; she's not
a safe neighbour, an' her own husband suspects her to be as
bad as the worst among them. Ay, an' he'll catch her yet
known as she thinks herself."

" Be the book, I'll turn another pin in *your* nose, my
lady," said Harry, addressing Bid; "never fear but I will.
I'll make you that you won't have yourself the talk o' the
neighbours, an' me, too, that doesn't desarve it. The curse
o' Cromwell on me if I don't. Now!"

" Why thin now," said Bid, calmly turning to Betty, "in
the name of all that's beautiful, what are these two dunghill
cocks at? are they mad? or is it only dhrunk they
are?"

" No," replied Betty, " but goin' to bate us I suppose!"

" Ay, very likely," returned the other; "any how they
may be proud o' themselves, to join two women as if we
wor fit to fight them. Throth I'm glad their own childhre's
not to the fore to see their fine manly behaviour. Come,
Betty, are you goin' up to Ailey's? Whether the child's
sick or not, the crathur's lonely, as Barney's from home, an'
it's a charity to sit awhile wid her. Are you comin'?"

" No, nor you aither; the divil a one toe," said her
husband.

"The divil take them that says to the conthrary ; come, Betty."

"Ay if *I* like," said he.

"Ay, whether you like or not, dear ; the sarra wan o' me 'ill be stopped by you this day."

"You won't ? "

"I won't, now."

"Never heed her, Harry," said Dick : "let her go to ould Nick her own way ; ay, both o' them ; off wid you now ; but you'll see what'll come of it at the long run."

"Where's the Catechiz ? " said Harry : "I'll take my book oath this minute, that for a month to come, I'll not let you on the one side of the house wid me any how. Will no one tell me where the Catechiz is ? "

"An' is that to vex me, Harry ? arra, why don't you make it twelve months while your hand's in ? It wouldn't be worth your while to switch the primer for a bare four weeks, man alive ? "

"Be my soul, it's you ought to be switched instead o' the primer."

"Very well," replied his imperturbable and provoking spouse ; "I suppose the next thing you'll do will be to bate us sure enough—but sure we can't help it, only it will be a fine story to have to tell the neighbours. You'll look well afther it ; you may then hould up your head like a man ! Oh, ye—but I won't let myself down to scould wid ye. Come, Betty."

"No," said Betty, "I wouldn't be squabblin' wid them about goin'. It's nothin' to uz one way or the other, so we'll sit here. Oh, thin, God he knows but we're the well-matched women at all evints. Sure if we wor the worst that ever riz this day—ay, if we wor so bad that the very dogs wouldn't lap our blood, we couldn't be thrated worse than we are by thim two men."

"I say again," observed Harry, seeing his wife somewhat

13

irresolute, " that if you go, your breath won't come near me in haste."

" Oh, hould you tongue, man," replied Bid, " I seen the day you thought enough about my breath."

" Faith, an' that was becase I didn't know you then as well as I do now."

" That's not what you thought, or what you said aither, when I was ill last harvest, and goin' to die. Sure you wor roarin' about the house like a suckin' calf that has lost its mother, wid your two eyes as red as a pair of sunburnt onions."

" Never heed her," said his brother; " you know she'd bate both of us at the tongue ; she's now in her glory."

" Betty," said Bid, addressing her sister-in-law, in a voice exceedingly calm and quiet ; that is to say, in the voice of a woman whose contempt alone prevented her from continuing the controversy ; " go out, alanna, an' cut me a bit o' greens to put down wid that bacon for the dinner; after that we'll clane ourselves up, an' be in time for the twelve o'clock mass."

" But what if somebody would run away wid us ? " said Betty, laughing.

" Oh, sure," said the other, " that's all they'd want. They'd thin get shut of the two sich villains as we are. Go, alanna, and never mind them—they're not worth our breath, little as they think about it."

" A purty Sunday mornin' they've made us spind—but no matther—God forgive them for wrongin' us as they're doin' ! "

Their two husbands did not go to mass that day, having in fact devoted it to the purpose of ferreting out evidence against their wives. Their exertions, however, were fruitless, although we are bound honestly to state that they left no stone unturned to procure it. The children were taken to task and severely interrogated, but they could prove nothing, except that their mothers were sometimes out for a considerable time, and that they themselves were often sent to play, and that on returning of an odd time sooner than was expected, they found the doors bolted, and heard strange voices within. Of these facts, however, the good men had been apprised before; so that the sum of all they obtained was nothing more than an accession to their uneasiness, without any addition to their knowledge. Both men, indeed, were unusually snappish the whole day, especially after the hour of dinner; for each of their wives could observe that her husband often put his hand quietly over to the hole of the hob, and finding that his pipe was not there, vented his spleen upon the cat or dog, if either came in his way, and not unfrequently even upon his own children.

At length Dick got up and was about to go out, when Betty asked in her turn, "Where he was goin'?"

"Not far," he replied. "I'll be back in a quarther of an hour—too soon for you to have an opportunity of bein' at your ould work."

"If you're afeard o' that," she replied, "hadn't you betther not go at all?"

To this he made no reply, but putting his hands over his brows, he stalked gloomily out of the house.

Almost precisely similar was the conduct of his brother, who, after exchanging a random shot or two with Bid, slunk out soon after Dick, but each evidently attempted to conceal from the wife of the other that he had gone out—a circumstance that was clearly proved by Dick declining to pass Harry's door, and Harry Dick's.

Alas! and must I say it?—I must—I must—unhappily the interests of truth compel me to make the disclosure. The two men were no sooner gone, than their irreclaimable wives had an immediate consultation.

"Where's Dick?" asked Bid.

"Why sure, I thought I'd split," replied Betty, "to see

him frettin' the heart out of himself after his pipe. The norra be in me, but it was a'most too much for me to look at him searchin' the hob every five minutes for the dudeen he broke upon the wall in his tantrems this mornin'. I know he's away over to Billy Fulton's to buy one."

"'Twas the same wid Harry," said Bid ; " he didn't know which end of him he was sittin' on. He's off, too, to the same place, for I watched him through the windy : an' now that the coast's clear, let's be off to Ailey, an' have all over afore our two gintlemen comes back ; or, in troth they'll skiver us clane."

" The never a lie in that ; the house wouldn't hould them if they found us out. But wasn't it lucky that they lost their temper and broke their pipes ? If they had kept cool, we would have now no opportunity—come."

And so they proceeded once more to Ailey Brady's ; and again the door was locked and bolted ; and, as before, the mysteries, whatever they may have been, were re-enacted, and the vigilance and terrors of their husbands became the subject of open ridicule, and much mirth went forward, as might easily be conjectured from the hearty, but somewhat suppressed laughter which an experienced ear might have heard through the door—we say suppressed, for their mirth was expressed, notwithstanding the high spirit of enjoyment which ran through it, in that timid and cautious undertone that dreads discovery.

As their object was now to reach home before the return of their husbands, so was the period of their enjoyments on this evening much more brief than on the preceding. They had very little time to spare, however, for scarcely were the cloaks and bonnets thrown aside, and an air of the most decorous and matronly composure assumed, when the good men entered.

"Musha, but that's a long quarther of an hour you stayed," said Betty ; " where on airth wor you all this time?"

"I was upon business," returned Dick, "gettin' somethin' to keep me cool against your behaviour. Hand me a double sthraw out of the bed there, till I light my pipe. Wor you out since?"

"Was I out since!" returned his wife, with the look of a deeply offended woman; "hut, ay, to be sure—Bid an' myself wor up at Ailey Brady's, an' you niver saw such a piece o' fun as we had. Sure we're only come in this minnit. Why, upon my throth, Dick, you'd vex an angel from heaven. Was I out!—arra, don't I look very like a woman that was out?"

"Well, well," rejoined her husband, whiffing away rather placidly from his new pipe, "don't be flyin' out at us like Bid; I'm not sayin' you wor out *this* evenin'; so hould your whisht about it."

"No, but to think—the sorra one——"

"Very well—that's enough—be done."

And so the adroit wife grumbled gradually into silence.

The skirmish between Harry and Bid was of a brisker and more animated description, but we need not say on which side the victory settled. The pipe, however, soon produced something like tranquillity, and after a hard bout at a united prayer in the shape of a Rosary between the deceiver and the deceived, both went to bed on very good terms with each other, as indeed, after all, did Dick and Betty, not, any more than the others, forgetting their devotions.

The next morning was that on which our absent friend, Barney Brady, was expected home, and about ten or eleven o'clock, Ailey was descanting in conversation with a neighbour upon the kindness and generosity of Aunt Madge, and the greater warmth of affection which, on all occasions, she had manifested towards her and Barney, than ever she had shewn to that sleeveen pack of cabogues, the Finnegans, when who should appear but the redoubtable Barney himself, bearing, under his right arm, a fat grey goose, alive and kicking.

"Musha, Barney, what is this?" exclaimed Ailey, as her husband laid the goose down on the floor.

"Why," he replied good humouredly, "don't you see it's a leg o' mutton that Aunt Madge sent for our dinner on Sunday next. What's that, indeed!"

The goose was immediately taken up—handled like a wonder—balanced, that they might guess its weight—felt, that they might know how fat it was, and examined from beak to claw with the most minute inspection. The children approached it with that eager but fearful curiosity for which childhood is remarkable. They touched it, retreated with apprehension, took fresh courage, patted it timidly on the back, and after many alternations of terror and delight, the eldest at length ventured to take it up in his arms. This was a disastrous attempt; for the goose, finding him unable to hold it firmly, naturally fluttered its pinions, and the young hero threw it hastily down, and ran screaming behind his mother, where his little sister joined the chorus.

Barney and his wife then entertained the neigbour we spoke of with a history of Aunt Madge's wealth, assuring him confidentially, that they themselves were *down* for every penny and penny's worth belonging to her, pointing to the goose at the same time as a triumphant illustration of their expectations.

No sooner had their friend left them, than Barney, having given Ailey a faithful account of every thing respecting Aunt Madge, said he hoped she had not forgotten his parting advice on Saturday, that she had kept aloof from the tainted wives of the Maguigans, and "neither coshered or harboured with them," in his absence.

"Musha, throth, Barney, afore I'd lead this life, an' be catechized at every hand's turn, I'd rather go out upon the world, and airn my bread honestly, wid my own two hands,

as I did afore I met you. The wives o' the Maguigans!
Why, what 'ud I be doin' wid the wives o' the Maguigans?
or what 'ud the wives o' the Maguigans be doin' wid me?
It's little thim or their consarns throubles me—I have my
house an' childhre to look afther, an' that's enough for any
one woman, I'm thinkin'."

"Well, but sure you needn't be angry wid me for
puttin' you on your guard."

"It's not to say that I'm angry wid you—but sure wanst
to say a thing ought to be enough—but here you keep
gnawin' an aiten at me about the wives o' the Maguigans.
Musha, I wish to marcy, the same wives o' the Maguigans
wor far enough out o' the counthry, for they're the heart-
scald to me anyhow."

"Well, well, Ailey; to the sarra wid them; but about
another thing,—what'll we do wid this goose? Whether is
it betther to roast it or boil it?"

"Arra, Barney, what if we'd not kill it at all, but keep it
an' rear a flock ourselves. There's plinty o' wather an'
grazin' for them about the place."

"Throth, you're right; come or go what will, we had
betther not kill it, the crathur."

"Throth, we won't; I don't stand blood well myself;
an' I'd as soon, to tell you the thruth, you'd *not* ax me to
kill this one *now*, Barney. I don't think it 'ud sarve me."

"Very well," said her husband, yielding to her suggestion with singular good humour; "as it is your wish, the
divil resave the drop will lave its carcase this bout—so let
it be settled that we'll rear a flock ourselves; an' as you
say, Ailey, who knows but the same goose may be sent to
us for good luck."

It was so arranged: but as a solitary fowl of that species
is rather an unusual sight about a countryman's house, they
soon procured it a companion, as they had said, after
which they went to bed every night anxious to dream that

all its eggs might turn out golden ones to them and their children.

Now, perhaps, the sagacious reader may have already guessed that the arrival of the goose, whatever it might have been to honest Barney, was an excellent apology for a capital piece of by-play to his wife. The worthy fowl had not, in fact, been twenty-four hours at their place, when in came " the two tainted wives of the Maguigans!" This visit was an open one, and paid in the evening, a little before the men returned from their daily labour. Great was Barney's astonishment then, when on reaching home, he found Bid and Betty Maguigan in conference with Ailey; and what appeared to him remarkably strange, if not rather hardy on their part, was the fact that they carried on the conversation without evincing the slightest consciousness of offence. It is true this had not hitherto been actually proved, but it is needless to say that the suspicion entertained against them was nearly tantamount to proof. Their absences were so difficult to be accounted for, and the situations in which they were found so critical, that it was impossible even for their warmest friends to assert that they were blameless. As Barney entered the house, they addressed him with singular good humour and kindness, but it was easy to infer from his short monosyllabic replies that they had in his case a strong prejudice to overcome.

" Musha, how are you, Barney?"

" At the present time not comfortable."

This was accompanied by a quick suspicious glance from them to his wife.

" Why, there's nothing wrong wid you, we hope?"

" Maybe that's more than I can say."

" You're not unwell, sure?"

" No."

" Barney," said the wife; " Bid and Betty came runnin' up

to look at the goose ; an' the sorra one o' them but says it's the greatest bully they seen this many a day."

This was meant as a soother ;—" for Barney himself," to to use the words of Ailey, " was as proud as e'er a one o' the childhre out of the same goose."

His brow cleared a little at this adroit appeal to his vanity, and he sat down with a look of more sauvity.

" Why, thin, Barney, it's a nice present all out."

" It's more than the Finnigans would get from Aunt Madge, any way," said Ailey, " for Barney's her favourite.

" Is that by way of news," asked Barney, whose vanity was highly tickled, notwithstanding his assumed indifference. " Every fool knows I was always that."

" It's no secret," observed Betty, who, as well as Bid, knew his weakness here ; " an' it's only a proof of her own sinse into the bargain. They're a mane pack, thim Finnigans."

" Oh, the scruff o' the airth," exclaimed Bid ; " why would you mintion thim an' a dacent man in the one day ? "

" Come, Betty," said the other ; " my goodness, we haven't a minute now, the good men 'll swear we're about no good if they find us out when they come home."

" Hut," said Barney, " sit a while can't yez ? You can do no harm here any how."

" Nor anywhere else, I hope," said Bid ; " but, indeed, Barney, you don't know the men they are, or you'd hunt us home like bag-foxes."

" Don't be axin' them to stay, thin," said Ailey ; " what they say I believe is thrue enough ; an' for my part, I wouldn't wish to have our little place mintioned one way or other, in any dispute that yez may have, Betty."

" Troth," said Bid, " I don't b'lieve they'd think us safe in a chapel ; an' God forgive them for it. Come, Betty, if we wish to avoid a battle, we have not a minute to spare. Oh thin Ailey Brady, it's you that has the good-nathur'd sinsible husband, that doesn't keep you night and day in a state of heart-scald.   Throth you're a happy woman.   May God spare him to you ! "

" Throth, not that he's to the fore, himself," rejoined his wife, " I'll say this, that a betther husband never drew breath this day.   Divil a word he turns on me wanst in the twelve months."

" We believe it," they replied ; " the dacent man's above it ; he wouldn't demane himself by skulkin' about, an' watchin' and pokin' his nose into every hole an' corner the way our mane fellows does be doin', till we can't——bless ourselves for them."

" No, the sorra thing o' the kind he does ; sure I must tell the truth any way."

" Well, God be wid yez ; we must be off.   Good bye, Barney, sure you can bear witness for us this bout."

" That I can, Bid, an' will too ; God bless yez ! "

As they apprehended, their husbands, on returning from their work, were once more in a fume, on finding the good women absent.

" Soh ! " said Dick, " is it a fair question to ax where yez war ? "

" Fair enough," said Bid.

" You wor at the ould work," observed Harry ; " but I tell you what, by the holy St. Countryman ! we won't suffer this much longer—that's one piece o' truth for yez ! "

" Where war yez I say ? " asked his brother sternly ; " no desate, now ; tell us plump an' at wanst where yez war ? "

" Why, then, if you want to know," replied Betty, " we wor up seein' Barney Brady's goose."

" Barney Brady's goose ! " exclaimed Harry, with a look as puzzled as ever was visible on a human face.

" Barney Brady's goose ! " repeated Dick, with a face quite as mystified.   The two brothers looked at each other for nearly a minute, but neither could read in the other's coun- tenance any thing like intelligence.

"What are they at?" asked Dick.

"Why, that they have their tongues in their cheeks at us, to be sure!" replied the other.

"Why, where else would we have them," said Bid; "it isn't in our pockets you'd have us to carry them?"

"I wish to Jamini they wor any where but where they are," returned her husband. "What do you mane?"

"Jist what we say, that we wor up takin' a look at Barney Brady's goose."

"Why, the curse o' the crows upon you, don't you know that Barney Brady never had a goose in his life?"

"He has one now then," replied Bid.

"Ay," added her sister, "an' as fine a bully of a goose as ever I seen wid my two livin' eyes."

"Sure," said Bid, "if you won't believe us, can't yez go up an' see?"

This, after all, was putting the matter to a very fair issue, and the two men resolved to take her at her word, each feeling quite satisfied of the egregious falsehood their wives had attempted to make them swallow.

"Come, Dick," said Harry, "put on your hat: the sorra step further we'll let this go till we see it out; an' all I can say is," he added, addressing the women, "that you had betther not be here before us when we come back, if we find you out in a falsity."

They had not gone fifty yards from the door when the laughter of the two women was loud and vehement at the scene which had just occurred, especially at the ingenuity with which Bid had sent them abroad, and thus got the coast clear for their purposes.

"Out wid yez, childre, and play awhile—*honom-an-dioual!* Is it ever an' always burnin' your shins over the fire yez are? Away out o' this, an' don't come back till we call yez."

When the children were gone, they brought in two neigh-

bours' wives, who lived immediately beside them, shut and
bolted the door, and again did the mysterious rites of
which we have so often written, proceed as before. On
this occasion, however, there was much caution used, every
now and then the door was stealthily opened, and a face
might be seen peeping out to prevent a surprise. The conversation was carried on in a tone unusually low, and the
laughter, which was frequent, and principally at the expense
of their husbands, could scarcely be heard through the
door.

In due time, however, the parties dispersed ; and when
Dick and Harry returned, they found their wives each in-
dustriously engaged in the affairs of the household, which,
indeed, they went through with an air of offended dignity,
and a tartness of temper that contrasted strongly with the
sheepish and somewhat crest-fallen demeanour of their
spouses.

"Musha bad luck to you for a dog an' lave my way, you
dirty crooked cur, you," exclaimed Bid, to the dog that
innocently crossed her path ; "it's purty lives we lead one
way or other. We have enough, dear knows, to try our
temper widout you comin' acrass us—ha ! you divil's limb !
out wid you ! Well," she added, after a short pause, "you
see we're here before you for all your big threats ; but I'll
tell you what it is, Harry, upon my sowl you must turn a
new leaf or I'll lose a fall. If you or Dick have any thing
against us, why don't you prove it manfully at wanst, and
not be snakin' about the bush the way yez do. The sorra
aither of us will lie undher your low, mane thoughts any
longer. I hope you seen Barney Brady's goose on your
thravels? Faugh upon ye ! Troth you ought to be
ashamed to rise your head this month to come !"

"Ay, now you're at it," exclaimed Harry, rising and
putting on his hat ; "but for my part I'll lave you to fight
the walls till your tongue tires. All you want is some one

to jaw back to you, just to keep the ball goin'. *Bannaght latht* for a while ! "

Outside the door he met his brother.

" I was goin' to sit awhile wid you," said Dick ; " I can't stand that woman's tongue good or bad."

" Faith, an' I was jist goin' into *you*," replied the other, " Bid's in her glory ; there's no facin' her. Let us go an' sit awhile wid Charley Magrath."

" Bad luck to Barney Brady's goose, any how ; it'll be a long day till we hear the end of it."

" The curse o' Cromwell on it, but it's the unlucky bird to us this night, sure enough," re-echoed his brother. "Come an' let us have a while's shanahas wid Charley till these women settle."

They accordingly went, and ere a lapse of many minutes their wives were together again for the purpose of comparing notes, and of indulging in another hearty laugh at their husbands.

Barney Brady's goose now began to be a goose of some eminence. In short, it was much talked of, and had its character and qualities debated *pro* and *con.* One thing, however, was very remarkable in this business ; and that thing was, that the male portion of the neighbours hated it with a cordiality which they could not disguise, whilst their wives, on the other hand, defended it most strenuously against all the calumnious attacks of its enemies. The dreaded change, to which we have before alluded, was now going on rapidly, and it somehow happened that scarcely a family feud connected with it took place within a certain circle of Barney Brady's house, in which his goose was not either directly or indirectly concerned.

Barney himself, whose suspicions had been for a long time lulled by the interest he took in a bird of his own procuring, at length began to look queer at certain

glimpses which he caught of what was going forward.

"Ailey," said he, with a good deal of uneasiness, "what
brings up them wives o' the Maguigans here, that I spoke
so much about?"

"Why, throth, Barney, I thought there was something
wrong wid the poor goose, an' I sent down for them."

"By the mortial man, I wish," replied Barney, "that I
had never brought the dirty drab of a crathur about the
place. Why, if all you say about it is true, it never had a
day's health since it came to us, an' yet I'll take my oath
it's as fat a goose this minute as ever wagged."

"An' right well you know, Barney, it got delicate afthur
it came to us: an't stands to raison,—the crathur fretted
afther them it left behind it."

"No, confusion to the fret; it had no raison in life when
it got a comrade to keep it company. Be me sowl it's I
that fretted, an' I dunna but I'm the greatest goose o' the
two for not wringin' its head off, an' puttin' a stop to a crew
o' women comin' to the place on the head of it. What's
wrong wid it now?"

"Why, throth, I didn't know myself till Bid Maguigan
tould me. I thought it was sick, but it's not. Sure the
poor thing's goin' to clock. an' I must set the eggs for it
to-morrow."

"I hope you'll keep your word then," said Barney, "for
although it would go against me to harm the crathur, still,
I tell you, that if the crew I'm spaken of does be comin'
about the place undher pretence of it, be the crass I'll be
apt to give it a dog's knock sometime; an' take care, Ailey,
that more geese than one won't come in for a knock."

In this instance, however, it so happened that Ailey had
truth on her side, the fact, indeed, was unquestionable, and
enabled the good women of the neighbourhood to keep
their angry husbands quiet for a considerable time after-

wards. With some of the latter the report gained ground very slowly, but on ascertaining that it was a fact, many of them felt considerably relieved.

The reader already sees that Barney Brady's goose was really a goose of importance, whose out-goings and in-comings, whose health or illness, weal or woe, involved the ease and comfort, or the doubt and anxiety of a considerable number of persons in the surrounding district. Barney himself, however, felt that her incubation was rather a matter of discomfort to him than otherwise ; for had she been up and stirring, he knew that she might be liable to all the "skyey influences" that geese are heirs to. Now, however, Ailey had no apology arising from her to receive visits from the black sheep of the neighbourhood, and yet he often detected them, either in his house or leaving it. This troubled him very much, but still Ailey failed not in her excuse, and as he knew she seldom went out, he did not suspect, much less believe, that his own house would or could be made the scene of those private meetings, held by such women as the Maguigans, or others still farther sunk in the practices which were abroad.

Things, however, were ripening, for whilst Barney gravely meditated upon the moral prospect that presented itself in the country, the task of incubation was crowned by the birth of a fine brood of goslins, amounting to eleven out of twelve, every one of which appeared to be healthy, and to give promise in due time of arriving at the full proportion of a goodly goose, allowance being made as usual for fate and foxes.

Our readers are now to suppose two things, first, that the goodly brood is reared ; and, secondly, that the mysterious but predominant vice of the neighbourhood is fast increasing. Barney had promised himself a handsome return from the sale of the geese, and hoped in a year or two, to be able, from the proceeds, to buy a cow or a heifer, and never,

besides, to be without a good fat dinner at Michaelmas.
All this was creditable, and becoming an industrious man.
In the meantime he thought that, somehow, the flock
appeared lessened in his eye ; that is to say, that they
looked as a whole, to be rather diminished in number.
The thing had struck him before, but in that feeble and
indistinct manner in which, in easy minds, leaves not an
impression behind it which ever leads to the following up
of the suggestion.   But on this occasion, great was his
dismay and astonishment when, on reckoning them, he
found that three were most unaccountably missing.   Here
was more mystery ; and, unfortunately, this discovery was
made at a time when he had every reason to suspect that
Aileen had at length been drawn into the prevalent practices·
The fact was, that many secret and guarded movements had
been of late noticed by him, of which, from motives of deep
and sagacious policy, he had determined to take no open
cognizance, being resolved to allow Aileen to lull herself
into that kind of false security which is usually produced
by indifference or stupidity on the part of the husband.

Here was a matter, however, that could not be overlooked,
and accordingly he demanded an explanation ; but this in a
manner so exceedingly sage and cunning, that we are sure
our readers cannot withhold from him the mark of their approbation.

"Aileen," said he, without appearing to labour under any
suspicion whatsoever, "you had betther look afther them
crathurs o' geese this mornin' ; there's three o' them missin'
I can reckon only eight, not countin' the gandher."

"Bad cess to your curiosity, Barney : you're as bad as a
woman, so you are, countin' the geese ! Musha go to
heaven."

"No, divil a foot," said her husband, starting up in a passion, an' be the holy vestment, if you don't tell me on the
nail what bekem of them, I won't lave a goose o' them alive

in twinty minnits. An' more than that, take care an' don't
—take care I say—don't exaggrawate me, I tell you."

"Well, throth, Barney, this is good! afore your own
childre too. An' now if you want to know, I did nothin'
wrong wid thim, in regard that I knew well enough you'd
bring me over the coals about it; ay did I. You gave me
two an' sixpence to pay my Aisther dues; an' I met my
aunt, and my sisther an' her bachelor, Charley Cleary, an' I
axed thim in an' thrated them dacently wid your money, an'
of coorse I had to sell *one* o' the geese to make it up."

"Then of coorse, too, you ped your dues."

"Divil send you news whether I did or not. I'll tell you
what, Barney, sooner than I'd lead such a life, I'd——"

"You'd what? you'd what? But I curb myself. To-
morrow's market day. Now I tell you, out you'll trudge
step for step along wid myself; an' be the mortual man,
two o' the same geese must go afore you lave the town.
At your elbow I'll stay till they're sould; an' every market
day till they're gone, a pair o' them must go."

"Why, then, you mane-spirited *pittiouge*, is it to sell geese
—arra what'll you come to at last, you blanket, you? Sure
if I did wrong, can't you beat me? So you'll stand at my
elbow till I sell my geese? Be me soul if you do I'll bring
a blush in your face, if there's such a thing in it, which
there's not, or you wouldn't make an ould woman—a *Molshy*
—of yourself as you're doin'. Upon my dickens I wondher
you didn't sit on the eggs yourself; but, sure, I'll say you did,
to-morrow, an' then they'll bring three prices! Saver above,
but I'm leadin' a happy life wid you an' you're geese!
Musha bad luck be from them every day they rise, but they
have been a bitther pill to me from the beginnin'. Sure
yourself an' them's a common by-word. Can either of us
go to mass or market that the neighbours doesn't be axin'
wid a grin, 'how is Barney Brady's goose?'"

It would be acting rather unbecoming the dignity of a

14

historian were we to dwell too minutely on the bitter feuds which followed the sale of every goose until the last of the clutch was disposed of. The truth is, that Barney, in spite of all his authority and watchfulness and conscious wisdom to boot, was never able to lay a finger upon a single penny of the proceeds, nor could he with all his acuteness of scent, smell out the purpose to which Aileen applied it. No: we are wrong in this. He did find it out, and, as we have said, strongly suspect it too; but he was hitherto able in no instance to detect Aileen so as perfectly to satisfy himself and bring the proof home against her.

A circumstance, however, now occurred which brought the whole dark secrecy of this proceeding to light. Barney, one day, while searching in some corner for a hatchet, which he wanted, stumbled upon a smooth round vessel with a handle on one side, a pipe on the other, and a close-fitting lid on the top. Cruikshank or Brooke would have enjoyed the grin of malignant triumph which played upon his features, as with one hand stretched under the bed, he lay curiously feeling and examining the vessel in question. Very fortunately for him Aileen was cutting some greens in the garden for their dinner, and was consequently totally ignorant of the discovery. The opportunity was too good to be lost, and Barney, who, although he knew not the use to which the vessel was applied, having never seen one before, yet suspecting that it was part and parcel of the wicked system which prevailed, resolved, now that the coast was clear, to carry it to those who could determine its use and application. He immediately whipped it out, took a hasty glance, and, hiding it under his big coat, stole off, unperceived by Aileen, to consult the two Maguigans. Here, however, was no chance of solving the mystery, the Maguigans never having, any more than himself, seen to their knowledge any vessel of the kind before. Long and serious was their deliberation respecting the steps necessary to be taken upon this important occasion ; one suggesting one thing, another an-other.   At length it occurred to them, that their best plan would be to consult Kate Doorish, an old woman who was considered an infallible authority.   Barney, accordingly, once more putting this delfic enigma under his coat, set off to Kate's house, with something like a prophetic assurance of success.   In this again he was doomed to be disappointed, Kate, in truth, was the very last person with whom, had he known as much as his wife, he would or ought to have ex-pected information.   She it was who had chiefly corrupted the good wives of the village, both by precept and example and on her head of course did the original sin of the whole neighbourhood lie.   Barney found her at home, and took it for granted that the difficulty must now be solved without further trouble.

"God save you, Kate."

"God save you kindly, Barney.   How is Aileen and the childher ? "

"All as tight as tuppence, Kate.   What's the news ? any births or marriages abroad ? "

"Ay is there, as many as ever ; an' will be, plase God, to the end o' the chapther, man."

"Why, thin, I believe you're right, Kate.   While the sun shines an' the wind blows, the world will still be goin' ; but, Kate, betuxt you an' me, is it thrue that there's a dale o' bad work goin' on among ourselves ? "

"Faix, I suppose so ; you men never wor good."

"Don't lift me till I fall, Kate ; I mane among the women, I'm tould there's hardly one of them what she ought to be."

"Why, barrin' the grace o' God that's thrue ; for, Barney, where's the man or woman aither that is as they *ought* to be ? glory be to God ! "

"To tell the thruth, Kate, I'm afeard my own wife's not much betther than the rest."

" Faith, if she's as good, man, you have no right to complain. Isn't she good enough for *you* anyhow ? Is it a lady you want ? Musha, cock you up, indeed ! "

" There's thim eleven geese, they're gone now, and not a farden ever I touched of the price of any one of them, only two hogs I got to help to buy leather for a pair of brogues."

" Well ! "

" But I say, Kate, it's not well. Now where did it go to? —answer me that, I tell you she's as bad as the Maguigans, an' of the three, worse. I can't keep them asundher, and the lies they tell us is beyant belief. An' not only that, but when they get together, we're their sport and maygame, an' you know that very well."

" No, nor you don't."

" Don't I ? I tell you I *cotch* them."

" Cotch them ! at what? pullin' down churches ? eh ? "

" Any way I as good as cotch them ; an' here's a piece o' their villany," he added, producing the mystery from under his coat. " Now, Kate, I'll give you share of half a pint if you tell me the right name of this consarn."

" Why," replied Kate, " did you never see one o' these before ; an' is it possible you don't know the name of it ? "

" No ; but I suspect."

" An' so you came here to know the name of it, an' what it's for ? "

" Divil a thing else brought me."

" An' you expect me to turn informer against the dacent woman to satisfy your curiosity ! Get out, you mane-spirited blaggard, how dare you come to me on sich a business? It's a salt herrin' you ought to have tied to your tail, an' be turned out before a drag-hunt, you skulkin' vagabone. Begone out o' this ! "

Discomfitted and grieved he returned home, almost despairing of ever ascertaining the purpose for which the mysterious and strangely-shapen vessel was employed.

Now it so happened that the priest of the parish, Father O'Flaherty, held a station that day in the next townland, and thither did honest Barney repair, that he might have his reverence's opinion upon the vessel which he carried under his coat. He accordingly bent his steps in that direction, and arrived just as the priest had concluded the business of the day.

"Well, Barney," said the priest, "I hope there's nothing wrong."

Barney shook his head with a good deal of solemnity, and replied—

"It's hard to say, your reverence, but I'd be glad to have a word or two in private wid you, if it's agreeable."

The priest brought him into the room where he had been confessing, and inquired what was the matter.

"But first sit down, Barney," said he; "and how is the wife and children?"

"I'm much obliged to you, sir," replied Barney; "but it's not jist convanient to me to sit, in regard of what I'm carryin'—the childre's all well, sir, thank God and your reverence; an' Aileen too, sir, as far as health is consarned."

"But why don't you sit down, man?"

"The divil a one of me can, sir, as I said; I've a thing here that I want to ax your reverence's opinion on; for to tell you the truth, sir, I suspect it to be nothing more or less than a piece of the divil's invintion."

"Where did you get it?"

"Why, sir, I was gropin' about to-day looking for a hatchet, an' I stumbled on it by accident."

As he spoke, he slowly unfolded the skirts of his cothamore, and produced the "mystery of iniquity" to the priest.

The priest, who was a bit of a humorist in his way, cn seeing what Barney carried with such secrecy, laughed

heartily, and commenced a stave or two of the old song,
familiar by the name of—" Oh, Tea-pot, are you there ? "

Oh for the muse of old Meonides, or that tenth lady
from Helicon who jogged the poetic elbow of our own
Mark Bloxam ! Oh for—but this is useless—one line of
Virgil will paint honest Barney, on ascertaining from the
priest, that the utensil he bore about with all the apparent
importance and caution of an antiquarian, was after all the
damnable realization of his worst terrors, and the confirma-
tion of his unprincipled wife's guilt, an accursed tea-pot :—

" Obstupuit, steteruntque comæ, et vox faucibus hæsit."

Truly his dismay and horror could scarcely be painted ; he
started as if he had seen a spirit, his fingers spread, his eyebrows were uplifted, and his eyes protruded almost out of
their sockets ; his very hair, as the poet says, stood upright,
and speech for nearly a minute was denied him.

But this paroxysm of Barney's on discovering what the
mystic vase actually was, demands a few words of explanation. We believe it is pretty well known to most of our
aged readers (if it so happen that any old lady or gentleman will condescend to peruse us), that about half a
century ago, or even later, ere civilization had carried many
of its questionable advantages so far into the remote
recesses of humble life as it does in the present day, there
existed among the lower classes a prejudice against tea-
drinking, that was absolutely revolting, It is, to be sure,
difficult properly to account for this ; but the reader may
rest assured that so it was. In the time of which we speak,
any woman, especially a married one, suspected of "tay-
dhrinkin'," was looked upon as a marked sheep, and if
detected in the act, she was considered a disgrace to her
sex, and her name a reproach to her connexions. Many
circumstances went to create this not unwholesome prejudice, and we shall mention a few of them.

In the first place, tea at that time was by no means so cheap a luxury as it is now ; and, besides, it brought still more luxuries in its train. They could not use tea without sugar ; and it was found that a loaf of "white bread " and butter were a decided improvement. This costly indulgence was naturally and justly looked upon as an act of domestic profligacy, altogether unjustifiable on the part of the poor and struggling classes, who must have distressed themselves and wasted their means in striving to procure it. Nor was this all. It was too frequently found that wives and daughters did not scruple to steal, or otherwise improperly make away with the property of their husbands and fathers, rather than live without this fascinating beverage, which had then the zest of novelty to recommend it. Neither did its injurious consequences, in a moral point of view, end here. Wives and daughters have been known to entail still deeper disgrace upon their families, in order to obtain it. The sons of half-sirs, and of independent farmers, might have been less successful in their gallantries among the females of their father's tenantry, were it not for the silly weakness which often yielded to temptation in this shape. These facts of themselves were sufficient to create an abhorrence against tea among the male portion of the lower classes, and to render it almost infamy for any woman to be known to drink it. Our catalogue of prejudices, however, does not end even here. It was reported—by the husbands, we presume—that tea was every way unlucky about a house, and that no poor family in which it was drunk was ever known to thrive,—and for this reason, that the devil was worshipped in the country from whence it came, and that it was consequently " *the devil's plant.*" But independently of this, did not they all know the wickedness that took place in the high families, when men and women, married and single, from the lord-lieutenant to the squire, met in the middle of night, and in the pitch dark, to drink,

every two of them—that is man and woman—their RAKING
POT OF TEA!   Sure it was well known that the devil was
always present, and made the " tay" himself ; and as most
of the lords and gentlemen were members of the Hell-fire
Club, it stood to reason that the devil and they were all in
their glory.

Now, all this came of "tay dhrinking ; " and how, then,
could it happen but that the old boy must have had a hard
grip of any woman that took it.   Our readers, we trust,
can now understand not only our friend Barney's horror,
on discovering that the vessel he carried about with him
was nothing more nor less than an unholy tea-pot, but also
the distress, and indignation, and jealous vigilance with
which he and the Maguigans kept watch upon the motions
of their inoffensive wives.   Indeed, much of the simplicity
of character which then existed, is now gone, and we have
every reason to regret it, although not more than the unhappy people themselves.   It was truly amusing to witness
the harmless but covert warfare which went on between the
husbands and wives of a village, who assailed each other as
if from masked batteries, whilst a firm and incorruptible
espirit du corps knit the individuals on each side together—
thus joining themselves into a most cunning league for the
purpose of circumventing the opposite party.   And in
later times, when tea was sanctioned at least once a week
—to wit, on Sunday morning—it was highly diverting to
witness the manœuvres resorted to by the good-wife or her
daughters, in order to have a cup of it more frequently.
Sometimes they salted the porridge made for breakfast so
villanously, that there was nothing for it but the "cup o'tay;"
sometimes the schoolmaster was to breakfast with them, and
when the strongest and most fragrant was ready drawn and
awaiting him, it was discovered that the whole matter was
a hoax, got up by the females of the family, that they
might secure it to themselves.   But alas! those good

innocent days are gone, and we fear for ever !—But to return—

"Heaven and earth, your reverence !" exclaimed Barney, when he had recovered himself, "what's to be done ? I'm a ruined man, an' my wife's worse."

Now nobody living understood the nature of Barney's grievance better than the priest, to whom, upon the woful subject of tea-drinking, many a sore complaint, heaven knows, had been carried.

"Why, Barney," said he, pretending ignorance, "what is wrong ? "

"Wrong ! By the mortual man, your reverence—God pardon me for swearin' in your presence—she's at it hard and fast for the last nine months."

"Nine months ! how is that ? what do you mean ? "

"The devil's plant, the tay, sir. Aileen, my wife's to the back bone into it. She an' them two rotten sheep, the Maguigans' wives. Ay are they ; an' the truth, the naked truth, is, sir, that they're all roddled wid the same stick— divil a thing but truth I'm tellin' you."

"Tut ! you're dreaming, Barney. How could your wife afford to drink tea ? Where could she get the money for it ? You have none to spare, I believe ; and if you had, I don't think you'd allow it to her for such a purpose."

"It ariz all along out of a damnable—heaven forgive me agin' for taking its name afore you, sir—out of a damnable goose I got from an aunt o' mine ; and may all the plagues of Aygip light upon her, an' on the dotin' ould goose of a gandher that's along wid her ! "

"Why, what has the goose to do with your wife's tea-drinking ? "

"Every thing, and be cursed to her—the dirty black-guard fowl made me a laughin'-stock to the neighbours in the beginnin', and now my wife has made me worse. God only knows what she has made me; a tay-dhrinker, your reverence knows, will do any thing."

"But the goose, Barney? I can't connect the goose with your wife's tea-drinking."

"*Thonom an dioual*, sir—the same goose brought us a clackin' of eleven as fine fat birds as ever you tasted in your life; an' confusion to the one of them but she drank in tea, barrin' two shillings she gave me to buy leather for a pair o' brogues, when my heels were on the stones."

"Is it the goose or your wife you're speaking of?"

"My wife, the thief."

"You don't mean that it was she brought you the clackin' of——"

"No, sir," replied Barney with a grin, which he could not suppress; "nor, be me sowl, it wasn't the goose drank the tay aither. But what's to be done, your reverence?"

"Is the goose fat now, Barney?"

"Faith, sir, Squire Warnock's a skilleton to her; she'd want an arm chair to be rolled about in."

"Well, Barney, to get out of trouble, send me the goose and gander, and make your mind easy. I'll cure the tea-drinking; or at all events, I'll undertake that your wife won't taste a single cup without you knowing it."

"You shall have them, sir; but faith I say it's a bould undertaking. God grant you may succeed in it—hopin' always that it mayn't be too late, so far as *I'm* consarned; for they say that a tay-dhrinker has no scruples good or bad. Oh murdher! God pity the man that has a tay-dhrinkin' wife, an' undhertakes to rear geese! I'm nothing but a marthyr to them."

"Barney, I'll tell you what you'll do," says the priest. "Take this same tea-pot back to your own house, and leave it, unknown to your wife, exactly in the spot where you got it. After this, keep singing, 'Tea-pot, are you there?' during the remainder of the day; and you may throw out a hint to her that you have lately seen such a thing; then watch her well, and in a day or two let me know how she'll act. Come now, put it under your tail and be off. I have given you proper instructions."

Barney thanked the priest, rolled it up in the tail of his great-coat as before, and made towards home; but not without a determination first to see and consult with the Maguigans. This, indeed, was a bitter meeting. No sooner had his two neighbours satisfied themselves that it was a *bona fide* tea-pot, than they solemnly pledged themselves, heart and hand, to support Barney in any plan that might enable them to put an end to tea-drinking for ever. They then separated, having as good as sworn an oath that they would mutually sustain and back one another in this severe and opprobrious trial.

It was very fortunate for Barney that Aileen had gone to bring in a pitcher of water for the supper, when he reached home, as by that means he had an opportunity of replacing the tea-pot without the possibility of her seeing him. Great, however, was her astonishment, or rather consternation, when on entering the house she heard Barney singing, "O tea-pot, are you there?" in a tone so jolly and full of spirits, that she knew not in what light to consider this unusual inclination to melody—whether as the result of accident or design.

"Barney, dear," said she, with more affection than usual, "where wor you?"

"In several places, Aileen my honey, I seen many strange sights to-day, Aileen."

"What wor they, Barney, darling? Tell us one o' them."

"Why, I was lookin' about to-day, Aileen, for an article I wanted—a hatchet, it was to mend a gate—and, upon my throth, I found a jinteel tea-pot in anything but jinteel company. 'O tea-pot, are you there?'" &c, &c., and he gave her very sturdily a second stave of the same melody.

This melodious system of bitter jocularity he continued like a man on the rack for two or three days, during which period he observed that several secret conferences took place between Aileen and the tainted wives of her neighbours, as was evident from her occasional absence and the rapid expresses that passed from time to time between them. The fact was, that the finding of the tea-pot proved a very fortunate discovery, and was attended by a no less important result than the breaking up of the tea-drinking confederacy that existed in the village.

We have now solved and explained this great mystery —and, like all other mysteries, discovery put an end to it. Aileen made humble and sufficient apologies for having been drawn into the grievous immorality of tea-drinking. As a token that the wickedness was for ever abandoned, the tea-pot was brought out and smashed with all due ceremony. Father O'Flaherty too was induced to issue from the altar so severe an interdict against the forbidden beverage, as altogether suppressed the practice throughout the parish.

CONDY CULLEN:

and how he defeated the Exciseman.

YOUNG Condy Cullen was descended from a long line of private distillers, and of course, exhibited in his own person all the practical wit, sagacity, cunning, and fertility of invention, which the natural genius of the family, sharpened by long experience, had created from generation to generation, as a standing capital to be handed down from father to son. There was scarcely a trick, evasion, plot, scheme, or manœuvre that had ever been resorted to by his ancestors, that Condy had not at his finger ends ; and though but a lad of sixteen at the time we present him to the reader, yet be it observed, that he had had his mind, even at that age, admirably trained by four or five years of keen vigorous practice, in all the resources necessary to meet the subtle vigilance and stealthy circumvention of that prowling animal—the gauger. In fact, Condy's talents did not merely consist in an acquaintance with the hereditary tricks of his family. These, of themselves, would prove but a miserable defence against the ever-varying ingenuity with which the progressive skill of the still-hunter masks his approaches, and conducts his designs. On the contrary every new plan of the gauger must be met and defeated by a counter-plan equally novel, but with this difference in the character of both, that whereas the exciseman's devices are the result of mature deliberation—Paddy's, from the very nature of the circumstances, must be necessarily extemporaneous and rapid. The hostility between the parties, being, as it is, carried on through such varied stratagem on both sides, and characterised by such adroit and able duplicity, by so many quick and unexpected turns of incident—it would be utter fatuity in either, to rely upon obsolete tricks and stale manœuvres. Their relative position and occupation do not, therefore, merely exhibit a contest between Law and that mountain nymph, Liberty, or between the Excise Board and the Smuggler—it presents a more interesting point for observation, namely, the struggle between mind and mind—between wit and wit—between roguery and knavery.

It might be very amusing to detail from time to time, a few of those keen encounters of practical cunning, which take place between the potheen distiller and his lynx-eyed foe, the gauger. They are curious as throwing light upon the national character of our people, and as evidences of the surprising readiness of wit, fertility of invention, and irresistible humour, which they mix up with almost every actual concern of life, no matter how difficult or critical it may be. Nay, it mostly happens that the character of the peasant in all its fulness, rises in proportion to what he is called upon to encounter, and that the laugh at, or the hoax upon the gauger, keeps pace with the difficulty that is overcome. But now to our short story.

Two men in the garb of gentlemen were riding along a remote by-road, one morning in the month of October, about the year 1827, or '28, I'm not certain which. The air was remarkably clear, keen, and bracing ; a hoar frost for the few preceding nights had set in, and then lay upon the fields about them, melting gradually, however, as the sun got strength, with the exception of the sides of such hills and valleys as his beams could not reach, until evening chilled their influence too much to absorb the feathery whiteness which covered them. Our equestrians had nearly reached a turn in the way, which we should observe in this place skirted the brow of a small declivity that lay on the right. In point of fact, it was a moderately inclined plane or slope rather than a declivity ; but be this as it may, the flat at its foot was studded over with furze bushes, which grew so close and level, that a person might almost imagine it possible to walk upon their surface. On coming within about two hundred and fifty yards of this angle the horsemen noticed a lad, not more than sixteen, jogging on towards them, with a keg upon his back. The eye of one of them was immediately lit with that vivacious sparkling of habitual sagacity, which marks the practised gauger among ten thousand. For a single moment he drew up his horse, an action which, however slight in itself, intimated more plainly than he could have wished, the obvious interest which had just been excited in him. Short as was the pause, it betrayed him, for no sooner had the lad noticed it, than he crossed the ditch and disappeared round the angle we have mentioned, and upon the side of the declivity.   To gallop to the spot, dismount, cross the ditch also, and pursue him, was only the work of a few minutes.

"We have him," said the gauger, "we have him—one thing is clear, he cannot escape us."

"Speak for yourself, Stinton," replied his companion—"as for me, not being an officer of his Majesty's Excise, I decline taking any part in the pursuit—it is a fair battle, so fight it out between you—I am with you now only through curiosity."   He had scarcely concluded, when they heard a voice singing the following lines, in a spirit of that hearty hilarity which betokens a cheerful contempt of care, and an utter absence of all apprehension :

> "Oh ! Jemmy, she sez, you are my true lover,
> You are all the riches that I do adore ;
> I solemnly swear now, I'll ne'er have anoder,
> My heart it is fixed to never love more."

The music then changed to a joyous whistle, and imme-diately they were confronted by a lad, dressed in an old red coat patched with grey frieze, who, on seeing them, ex-hibited in his features a most ingenuous air of natural sur-prise.   He immediately ceased to whistle, and with every mark of respect, putting his hand to his hat, said in a voice, the tones of which spoke of kindness and deference,—

"God save ye, gintlemen."

"I say, my lad," said the gauger, "where is the customer with the keg on his back ?—he crossed over there this moment."

"Where, when, sir ?" said the lad with a stare of sur-prise.

"Where? when ? why this minute, and in this place."

"And was it a whisky keg, sir ?"

"Sir, I am not here to be examined by you," replied Stinton, "confound me if the conniving young rascal is not sticking me into a cross-examination already—I say, red coat, where is the boy with the keg, sir?"

"As for a boy, I did see a boy, sir; but the never a keg he had—hadn't he a grey frieze coat, sir?"

"He had."

"And wasn't it a dauny bit short about the skirts, plase your honour?"

"Again he's at me. Sirra, unless you tell me where he is in half a second, I shall lay my whip to your shoulders!"

"The sorra a keg I seen, then, sir—the last keg I seen was——"

"Did you see a boy without the keg, answering to the description I gave you?"

"You gave no description of it, sir—but even if you did, when I didn't see it, how could I tell your honour any thing about it?"

"Where is the fellow, you villain?" exclaimed the gauger in a fury, "where is he gone to? You admit you saw him; as for the keg, it cannot be far from us—but where is he?"

"Dad I saw a boy wid a short frieze coat upon him, crassing the road there below, and runnin' down the other side of that ditch."

This was too palpable a lie to stand the test even of a glance at the ditch in question; which was nothing more than a slight mound that ran down a long lea field, on which there was not even the appearance of a shrub.

The gauger looked at his companion—then turning to the boy—"Come, come, my lad," said he, "you know that lie is rather cool. Don't you feel in your soul that a rat could not have gone in that direction, without our seeing it?"

"Bedad an' I saw him," returned the lad, "wid a grey coat upon him, that was a little too short in the tail—it's better than half an hour agone."

"The boy I speak of you must have met," said Stinton; "it's not five minutes—no, not more than three, since he came inside the field?"

"That my feet may grow to the ground then if I seen a boy in or about this place, widin the time, barrin' myself."

The gauger eyed him closely for a short space, and pulling out half-a-crown, said—"Harkee, my lad, a word with you in private."

The fact is, that during the latter part of this dialogue, the worthy exciseman observed the cautious distance at which the boy kept himself from the grasp of him and his companion. A suspicion consequently began to dawn upon him, that in defiance of appearances, the lad himself might be the actual smuggler. On re-considering the matter, this suspicion almost amounted to certainty; the time was too short to permit even the most ingenious cheat to render himself and his keg invisible in a manner so utterly unaccountable. On the other hand, when he reflected on the open, artless character of the boy's song; the capricious change to a light-hearted whistle, the surprise so naturally, and the respect so deferentially expressed, joined to the dissimilarity of dress, he was confounded again, and scarcely knew on which side to determine. Even the lad's reluctance to approach him might proceed from fear of the whip. He felt resolved, however, to ascertain this point, and with the view of getting the lad into his hands, he showed him half-a-crown, and addressed him as already stated.

The lad on seeing the money, appeared to be instantly caught by it, and approached him, as if it had been a bait he could not resist; a circumstance which again staggered the gauger. In a moment, however, he seized him.

15

"Come, now," said he, unbuttoning his coat, "you will oblige me by stripping."

"And why so?" said the lad, with a face which might have furnished a painter or sculptor with a perfect notion of curiosity, perplexity, and wonder.

"Why so?" replied Stinton—"we shall see—we shall soon see."

"Surely you don't think I've hid the keg about me," said the other, his features now relaxing into such an appearance of utter simplicity, as would have certainly made any other man but a gauger give up the examination as hopeless, and exonerate the boy from any participation whatsoever in the transaction.

"No, no," replied the gauger, "by no means, you young rascal.   See here, Cartwright," he continued, addressing his companion—"the keg, my precious;" again turning to the lad—"Oh! no, no, it would be cruel to suspect you of any thing but the purest of simplicity."

"Look here, Cartwright," having stripped the boy of his coat and turned it inside out, "there's a coat—there's thrift —there's economy for you—Come, sir, tuck on, tuck on instantly; here, I shall assist you—up with your arms— straighten your neck; it will be both straightened and stretched yet, my cherub.   What think you now, Cartwright?   Did you ever see a metamorphosis in your life so quick, complete, and unexpected?"

His companion was certainly astonished in no small degree on seeing the red coat, when turned, become a comfortable grey frieze, one precisely such as he who bore the keg had on.   Nay, after surveying his person and dress a second time, he instantly recognised him as the same.

The only interest, we should observe, which this gentleman had in the transaction, arose from the mere gratification which a keen observer of character, gifted with a strong relish for humour, might be supposed to feel.   The gauger, in sifting the matter, and scenting the trail of the keg, was now in his glory, and certainly when met by so able an opponent as our friend Condy, for it was indeed himself, furnished a very rich treat to his friend.

"Now," he continued, addressing the boy again—"lose not a moment in letting us know where you've hid the keg."

"The sorra bit of it I hid—it fell of a' me, an' I lost it; sure I'm lookin' afther it myself, so I am;" and he moved over while speaking, as if pretending to search for it in a thin hedge, which could by no means conceal it.

"Cartwright," said the gauger, "did you ever see any thing so perfect as this, so ripe a rascal—you don't understand him now. Here, you simpleton; harkee, sirra, there must be no playing the lapwing with me; back here to the same point. We may lay it down as a sure thing that whatever direction he takes from this spot is the wrong one; so back here, you, sir, till we survey the premises about us for your traces."

The boy walked sheepishly back, and appeared to look about him for the keg, with a kind of earnest stupidity, which was altogether inimitable.

"I say, my boy," asked Stinton ironically, "don't you look rather foolish now? can you tell your right hand from your left?"

"I can," replied Condy, holding up his left, "there's my right hand."

"And what do you call the other?" said Cartwright.

"My left, bedad, any how, an' that's true enough."

Both gentlemen laughed heartily.

"But it's carrying the thing a little too *far*," said the gauger: "in the meantime let us hear how you prove it?"

"Aisy enough, sir," replied Condy, "bekase I am left-handed—this," holding up the left, "is the right hand to me, whatever you may say to the conthrary."

Condy's countenance expanded, after he had spoken, into a grin so broad and full of grotesque sarcasm, that Stinton and his companion both found their faces, in spite of them, get rather blank under its influences.

"What the deuce!" exclaimed the gauger, "are we to be here all day? Come, sir, bring us at once to the keg."

He was here interrupted by a laugh from Cartwright, so vociferous, loud, and hearty, that he looked at him with amazement—"Hey, dey," he exclaimed, "what's the matter, what's the matter; what new joke is this?"

For some minutes, however, he could not get a word from the other, whose laughter appeared as if never to end; he walked to and fro in absolute convulsions, bending his body and clapping his hands together, with a vehemence quite unintelligible.

"What is it, man?" said the other, "confound you, what is it?"

"Oh!" replied Cartwright, "I am sick, perfectly feeble."

"You have it to yourself at all events," observed Stinton.

"And shall keep it to myself," said Cartwright, "for if your sagacity is over-reached, you must be contented to sit down under defeat—I won't interfere."

Now, in this contest between the gauger and Condy, even so slight a thing as one glance of an eye by the latter, might have given a proper cue to an opponent so sharp as Stinton. Condy, during the whole dialogue, consequently preserved the most vague and indefinable visage imaginable, except in the matter of his distinction between right and left; and Stinton, who watched his eye with the shrewdest vigilance, could make nothing of it. Not so was it between him and Cartwright; for during the closing paroxysms of his mirth, Stinton caught his eye fixed upon a certain mark barely visible upon the hoar frost, which mark extended down to the furze bushes that grew at the foot of the slope where they then stood.

As a staunch old hound lays his nose to the trail of a hare or fox, so did the gauger pursue the trace of the keg down the little hill ; for the fact was, that Condy, having no other resource, trundled it off towards the furze, into which it settled perfectly to his satisfaction ; and with all the quickness of youth and practice, instantly turned his coat, which had been made purposely for such rencounters. This accomplished, he had barely time to advance a few yards round the angle of the hedge, and changing his whole manner as well as his appearance, acquitted himself as the reader has already seen. That he could have carried the keg down to the cover, then conceal it, and return to the spot where they met him, was utterly beyond the reach of human exertion, so that in point of fact they never could have suspected that the whisky lay in such a place.

The triumph of the gauger was now complete, and a complacent sense of his own sagacity sat visible on his features. Condy's face, on the other hand, became considerably lengthened, and appeared quite as rueful and mortified as the other's was joyous and confident.

" Who's sharpest now, my knowing one ? " said he, "who is the laugh against, as matters stand between us ? "

" The sorra give you good of it," said Condy sulkily.

" What is your name ? " inquired Stinton.

" Barney Keerigan's my name," replied the other indignantly ; "an' I'm not ashamed of it, nor afeard to tell it to you or any man."

" What, of the Keerigans of Killoghan ? "

" Ay jist, of the Keerigans of Killoghan."

" I know the family," said Stinton, " they are decent *in their way*—but come, my lad, don't lose your temper, and answer me another question. Where were you bringing this whisky ? "

" To a betther man than ever stood in your shoes," replied Condy, in a tone of absolute defiance—" to a

gintleman any way," with a peculiar emphasis on the word
gintleman.

" But what's his name ? "

" Mr. Stinton's his name—gauger Stinton."

The shrewd exciseman stood and fixed his keen eye on
Condy for upwards of a minute, with a glance of such
piercing scrutiny as scarcely any consciousness of imposture
could withstand.

Condy on the other hand, stood and eyed him with an
open, unshrinking, yet angry glance ; never winced, but
appeared by the detection of his keg, to have altogether
forgotten the line of cunning policy he had previously
adopted, in a mortification which had predominated over
duplicity and art.

He is now speaking truth, thought the gauger ; he has
lost his temper, and is completely off his guard.

" Well, my lad," he continued, " that is very good so far,
but who sent the keg to Stinton ? "

" Do you think," said Condy, with a look of strong contempt at the gauger, for deeming him so utterly silly as to
tell him, " Do you think that you can make me turn
informer?   There's none of *that* blood in me, thank goodness."

" Do you know Stinton ? "

" How could I know the man I never seen," replied
Condy, still out of temper ; " but one thing I don't know,
gintlemen, and that is, whether you have any right to take
my whisky or not ? "

" As to that, my good lad, make your mind easy—I'm
Stinton."

" You, sir ! " said Condy, with well-feigned surprise.

" Yes," replied the other, " I'm the very man you were
bringing the keg to.   And now I'll tell you what you must
do for me ; proceed to my house with as little delay as
possible ; ask to see my daughter—ask for Miss Stinton—

take this key and desire her to have the keg put into the cellar ; she'll know the key, and let it also be as a token, that she is to give you your breakfast ; say I desired that keg to be placed to the right of the five-gallon one I seized on Thursday last, that stands on a little stillion under my blunderbuss."

" Of coorse," said Condy, who appeared to have misgivings on the matter, " I suppose I must, but somehow—"

" Why, sirra, what do you grumble now for ? "

Condy still eyed him with suspicion—" And, sir," said he, after having once more mounted the keg, "am I to get nothing for such a weary trudge as I had wid it, but my breakfast ? "

" Here," said Stinton, throwing him half-a-crown, " take that along with it, and now be off—or stop—Cartwright, will you dine with me, to-day, and let us broach the keg ? I'll guarantee its excellence, for this is not the first I have got from the same quarter—that's *entre nous*."

" With all my heart," replied Cartwright, " upon the terms you say, that of a broach."

" Then, my lad," said Stinton, " say to my daughter, that a friend, perhaps a friend or two, will dine with me to-day —that is enough."

They then mounted their horses and were proceeding as before, when Cartwright addressed the gauger as follows :—

" Do you not put this lad, Stinton, in a capacity to over-reach you yet ? "

" No," replied the other, " the young rascal spoke the truth after the discovery of the keg, for he lost his temper, and was no longer cool."

" For my part, hang me if I'd trust him."

" I should scruple to do so, myself," replied the gauger, " but, as I said, these Keerigans—notorious illicit fellows, by the way—send me a keg or two every year, and almost always about this very time. Besides I read him to the heart and he never winced. Yes, decidedly, the whisky was for me; of that I have no doubt whatsoever."

"I most positively would not trust him."

"Not that perhaps I ought," said Stinton, "on second thought, to place such confidence in a lad who acted so adroitly in the beginning. Let us call him back and re-examine him at all events."

Now Condy had, during this conversation, been discussing the very same point with himself.

"Bad cess for ever attend you, Stinton agra," he exclaimed, "for there's surely something *over you*—a lucky shot from behind a hedge, or a break-neck fall down a cliff, or something of that kind. If the ould boy hadn't his croubs hard and fast in you, you wouldn't let me walk away wid the whisky, any how. Bedad it's well I thought o' the Keeri-gans; for sure enough I did hear Barney say, that he was to send a keg in to him this week, some day: and he didn't think I knew him aither. Faix it's many a long day since I knew the sharp *puss* of him, wid an eye like a hawk. But what if they follow me, and do up all? Any way, I'll pre-vint them from having suspicion of me, before I go a toe further, the ugly rips."

He instantly wheeled about, a moment or two before Stinton and Cartwright had done the same, for the purpose of sifting him still more thoroughly—so that they found him meeting them.

"Gintlemen," said he, "how do I know that aither of yous is Mr. Stinton, or that the house you directed me to is his? I know that if the whisky doesn't go to him, I may lave the counthry!"

"You are either a deeper rogue, or a more stupid fool than I took you to be," observed Stinton—"but what security can you give us, that you will leave the keg safely at its destination?"

"If I thought you were Mr. Stinton, I'd be very glad to

lave you the whisky where it is, and even to do widout my breakfast—Gintlemen, tell me the truth, bekase I'd only be murdhered out of the face."

"Why, you idiot," said the gauger, losing his temper and suspicions both together, "can't you go to the town and inquire where Mr. Stinton lives?"

"Bedad thin, thrue enough, I never thought of that at all at all, but I beg your pardon, gintlemen, an' I hope you won't be angry wid me, in regard that it's kilt and quartered I'd be if I let myself be made a fool of by any body."

"Do what I desire you," said the exciseman; "inquire for Mr. Stinton's house, and you may be sure the whisky will reach him."

"Thank you, sir. Bedad I might have thought of that myself."

This last clause, which was spoken in a soliloquy, would have deceived a saint himself.

"Now," said Stinton, after they had recommenced their journey, "are you satisfied?"

"I am at length," said Cartwright; "if his intentions had been dishonest, instead of returning to make himself certain against being deceived, he would have made the best of his way from us—a rogue never wantonly puts himself in the way of danger or detection."

That evening, about five o'clock, Stinton, Cartwright, and two others arrived at the house of the worthy gauger, to partake of his good cheer. A cold frosty evening gave a peculiar zest to the comfort of a warm room, a blazing fire, and a good dinner. No sooner were the viands discussed, the cloth removed and the glasses ready, than their generous host desired his daughter to assist the servant in broaching the redoubtable keg.

"That keg, my dear," he proceeded, "which the country lad, who brought the key of the cellar, left here to-day."

"A keg!" repeated the daughter, with surprise.

"Yes, Maggy, my love, a keg; I said so, I think."

"But, papa, there came no keg here to-day!"

The gauger and Cartwright both groaned in unison.

"No keg!" said the gauger.

"No keg!" echoed Cartwright.

"No keg, indeed," re-echoed Miss Stinton—"but there came a country boy with the key of the cellar, as a token that he was to get the five gallon—"

"Oh!" groaned the gauger, "I'm knocked up, outwitted, —oh!"

"Bought and sold," added Cartwright.

"Go on," said the gauger, "I must hear it out?"

"As a token," proceeded Miss Stinton, "that he was to get the five gallon keg on the little stillion, under the blunderbuss, for Captain Dalton."

"And he got it?"

"Yes, sir, he got it; for I took the key as a sufficient token."

"But, Maggy—hell and fury, hear me, child—surely he brought a keg here, and left it; and of course it's in the cellar?"

"No, indeed, papa, he brought no keg here; but he did bring the five gallon one that *was* in the cellar away with him."

"Stinton," said Cartwright, "send round the bottle."

"The rascal," ejaculated the gauger, "we shall drink his health."

And on relating the circumstances, the company drank the sheepish lad's health, that bought and sold the gauger.

PHIL PURCEL,

The Connaught Pig-Driver.

PHIL PURCEL was the son of a man who always kept a pig. His father's house had a small loft, to which the ascent was by a step-ladder through a door in the inside gable. The first good thing ever Phil was noticed for, was said on the following occasion. His father happened to be called upon, one morning before breakfast, by his landlord, who it seems occasionally visited his tenantry to encourage, direct, stimulate, or reprove them, as the case might require. Phil was a boy then, and sat on the hob in the corner, eyeing the landlord and his father during their conversation. In the meantime the pig came in, and deliberately began to ascend the ladder with an air of authority that marked him as one in the exercise of an established right. The landlord was astonished at seeing the animal enter the best room in the house, and could not help expressing his surprise to old Purcel.

"Why, Purcel, is your pig in the habit of treating himself to the comforts of your best room?"

"The pig is it, the crathur? Why, your haner," said Purcel, after a little hesitation, "it sometimes goes up of a mornin' to waken the childhre, particularly when the buck-whist happens to be late. It doesn't like to be waitin'; and sure none of us like to be kept from the male's mate, your haner, when we want it, no more than it, the crathur.'

"But I wonder your wife permits so filthy an animal to have access to her rooms in this manner."

"Filthy!" replied Mrs. Purcel, who felt herself called upon to defend the character of the pig, as well as her own, "why, one would think, sir, that any crathur that's among Christyeen childhre, like one o' themselves, couldn't be filthy. I could take it to my dyin' day, that there's not a

claner or dacenter pig in the kingdom than the same pig.
It never misbehaves, the crathur, but goes out, as wise an'
riglar, jist by a look, your haner, the poor crathur!"

"I think," observed Phil, from the hob, "that nobody
has a betther right to the run of the house, wedher upstairs
or downstairs, *than him that pays the rint.*"

"Well said, my lad!" observed the landlord, laughing at
the quaint ingenuity of Phil's defence. "His payment of
the rent is the best defence possible, and no doubt should
cover a multitude of his errors."

"A multitude of his shins you mane, sir," said Phil, "for
thrath he's all shin."

In fact, Phil from his infancy had an uncommon attachment to these animals, and by a mind naturally shrewd and
observing made himself as intimately acquainted with their
habits and instincts, and the best modes of managing them,
as ever the celebrated *Cahir na Cappul* did with those of
the horse. Before he was fifteen he could drive the most
vicious and obstinate pig as quietly before him as a lamb;
yet no one knew how nor by what means he had gained the
secret that enabled him to do it. Whenever he attended a
fair, his time was principally spent among the pigs, where
he stood handling and examining, and pretending to buy
them, although he seldom had half a crown in his pocket.
At length, by hoarding up such small sums as he could
possibly lay his hands on, he got together the price of a
"slip," which he bought, reared, and educated in a manner
that did his ingenuity great credit. When this was brought
to its *ne plus ultra* of fatness he sold it, and purchased two
more, which he fed in the same way. On disposing of
these, he made a fresh purchase, and thus proceeded, until
in the course of a few years, he was a well-known pig-
jobber.

Phil's journeys as a pig-driver to the leading sea-port
town nearest him were always particularly profitable. In

Ireland swine are not kept in sties, as they are among English feeders, but permitted to go at liberty through pasture fields, commons, and along roadsides, where they make up as well as they can for the scanty pittance allowed them at home during meal-times. We do not, however, impeach Phil's honesty ; but simply content ourselves with saying that when his journey was accomplished he mostly found the original number with which he had set out increased by three or four, and sometimes by half a dozen. Pigs in general resemble each other, and it surely was not Phil's fault if a stray one, feeding on the roadside or common, thought proper to join his flock and see the world. Phil's object, we presume, was only to take care that his original number was not diminished, its increase being a matter in which he felt little concern.

He now determined to take a professional trip to England, and that this might be the more productive, he resolved to purchase a drove of the animals we have been describing. No time was lost in this speculation. The pigs were bought up as cheaply as possible, and Phil set out, for the first time in his life, to try with what success he could measure his skill against that of a Yorkshireman. On this occasion he brought with him a pet, which he had with considerable pains trained up for purposes hereafter to be explained.

There was nothing remarkable in the passage, unless that every creature on board was sea-sick, except the pigs ; even to them, however, the change was a disagreeable one ; for to be pent up in the hold of a ship was a deprivation of liberty which, fresh as they were from their native hills, they could not relish. They felt, therefore, as patriots, a loss of freedom, but not a whit of appetite ; for, in truth, of the latter no possible vicissitude short of death could deprive them.

Phil, however, with an assumed air of simplicity abso-

lutely stupid, disposed of them to a Yorkshire dealer at
about twice the value they would have brought in Ireland,
though, as pigs went in England, it was low enough. He
declared that they had been fed on *tip-top* feeding ; which
was literally true, as he afterwards admitted that the tops
of nettles and potato stalks constituted the only nourish-
ment they had got for three weeks before.

The Yorkshireman looked with great contempt upon
what he considered a miserable essay to take him in.

" What a fule this Hirishmun mun bea," said he, " to
think to teake me in !   Had he said that them there Hirish
swoine were *badly* feade, I'd ha' thought it fairish enough
on un ; but to seay that they was oll weal feade on *tip-top*
feadin' !   Nea, nea !   I knaws weal enough that they was
noat feade on nothin' at oll, which meakes them looak so
poorish !   Howsomever, I shall fatten them, I'se warrant—
I'se warrant I shall ! "

When driven home to sties somewhat more comfortable
than the cabins of unfortunate Irishmen, they were well
supplied with food which would have been very often considered a luxury by poor Paddy himself, much less by his
pigs.

" Measther," said the boor who had seen them fed, " them
there Hirish pigs ha' not teasted nout for a moonth yet ;
they feade like nout I never seed o' my laife ! "

" Ay ! ay ! " replied the master, " I'se warrant they'll soon
fatten—I'se warrant they shall, Hodge—they be praime
feeders—I'se warrant they shall ; and then, Hodge, we've
bit the soft Hirishmun."

Hodge gave a knowing look at his master and grinned
at this observation.

The next morning Hodge repaired to the sties to see
how they were thriving ; when, to his great consternation,
he found the feeding troughs clean as if they had been
washed, and not a single Irish pig to be seen or heard about

the premises; but to what retreat the animals could have betaken themselves was completely beyond his comprehension.   He scratched his head, and looked about him in much perplexity.

"Dang un!" he exclaimed, "I never seed nout like this."

He would have proceeded in a strain of cogitation equally enlightened, had not a noise of shouting, alarm, and confusion in the neighbourhood excited his attention.   He looked about him, and to his utter astonishment saw that some extraordinary commotion prevailed, that the country was up, and the hills alive with people, who ran, and shouted, and wheeled at full flight in all possible directions. His first object was to join the crowd, which he did as soon as possible, and found that the pigs he had shut up the preceding night in sties whose enclosures were at least four feet high had cleared them like so many *chamois*, and were now closely pursued by the neighbours, who rose *en massa* to hunt down and secure such dreadful depredators.

The waste and mischief they had committed in one night were absolutely astonishing.   Bean and turnip-fields, and vegetable enclosures of all descriptions, kitchen-gardens, corn-fields, and even flower-gardens, were rooted up and destroyed with an appearance of system which would have done credit to Terry Alt himself.

Their speed was the theme of every tongue.   Hedges were taken in their flight, and cleared in a style that occasioned the country people to turn up their eyes and scratch their thick, incomprehensive heads in wonder. Dogs of all degrees bit the dust, and were caught up dead in stupid amazement by their owners, who began to doubt whether or not these extraordinary animals were swine at all.   The depredators in the meantime had adopted the Horatian style of battle.   Whenever there was an ungenerous advantage taken in the pursuit, by slipping dogs

across or before their path, they shot off at a tangent
through the next crowd, many of whom they prostrated in
their flight ; by this means they escaped the dogs until the
latter were somewhat exhausted, when, on finding one in
advance of the rest, they turned, and with standing bristles
and burning tusks, fatally checked their pursuer in his full
career.   To wheel and fly until another got in advance was
then the plan of fight ; but, in fact, the conflict was conducted on the part of the Irish pigs with a fertility of ex-
pediency that did credit to their country, and established
for those who displayed it the possession of intellect far
superior to that of their opponents.   The pigs now began
to direct their course towards the sties in which they had
been so well fed the night before.   This being their last
flight, they radiated towards one common centre with a
fierceness and celerity that occasioned the women and
children to take shelter within doors.   On arriving at the
sties, the ease with which they shot themselves over the
four-feet walls was incredible.   The farmer had caught the
alarm, and just came out in time to witness their return ;
he stood with his hands driven down into the pockets of
his red, capacious waistcoat, and uttered not a word.   When
the last of them came bounding into the sty, Hodge approached, quite breathless and exhausted.

"Oh, measter," he exclaimed, "these be not Hirish pigs
at oll, they be Hirish deevils ; and you mun ha' bought 'em
fra a cunning mon!"

"'Hodge," replied his master, "I'se be bit— I'se heard
feather talk about un.   That breed's *true* Hirish ; but I'se
try and sell 'em to Squoire Jolly to hunt wi' as beagles, for
he wants a pack.   They do say all the swoine that the
deevils were put into ha' been drawned ; but for my peart,
I'se sure that some on un must ha' escaped to Hireland."

Phil, during the commotion excited by his knavery in
Yorkshire, was traversing the country in order to dispose

of his remaining pig ; and the manner in which he effected his first sale of it was as follows :—

A gentleman was one evening standing with some labourers by the wayside, when a tattered Irishman approached, equipped in a pair of white dusty brogues, stockings without feet, old patched breeches, a bag slung across his shoulder, his coarse shirt lying open about a neck tanned by the sun into a reddish yellow, a hat nearly the colour of the shoes, and a hay-rope tied for comfort about his waist: in one hand he also held a straw-rope, that depended from the hind leg of a pig which he drove before him ; in the other was a cudgel, by the assistance of which he contrived to limp on after it, his two shoulder-blades rising and falling alternately with a shrugging motion that indicated great fatigue.

When he came opposite where the gentleman stood he checked the pig, which instinctively commenced feeding upon the grass by the edge of the road.

" Och," said he, wiping his brow with the cuff of his coat, " my sorrow on you for a pig, but I'm kilt wit you. Musha, Gad bless yer haner, an' maybe ye'd buy a slip of a pig fwhrom me, that has my heart bruck, so she has, if ever anybody's heart was bruck wit the likes of her ; an' sure so there was, no doubt, or I wouldn't be as I am wit her. I'll give her a dead bargain, sir ; for it's only to get her aff av my hands I'm wantin', plase yer haner—*silence, pig ! silence you vagabond !*—Be asy, an' me in conwersation wit his haner here ! "

" You are an Irishman ? " the gentleman inquired.

" I am, sir, from Cannaught, yer haner, an' 'ill sell the crathur dag cheap, all out. Asy, you thief ! "

" I don't want the pig, my good fellow," replied the Englishman, without evincing curiosity enough to inquire how he came to have such a commodity for sale.

" She'd be the darlint in no time wit you, sir ; the run o'
16

your kitchen 'ud make her up a beauty, your haner, along wit no throuble to the sarwints about sweepin' it, or anything. You'd only have to lay down the *scrahag* on the flure, or the misthress, Gad bless her, could do it, an' not lave a crumblin' behind her, besides sleepin', yer haner, in the carner beyant, if she'd take the throuble."

The sluggish phlegm of the Englishman was stirred up a little by the twisted and somewhat incomprehensible nature of these instructions.

"How far do you intend to proceed to-night, Paddy?" said he.

"The sarra one o' myself knows, plase yer haner: sure we've an ould sayin' of our own in Ireland beyant—that he's a wise man can tell how far he'll go, sir, till he comes to his journey's ind. I'll give this crathur to you at more nor her value, yer haner."

"More!—why the man knows not what he's saying," observed the gentleman; "*less* you mean, I suppose, Paddy?"

"More or less, sir, you'll get her a bargain; an' Gad bless you, sir!"

"But it is a commodity which I don't want at present. I am very well stocked with pigs as it is. Try elsewhere."

"She'd flog the counthry side, sir; an' if the misthress herself, sir, ud shake the wishp o' straw fwhor her in the kitchen, sir, near the whoire. Yer haner could spake to her about it; an' in no time put a knife in her whin you plased. In regard o' the other thing, sir,—she's like a Christyeen, yer haner, an' no throuble, sir, if you'd be seein' company or anything."

"It's an extraordinary pig this of yours."

"It's no lie fwhor you, sir; she's as clane an' dacent a crathur, sir! Och, if the same pig ud come into the care o' the misthress, Gad bless her! an' I'm sure if she has as much gudness in her face as the hancrable *dinnha ousahl—*

the handsome gintleman she's married upon !—you'll have her thrivin' bravely, sir, shartly, plase Gad, if you'll take courage. Will I dhrive her up the aveny fwhor you, sir ? A good gintlewoman I'm sure, is the same misthress ! Will I dhrive her up fwhor you, sir ? "

"No, no ; I have no further time to lose ; you may go forward."

" Thank yer haner : is it whorid toarst the house abow, sir ? I wouldn't be standin' up, sir, wit you about a thrifle ; an' you'll have her, sir, fwhor anything you plase beyant a pound, yer haner ; an' 'tis throwin' her away it is : but one can't be hard wit a rale gintleman, anyway."

" You only annoy me, man ; besides I don't want the pig ; you lose time ; I don't want to buy it, I repeat to you."

" Gad bliss you, sir—Gad bliss you ! Maybe if I'd make up to the misthress, yer haner ! Thrath she wouldn't turn the crathur from the place, in regard that the tindherness ow the feelin' would come ower her—the rale gintlewoman, anyhow ! 'Tis dag chape you have her at what I said, sir ; an' Gad bliss you !"

" Do you want to compel me to purchase it whether I will or no ? "

" Thrath, it's whor next to nothin' I'm givin' her to you, sir ; but sure you can make your own price at anything beyant a pound. *Hurrish amuch—stadh ! anish*—be asy, you crathur, sure you're gettin' into good quarthers, any-how—goin' to the hanerable English gintleman's kitchen ; an' Gad knows it's a pleasure to dale wit 'em. Och, the world's differ there is betuxt thim an' our own dirty Irish buckeens, that 'ud shkin a bad skilleen, an' pay their debts wit the remaindher. The gateman ud let me in, yer haner, an' I'll meet you at the big house abow."

" Upon my honour, this is a good jest," said the gentle-man, absolutely teased into compliance ; "you are forcing me to buy that which I don't want."

"Sure you will, sir; you'll want more nor that yit, plase Gad, if you be spared. Come, amuck—come, you crathur; faix, you're in luck, so you are—gettin' so good a place wid his haner here, that you won't know yourself shortly, plase Gad."

He immediately commenced driving his pig towards the gentleman's residence with such an air of utter simplicity as would have imposed upon any man not guided by direct inspiration. Whilst he approached the house, its proprietor arrived there by another path a few minutes before him, and, addressing his lady, said:

"My dear, will you come and look at a purchase which an Irishman has absolutely compelled me to make? You had better come and see himself too, for he's the greatest simpleton of an Irishman I have ever seen."

The lady's curiosity was more easily excited than that of her husband. She not only came out, but brought with her some ladies who had been on a visit, in order to hear the Irishman's brogue and to amuse themselves at his expense. Of the pig, too, it appeared she was determined to know something.

"George, my love, is the pig also from Ireland?"

"I don't know, my dear; but I should think so from its fleshless appearance. I have never seen so spare an animal of that class in this country."

"Juliana," said one of the ladies to her companion, "don't go too near him. Gracious! look at the bludgeon, or beam, or something he carries in his hand, to fight and beat the people, I suppose: yet," she added, putting up her glass, "the man is actually not ill-looking; and though not so tall as the Irishman in Sheridan's Rivals, he is well made."

"His eyes are good," said her companion—"a bright grey and keen; and were it not that his nose is rather short and turned up, he would be human."

"George, my love," exclaimed the lady of the mansion,

" he is like most Irishmen of his class that I have seen ;
indeed, scarcely so intelligent, for he *does* appear quite a
simpleton, except, perhaps, a lurking kind of expression,
which is a sign of their humour, I suppose. Don't you
think so, my love ? "

" No, my dear ; I think him a bad specimen of the Irishman. Whether it is that he talks our language but im-
perfectly, or that he is a stupid creature, I cannot say ; but
in selling the pig just now he actually told me that he
would let me have it for *more* than it was worth."

" Oh, that was so laughable ! We will speak to him,
though."

The degree of estimation in which these civilised English
held Phil was so low that this conversation took place
within a few yards of him, precisely as if he had been an
animal of an inferior species, or one of the aborigines of
New Zealand.

" Pray what is your name ? " inquired the matron.

" Phadhrumshagh Corfuffle, plase yer haner : my fadher
carried the same name upon him. We're av the Corfuffles
av Leatheraum Laghy, my lady ; but my grandmudher
was a Dornyeen, an' my own mudher, plase yer haner,
was o' the Shudhurthaghans o' Ballymadoghy, my ladyship. *Stadh anish, amuck bradagh*—be asy, can't you, an'
me in conwershation wit the beauty o' the world that I'm
spakin' to."

" That's the Negus language," observed one of the young
ladies, who affected to be a wit and a blue-stocking ; "it s
Irish and English mixed."

" Thrath, an' but that the handsome young lady's so
purty," observed Phil, " I'd be sayin' myself that that's a
quare remark upon a poor unlarned man ; but Gad bless
her, she *is* so purty what can one say for lookin' an
her ! "

" The poor man, Adelaide, speaks as well as he can,"

replied the lady, rather reprovingly : "he is by no means so wild as one would have expected."

"Candidly speaking, much *tamer* than *I* expected," rejoined the wit. "Indeed, I meant the poor Irishman no offence."

"Where did you get the pig, friend? and how came you to have it for sale so far from home?"

"Fwhy it isn't whor sale, my lady," replied Phil, evading the former question ; "the masthcr here, Gad bless him an' spare him to you, ma'am!—thrath an' it's his four quarthers that knew how to pick out a wife, anyhow, whor beauty an' all hanerable whormations o' grandheur—so he did ; an' well he desarves you, my lady : faix, it's a fine houseful o' thim you'll have, plase God—an' fwhy not? whin it's all in the coorse o' Providence, bein' both so handsome ;—he gev me a pound note whor her, my ladyship, an' his own plisure aftherwards : an' I'm now watin' to be pcd."

"What kind of a country is Ireland, as I understand you are an Irishman?"

"Thrath, my lady, it's like fwhat maybe you never seen —a fool's purse, ten guineas goin' out whor one that gocs in."

"Upon my word, that's wit," observed the young blue-stocking.

"What is your opinion of Irishwomen?" the lady continued ; "are they handsomer than the English ladies, think you?"

"Murdher, my lady," says Phil, raising his caubeen, and scratching his head, in pretended perplexity, with his finger and thumb, "fwhat am I to say to that, ma'am, and all of yees to the fwhore? But the sarra one av me will give it agin the darlins beyant."

"But which do you think the more handsome?"

"Thrath, I do, my lady ; the Irish and English women would flog the world, an' sure it would be a burnin' shame to go to set them agin one another fwhor beauty."

"Whom do you mean by the 'darlins beyant'?" inquired the blue-stocking attempting to pronounce the words.

"Faix, miss, who but the crathurs ower the wather, that kills us entirely, so they do."

"I cannot comprehend him," she added to the lady of the mansion.

"Arrah, maybe I'd make bould to take up the manners from you fwhor a while, my lady, plase yer haner?" said Phil, addressing the latter.

"I do not properly understand you," she replied, "speak plainer."

"Throth, that's fwhat they do, yer haner; they never gos about the bush wit yees—the gintlemen, ma'am, of our counthry, fwhin they do be coortin' yees: an' I want to ax, ma'am, if you plase, fwhat *you* think of *thim*, that is, if ever any of them had the luck to come acrass you, my lady?"

"I am quite anxious to know how you came by the pig, Paddy?" said the wit.

"Arrah, miss, sure 'tisn't pigs you're thinkin' on, an' us discoorsin' about the gintlemen from Ireland, that you're all so fond ow here; faix, miss, they're the boys that can fwoight for yees, an' ud rather be bringin' an Englishman to the *sad* fwhor your sakes, nor atin' braad an' butther. Fwhy, now, miss, if you were beyant wit us, the sarra ounce o' gunpowdher we'd have in no time, for love or money."

"Upon my word, I should like to *see* Ireland!" exclaimed the blue-stocking; "and why would the gunpowder get scarce, pray?"

"Faix, fightin' about you, miss, an' all of yees sure; for myself sees no differ at all in your hanerable fwhormations of beauty an' grandeur, an' all high-flown admirations."

"But tell us where you got the pig, Paddy?" persisted the wit, struck naturally enough with the circumstance. "How do you come to have an Irish pig so far from home?"

"Fwhy thin, miss, 'twas to a brodher o' my own I was

bringin' it, that was livin' down the counthry here, an' fwhin I came to fwhere he lived, the sarra one o' me knew the place, in regard o' havin' forgot the name of it entirely, an' there was I wit the poor crathur an my hands, till his haner here bought it whrom me—Gad bless you, sir!"

"As I live, there's a fine Irish blunder," observed the wit; "I shall put it in my common-place book—it will be so genuine. I declare I'm quite delighted!"

"Well, Paddy," said the gentleman, "here's your money. There's a pound for you, and that's much more than the miserable animal is worth."

"Thrath, sir, you have the crathur at what we call in Ireland a bargain. Maybe yer haner ud spit upon the money fwhor luck, sir. It's the way we do, sir, beyant."

"No, no, Paddy, take it as it is. Good heavens! what barbarous habits these Irish have in all their modes of life, and how far they are removed from anything like civilization!"

"Thank yer haner. Faix, sir, this'll come so handy for the landlord at home, in regard o' the rint for the bit o' phatie ground, so it will, if I can get home agin widout brakin' it. Arrah, maybe yer haner ud give me the price o' my bed, an' a bit to ate, sir, an' keep me from brakin' in upon this, sir, Gad bless the money! I'm thinkin' o' the poor wife an' childher, sir—strivin', so I am, to do fwhor the darlins."

"Poor soul," said the lady, "he is affectionate in the midst of his wretchedness and ignorance."

"Here—here," replied the Englishman, anxious to get rid of him, "there's a shilling, which I give because you appear to be attached to your family."

"Och, och, fwhat can I say, sir, only that long may you reign ower your family an' the hanerable ladies to the fwhore, sir. Gad fwhor ever bliss you, sir, but you're the kind, noble gintleman, an' all belongin' to you, sir!"

Having received the shilling, he was in the act of departing, when, after turning it deliberately in his hand, shrugging his shoulders, two or three times, and scratching his head, with a vacant face he approached the lady.

"Musha, ma'am, an' maybe ye'd have the tindherness in your heart, seein' that the gudness is in yer hanerable face, anyway, an' it would save the skillyeen that the masther gev'd me for payin' my passage, so it would, jist to bid the steward, my ladyship, to ardher me a bit to ate in the kitchen below. The hunger, ma'am, is hard upon me, my lady; an' fwhat I'm doin', sure, is in regard o' the wife at home, an' the childher, the crathurs, an' me far fwhrom them, in a sthrange counthry, Gad help me!"

"What a singular being, George! and how beautiful is the economy of domestic affection exemplified, notwithstanding his half-savage state, in the little plans he devises for the benefit of his wife and children!" exclaimed the good lady, quite unconscious that Phil was a bachelor. "Juliana, my love, desire Simmons to give him his dinner. Follow this young lady, good man, and she will order you refreshment."

"Gad's blessin' upon your beauty an' gudness, my lady; an' a man might thravel far afore he'd meet the likes o' you for aither o' them. Is it the other handsome young lady I'm to folly, ma'am?"

"Yes," replied the young wit, with an arch smile; "come after *me.*"

"Thrath, miss, an' it's an asy task to do that, anyway; wit a heart an' half I go, acushla; an' I seen the day, miss, that it's not much o' mate an' dhrink ud trouble me, if I jist got lave to be lookin' at you, wit nothin' but yourself to think an. But the wife an' childher, miss, makes great changes in us entirely."

"Why, you are quite gallant, Paddy."

"Thrath, I suppose I am now, miss; but you see, my hanerable young lady, that's our fwhailin' at home; the counthry's poor, an' we can't help it, whedher or not. We're fwhorced to it, miss, whin we come ower here, by you, an' the likes o' you, mavourneen!"

Phil then proceeded to the house, was sent to the kitchen by the young lady, and furnished through the steward with an abundant supply of cold meat, bread, and beer, of which he contrived to make a meal that somewhat astonished the servants. Having satisfied his hunger, he deliberately, but with the greatest simplicity of countenance, filled the wallet, which he carried slung across his back, with whatever he had left, observing as he did it:—

"Fwhy, thin, 'tis sthrange it is that the same custom is wit us in Ireland beyant that is here; fwhor whinever a traveller is axed in, he always brings fwhat he doesn't ate along wit him. An' sure enough it's the same here amongst yees," he added, packing up the bread and beef as he spoke; "but Gad bliss the custom, anyhow, fwhor it's a good one!"

When he had secured the provender, and was ready to resume his journey, he began to yawn, and to exhibit the most unequivocal symptoms of fatigue.

"Arrah, sir," said he to the steward, "you wouldn't have e'er an ould barn that I'd throw myself in fwhor the night? The sarra leg I have to put undher me, now that I've got stiff wit the sittin' so lang; that, an' a wishp o' sthraw, sir, to sleep an, an' Gad bliss you!"

"Paddy, I cannot say," replied the steward; "but I shall ask my master, and if he orders it, you shall have the comfort of a hard floor and clean straw, Paddy—that you shall."

"Many thanks to you, sir: it's in your face, in thrath, the same gudness an' ginerosity."

The gentleman, on hearing Phil's request to be permitted a sleeping place in the barn, was rather surprised at his wretched notion of comfort than at the request itself.

"Certainly, Timmins, let him sleep there," he replied;

" give him sacks and straw enough.   I daresay he will feel
the privilege a luxury, poor devil, after his fatigue.   Give
him his breakfast in the morning, Timmins.   Good heavens,"
he added, " what a singular people !   What an amazing
progress civilization must make before these Irish can be
brought at all near the commonest standard of humanity ! "

At this moment Phil, who was determined to back the
steward's request, approached them.

" Paddy," said the gentleman, anticipating him, " I have
ordered you sacks and straw in the barn, and your breakfast in the morning before you set out."

" Thrath," said Phil, " if there's e'er a sthray blissin' goin',
depind an it, sir, you'll get it, fwhor your hanerable ginerosity to the sthranger.   But about the 'slip,' sir—if the
misthress herself ud shake the wishp o' sthraw fwhor her in
the far carner o' the kitchen below, an' see her gettin' her
supper, the crathur, before she'd put her to bed, she'd be
thrivin' like a salmon, sir, in less than no time ; an' to
ardher the sarwints, sir, if you plase, not to be defraudin'
the crathur of the big piatces.   Fwhor in regard it cannot
spake fwhor itself, sir, it frets as wise as a Christyeen, when
it's not honestly thrated."

" Never fear, Paddy ; we shall take good care of it."

" Thank you, sir.   But I aften heerd, sir, that you dunna
how to feed pigs in this counthry in ardher to mix the
fwhat an' lane, lair (layer) about."

" And how do you manage that in Ireland, Paddy ? "

" Fwhy, sir, I'll tell you how the mishthress, Gad bless
her, will manage it fwhor you.   Take the crathur, sir, an'
feed it to-morrow till it's as full as a tick—that's fwhor the
fwhat, sir ; thin let her give it nothin' at all the next day,
but keep it black fwhastin'—that's fwhor the *lane* (lean).
Let her stick to that, sir, keepin' it atin' one day an' fastin'
anodher, for six months, thin put a knife in it, an' if you
don't have the fwhat an' lane, lair about, beautiful all out,

fwhy niver bleeve Phadrumshagh Corfuffle agin. Ay, indeed !"

The Englishman looked keenly at Phil, but could only read in his countenance a thorough and implicit belief in his own recipe for mixing the fat and lean. It is impossible to express his contempt for the sense and intellect of Phil ; nothing could surpass it but the contempt which Phil entertained for him.

The next morning he failed to appear at the hour of breakfast, but his non-appearance was attributed to his fatigue, in consequence of which he was supposed to have overslept himself. On going, however, to call him from the barn, they discovered that he had decamped ; and on looking after the "slip" it was found that both had taken French leave of the Englishman. Phil and the pig had actually travelled fifteen miles that morning before the hour on which he was missed—Phil going at a dog's trot, and the pig following at such a respectful distance as might not appear to identify them as fellow-travellers. In this manner Phil sold the pig to upwards of two dozen intelligent English gentlemen and farmers, and after winding up his bargains successfully, both arrived in Liverpool, highly delighted by their commercial trip through England.

When Phil arrived at the vessel, he found the captain in a state of peculiar difficulty. About twelve or fourteen gentlemen of rank and property, together with a score or upwards of highly respectable persons, but of less consideration, were in equal embarrassment. The fact was, that as no other vessel left Liverpool that day, about five hundred Irishmen, mostly reapers and mowers, had crowded upon deck, each determined to keep his place at all hazards. The captain, whose vessel was small, and none of the stoutest, flatly refused to put to sea with such a number. He told them it was madness to think of it ; he could not risk the lives of the other passengers, nor even their own, by sailing with five hundred on the deck of so small a vessel. If one half would withdraw peaceably, he would carry the other half, which was as much as he could possibly accomplish. They were very willing to grant that what he said was true ; but, in the meantime, not a man of them would move, and to clear out such a number of fellows, who loved nothing better than fighting, armed, too, with sickles and scythes, was a task beyond either his ability or inclination to execute. He remonstrated with them, entreated, raged, swore, and threatened, but all to no purpose. His threats and entreaties were received with equal good humour. Gibes and jokes were broken on him without number, and as his passion increased, so did their mirth, until nothing could be seen but the captain in vehement gesticulation, the Irishmen huzzaing him so vociferously that his damns and curses, uttered against them, could not reach even his own ears.

"Gentlemen," said he to his cabin passengers, "for the love of Heaven, tax your invention to discover some means whereby to get one-half of these men out of the vessel, otherwise it will be impossible that we can sail to-day. I have already proffered to take one-half of them by lot, but they will not hear of it ; and how to manage I am sure I don't know."

The matter, however, was beyond their depth : the thing seemed utterly impracticable, and the chances of their putting to sea were becoming fainter and fainter.

"Bl—t their eyes !" he at length exclaimed, "the ragged, hungry devils ! If they heard me with decency, I could bear their obstinacy better : but no, they must turn me into ridicule, and break their jests and turn their cursed barbarous grins upon me in my own vessel. I say, boys," he added, proceeding to address them once more—"I say, savages, I have just three observations to make. The first is ——"

" Arrah, captain, avourneen, hadn't you betther get upon
a stool," said a voice, "an' put a text before it, thin divide
it dacently into three halves, an' make a sarmon of it."

" Captain, you wor intinded for the Church," added
another. " You're the moral of a Methodist preacher, if
you wor dressed in black."

" Let him alone," said a third ; " he'd be a jinteel man
enough in a wilderness, an' ud make an illigant dancin'-
masther to the bears."

" He's as graceful as a shaved pig on its hind legs,
dancin' the ' Baltihorum jig.' "

The captain's face was literally black with passion : he
turned away with a curse, which produced another huzza,
and swore that he would rather encounter the Bay of
Biscay in a storm than have anything to do with such an
unmanageable mob.

" Captain," said a little, shrewd-looking Connaught man,
" what ud you be willin' to give anybody, over an' abow his
free passage, that ud tell you how to get one half o' them out?"

" I'll give him a crown," replied the captain, "together
with grog and rations to the eyes : I'll be hanged if I don't."

"Then I'll do it fwhor you, sir, if you keep yor word wit me."

" Done," said the captain, " it's a bargain, my good
fellow, if you accomplish it ; and what's more, I'll consider
you a knowing one."

" I'm a poor Cannaught man, your haner," replied our
friend Phil, " but what's to prevint me thryin' ! Tell thim,"
he continued, " that you *must* go ; purtind to be fwhor
takin' thim wit you, sir. Put Munshther agin Cannaught,
one half an this side, an' the odher an that, to keep the
crathur of a ship steady, your haner ; an' fwhin you have
thim half an' half, wit a little room betuxt thim, ' Now,
says your haner, ' boys, you're divided into two halves ; if
one side kicks the other out o' the ship, I'll bring the cun-
quirors."

The captain said not a word in reply to Phil, but immediately ranged the Munster and Connaught men on each side of the deck—a matter which he found little difficulty in accomplishing, for each party, hoping that he intended to take themselves, readily declared their province, and stood together. When they were properly separated, there still remained about forty or fifty persons belonging to neither province; but, at Phil's suggestion, the captain paired them off to each division, man for man, until they were drawn up into two bodies.

"Now," said he, "there you stand: let one half of you drub the other out of the vessel, and the conquerors shall get their passage."

Instant was the struggle that ensued for the sake of securing a passage, and from the anxiety to save a shilling, by getting out of Liverpool on that day. The saving of the shilling is, indeed, a consideration with Paddy which drives him to the various resources of begging, claiming kindred with his resident countrymen in England, pretended illness, coming to be passed from parish to parish, and all the turnings and shiftings which his reluctance to part with money renders necessary. Another night, therefore, and probably another day in Liverpool would have been attended with expense. This argument prevailed with all; with Munster as well as with Connaught, and they fought accordingly.

When the attack first commenced each party hoped to be able to expel the other without blows. This plan was soon abandoned. In a few minutes the sticks and fists were busy. Throttling, tugging, cuffing, and knocking down—shouting, hallooing, huzzaing, and yelling gave evident proofs that the captain, in embracing Phil's proposal, had unwittingly applied the match to a mine whose explosion was likely to be attended with disastrous consequences. As the fight became warm, and the struggles more desperate, the hooks and scythes were resorted to; blood began to flow, and men to fall, disabled and apparently dying. The immense crowd which had now assembled to witness the fight among the Irishmen could not stand tamely by and see so many lives likely to be lost, without calling in the civil authorities. A number of constables in a few minutes attended ; but these worthy officers of the civil authorities experienced very uncivil treatment from the fists, cudgels, and sickles of *both* parties. In fact, they were obliged to get from among the rioters with all possible celerity, and to suggest to the magistrates the necessity of calling in the military.

In the meantime the battle rose into a furious and bitter struggle for victory, The deck of the vessel was actually slippery with blood, and many were lying in an almost lifeless state. Several were pitched into the hold, and had their legs and arms broken by the fall ; some were tossed over the sides of the vessel, and only saved from drowning by the activity of the sailors ; and not a few of those who had been knocked down in the beginning of the fray were trampled into insensibility.

The Munster men at length gave way; and their opponents, following up their advantage, succeeded in driving them to a man out of the vessel just as the military arrived. Fortunately their interference was unnecessary. The ruffianly captain's object was accomplished; and as no lives were lost, nor any injury more serious than broken bones and flesh wounds sustained, he got the vessel in readiness and put to sea.

FATHER PHILEMY:

OR

The Holding of the Station.

OUR readers are to suppose the Reverend Philemy M'Guirk, parish priest of Tir-neer, to be standing upon the altar of the chapel, facing the congregation, after having gone through the canon of the mass ; and having nothing more of the service to perform than the usual prayers with which he closes the ceremony.

"Take notice, that the Stations for the following week will be held as follows :—

"*On Monday, in Jack Gallagher's of Corraghnamoddagh.* Are you there, Jack ? "

"To the fore, yer reverence."

"Why, then, Jack, there's something ominous—something auspicious—to happen, or we wouldn't have you here ; for it's very seldom that you make part or parcel of the *present* congregation ; seldom are you here, Jack, it must be confessed : however, you know the old classical proverb, or if *you* don't, *I* do, which will just answer as well—*Non semper ridit Apollo*—it's not every day *Manus* kills a bullock ; so,, as you *are* here, be prepared for us on Monday."

"Never fear, yer reverence, never fear ; I think you ought to know that the grazin' at Corraghnamoddagh's not bad."

"To do you justice, Jack, the mutton was always good with you, only if you would get it better killed it would be an improvement."

"Very well, yer reverence, I'll do it."

"*On Tuesday, in Peter Murtagh's, of the Crooked Commons.* Are you there, Peter ? "

"Here, yer reverence."

"Indeed, Peter, I might know you are here ; and I wish

17

that a great many of *my* flock would take example by you: if they did, I wouldn't be so far behind in getting in my *dues.* Well, Peter, I suppose you know that this is Michaelmas ? "

" So fat, yer reverence, that they're not able to wag ; but, any way, Katty has them marked for you—two fine young crathurs, only last year's fowl, and the ducks isn't a taste behind them—she's crammin' them this month past."

" I believe you, Peter, and I would take your word for more than the condition of the geese—remember me to Katty, Peter."

" *On Wednesday, in Parrah More Slevin's of Mullaghfadh.* Are you there, Parrah More ? "—No answer. " Parrah More Slevin ? "—Silence. " Parrah More Slevin, of Mullaghfadh ? "—No reply. " Dan Fagan ? "

" Present, sir."

" Do you know what keeps that reprobate from mass ? "

" I bleeve he's takin' advantage, sir, of the frast, to get in his praties to-day, in respect of the bad footin', sir, for the horses in the bog when there's not a frast. Anyhow, betune that and a bit of a sore head that he got, yer reverence, on Thursday last in takin' part wid the O'Scallaghans agin the Bradys, I believe he had to stay away to-day."

" On the Sabbath day, too, without my leave ! Well, tell him from me that I'll make an example of him to the whole parish, if he doesn't attend mass better. Will the Bradys and the O'Scallaghans never be done with their quarrelling ? I protest, if they don't live like Christians I'll read them out from the altar. Will you tell Parrah More that I'll hold a station in his house on next Wednesday ? "

" I will, sir ; I will, yer reverence."

" *On Thursday, in Phaddhy Sheemus Phaddhy's of the Esker.* Are you there, Phaddhy ? "

" Wid the help of God, I'm here, sir."

"Well, Phaddhy, how is yer son Briney, that's at the Latin ?   I hope he's coming on well at it ? "

" Why, sir, he's not more nor a year and a half at it yet, and he's got more books amost nor he can carry—he'll break me buying books for him."

" Well, that's a good sign, Phaddhy, but why don't you bring him to me till I examine him ? "

" Why, never a one of me can get him to go, sir, he's so much afeard of your reverence."

"Well, Phaddhy, we were once modest and bashful our- selves, and I'm glad to hear that he's afraid of his *clargy* ; but let him be prepared for me on Thursday, and maybe I'll let him know something he never heard before ; I'll give him a Maynooth touch."

" Do you hear that, Briney," said the father, aside, to the son, who knelt at his knee—"ye must give up yer hurling and idling now, you see. Thank yer reverence, thank you, docthor."

" *On Friday, in Barny O'Darby's,* alias *Barny Butter's.* Are you there, Barny ? "

" All that's left of me is here, sir."

" Well, Barny, how is the butter trade this season ? "

" It's a little on the rise now, sir ; in a month or so I'm expecting it will be brisk enough ; *Boney,* sir, is doing that much for us, any way."

" Ay, and Barny, he'll do more than that for us ; God prosper *him* at all events—I only hope the time's coming, Barny, when everyone will be able to eat his own butter and his own beef, too."

" God send it, sir."

" Well, Barny, I didn't hear from your brother Ned these two or three months ; what has become of him ? "

" Ah, yer reverence, Pentland done him up."

" What, the gauger ? "

" He did, the thief ; but maybe he'll sup sorrow for it afore he's much oulder."

" And who do you think informed, Barny ? "

" Oh, I only wish we knew that, sir."

" I wish *I* knew it ; and if I thought any miscreant here would become an *informer* I'd make an example of him. Well, Barny, on Friday next ; but I suppose Ned has a drop still—eh, Barny ? "

" Why, sir, we'll be apt to have something stronger nor wather, anyhow."

" Very well, Barny : your family was always a dacent and spirited family, I'll say that for them : but tell me, Barny, did you begin to *dam* the river yet ?   I think the trouts and eels are running by this time."

" The creels are made, yer reverence, though we did not set them yet ; but on Tuesday night, sir, wid the help o' God, we'll be ready."

" You can *corn* the trouts, Barny, and the eels too ; but should you catch nothing, go to Pat Hartigan, Captain Sloethorn's gamekeeper, and if you tell him it's for me, he'll drag you a batch out of the fish-pond."

" Ah ! then, your reverence, it's 'imself that 'ill do that wid a heart an' a half."

Such was the conversation which took place between the Reverend Philemy M'Guirk and those of his parishioners in whose houses he had appointed to hold a series of stations for the week ensuing the Sunday laid in this, our account, of that hitherto undescribed portion of the Romish discipline.

Now, the reader is to understand that a station in this sense differs from a station made to any peculiar spot remarkable for local sanctity.   There, a station means the performance of a pilgrimage to a certain place, under peculiar circumstances, and the going through a stated number of prayers and other penitential ceremonies, for the purpose of wiping out sin in this life, or of relieving the soul of some relation from the pains of purgatory in the other ; here, it simply means the coming of the parish priest and his curate to some house in the townland, on a day publicly announced from the altar for that purpose on the preceding Sabbath.

Father Con, the curate, arrived first; Phaddhy and Kitty were instantly at the door to welcome him.

"Musha, and it's you that's welcome, from my heart out, to our house, Father Con, avourneen!" said Kitty, dropping him a low curtsy, and spreading her new brown quilted petticoat as far out on each side of her as it would go.

"I thank you," said honest Con, who, as he knew not her name, did not pretend to know it.

"Well, Father Con," said Phaddhy, "this is the first time you have ever come to us this-a-way; but plase God it won't be the last, I hope."

"I hope not, Phaddhy," said Father Con, who, notwithstanding his simplicity of character, loved a good dinner in the very core of his heart; "I hope not indeed, Phaddhy."

He then threw his eye about the premises, to see what point he might set his temper to during the remainder of the day; for it is right to inform our readers that a priest's temper, at a station, generally rises or falls according to the prospect of his cheer.

Here, however, a little vista or pantry, jutting out from the kitchen, and left ostentatiously open, presented him with a view which made his very nose curl with kindness. What it contained we do not pretend to say, not having seen it ourselves; we judge, therefore, only by its effect on his physiognomy.

Breakfast was laid in Katty's best style, and with an originality of arrangement that scorned all precedent. Two tables were placed, one after another, in the kitchen; for the other rooms were not sufficiently large to accommodate the company. Father Philemy filled the seat of honour at the head of the table, with his back to an immense fire. On his right hand sat Father Con; on his left, Phaddy himself, "to keep the *clargy* in company;" and, in due succession after them, their friends and neighbours, each taking precedence according to the most scrupulous notions of respectability. Beside Father Con sat "Pether Malone," a "young collegian," who had been sent home from Maynooth to try his native air for the recovery of his health, which was declining. He arrived only a few minutes after Father Philemy, and was a welcome reinforcement to Phaddy in the arduous task of sustaining the conversation with suitable credit.

With respect to the breakfast I can only say that it was super-abundant—that the tea was as black as bog water—that there were hen, turkey, and geese eggs—plates of toast soaked, crust and crumb, in butter, and, lest there might be a deficiency, one of the daughters sat on a stool at the fire, with her open hand, by way of a fire-screen, across her red, half-scorched brows, toasting another plateful ; and, to crown all, on each corner of the table was a bottle of whisky. At the lower board sat the youngsters, under the *surveillance* of Katty's sister, who presided in that quarter. When they were commencing breakfast, " Father Philemy," said Katty, "won't yer rev'rence bless the mate, if ye plase ? "

" If I don't do it myself," said Father Philemy, who was just after sweeping the top off a turkey egg, " I'll get them that will. Come," said he to the collegian, " give us grace, Peter, you'll never learn younger."

This, however, was an unexpected blow to Peter, who knew that an English grace would be incompatible with his " college breeding," yet was unprovided with any in Latin. The eyes of the company were now fixed upon him, and he blushed like scarlet on finding himself in a predicament so awkward and embarrassing. " *Aliquid, Petre, aliquid ; ' de profundis '—si habes nihil aliud*," said Father Philemy, feeling for his embarrassment, and giving him a hint. This was not lost, for Peter began, and gave them the *De profundis*, a Latin psalm which Roman Catholics repeat for the relief of the souls in purgatory. They forgot, however, that there was a person in company who considered himself as having an equal claim to the repetition of at least the one-half of it ; and accordingly, when Peter got up and repeated the first verse, Andy Lawlor got also on his legs, and repeated the response. This staggered Peter a little, who hesitated, as uncertain how to act.

"*Perge, Petre, Perge,*" said Father Philemy, looking rather wistfully at his egg—"*Perge, stultus est et asinus quoque.*" Peter and Andy proceeded until it was finished, when they resumed their seats.

The conversation during breakfast was as sprightly, as full of fun and humour, as such breakfasts usually are. The priest, Phaddy, and the young collegian had a topic of their own, whilst the rest were engaged in a kind of by-play until the meal was finished.

"Father Philemy," said Phaddy, in his capacity of host, "before we begin we'll all take a dhrop of what's in the bottle, if it's not displasing to yer reverence ; and, sure, I know 'tis the same doesn't come wrong at a station, anyhow."

This, *more majorum*, was complied with ; and the glass, as usual, went round the table, beginning with their reverences.

"Are you all ready now ?" said the priest, after breakfast, to a crowd of country people who were standing about the kitchen door, pressing to get the "first turn" at the tribunal, which, on this occasion, consisted of a good oak chair with his reverence upon it.

"Why do you crush forward in that manner, you ill-bred spalpeens ? Can't you stand back and behave yourselves like common Christians ?—back with you, or, if you make me get my whip, I'll soon clear you from about the dacent man's door. Hagarty, why do you crush them two girls there, you great Turk, you ? Look at the vagabonds !—Where's my whip ?" said he, running in, and coming out in a fury, when he commenced cutting about him, until they dispersed in all directions. He then returned into the house; and, after calling in about two dozen, began to catechise them as follows, still holding the whip in his hand, while many of those individuals, who, at a party quarrel in fair or market, or in the more inhuman crimes of murder or nightly depradations, were as callous and hardened specimens of humanity as ever set the laws of civilised society at defiance, stood trembling before him like slaves, absolutely pale and breathless with fear.

"Come, Kelly," said he to one of them, "are you fully prepared for the two blessed sacraments of Penance and the Eucharist, that you area bout to receive? Can you read, sir?"

"Can I read, is id?—my *brother Barney* can, yer reverence," replied Kelly, sensible, amid all the disadvantages around him, of the degradation of his ignorance.

"What's that to me, sir," said the priest, "what your brother Barney can do—can you not read yourself?—and, maybe," he continued, parenthetically, "your brother Barney's not much the holier for his knowledge."

"I cannot, your reverence," said Kelly, in a tone of regret.

"I hope you have your Christian Doctrine, at all events," said the priest—"Go on with the Confiteor."

Kelly went on—"*Confectur Dimniportenti batchy Mary semplar virginy, batchy Mickletoe Archy Angeloe batchy Johnny Bartisty, sanctris postlis—Petrum hit Paulum, omnium scantris, et tabby, pasture quay a pixavit minus coglety ashy hony verbum et offer him smaxy quilta smaxy quilta smaxy maxin in quilta.*"

"Very well, Kelly, right enough, all except the pronouncing, which wouldn't pass muster in Maynooth, however. How many kinds of commandments are there?"

"Two, sir."

"What are they?"

"God's and the Church's."

"Repeat God's share of them."

He then repeated the first commandment according to *his* catechism.

"Very good, Kelly, very good. Now you must know that the heretics split that into two, for no other reason in the world only to knock our blessed images on the head; but we needn't expect them to have much conscience. Well, now repeat the commandments of the Church."

"First—Sundays and holidays, Mass thou shalt sartinly hear;

Second—All holidays sanctificate throughout all the whole year.

Third—Lent, Ember days, and Virgils, thou shalt be sartin to fast;

Fourth—Fridays and Saturdays flesh thou shalt not, good, bad, or indifferent, taste.

Fifth—In Lent and Advent, nuptial fastes gallantly forbear;

Sixth—Confess your sins, at laste once dacently and soberly every year.

Seventh—Receive your God at confission about great Easter-day;

Eighth—And to his Church and his own frolicsome clargy neglect not tides to pay."

"Well," said his reverence, "now, the great point is, do you understand them?"

"Wid the help of God, I hope so, yer rev'rence—and I have also the three thriptological vartues."

"Theological, sirrah!"

"Theojollyological vartues; the four sins that cry to heaven for vingeance; the *five* carnal vartues—prudence, justice, timptation, and solitude; the six holy Christian gifts; the seven deadly sins; the eight grey attitudes——"

"Grey attitudes! Oh! the Bœotian!" exclaimed his reverence: "listen to the way in which he's playing havoc among them—stop, sir," for Kelly was going on at full

speed—"stop, sir ; I tell you it's not *grey* attitudes, but *bay*
attitudes—doesn't everyone know the eight beatitudes ? "

"The eight *bay* attitudes ; the nine ways of being guilty
of another's sins ; the ten commandments ; the twelve
fruits of a Christian ; the fourteen stations of the cross ; the
fifteen mystheries of the passion——"

"Kelly," said his reverence, interrupting him, and herald-
ing the joke, for so it was intended, with a hearty chuckle,
"you're getting fast out of you're teens, ma bouchal ! " and
this was, of course, honoured with a merry peal, extorted
as much by an effort at softening the rigour of examination,
as by the traditionary duty which entails upon the Irish
laity the necessity of laughing at a priest's jokes, without
any reference at all to their quality. Nor was his
reverence's own voice the first to subside into that gravity
which became the solemnity of the occasion ; for, even
whilst he continued the interrogatories, his eye was laughing at the conceit, with which it was evident the inner man
was not competent to grapple. "Well, Kelly, I can't say
but you've answered very well, as far as the *repeating* of
them goes : but do you perfectly *understand* all the
commandments of the Church ? "

"I do, sir," replied Kelly, whose confidence kept pace
with his reverence's good humour.

"Well, what is meant by the fifth ? "

"The fifth, sir," said the other, rather confounded—"I
must begin agin', sir, and go on till I come to it."

"Well," said the priest, "never mind that ; but tell us
what the eighth means ? "

Kelly stared at him a second time, but was not able to
advance. "First—Sundays and holidays, mass thou shalt
hear ; " but before he had proceeded to the second, a person
who stood at his elbow began to whisper to him the proper
reply, and, in the act of doing so, received a lash of the
whip across the ear for his pains.

"You blackguard. you!" exclaimed Father Philemy, "take that—how dare you attempt to prompt any person that I'm examining?"

Those who stood round Kelly now fell back to a safe distance, and all was silence, terror, and trepidation once more.

"Come, Kelly, go on—the eighth?"

Kelly was still silent.

"Why, you Ninny, you, didn't you repeat it just now. 'Eighth—And to his Church neglect not tithes to pay.' Now that I have put the words in your mouth, what does it mean?"

Kelly having thus got the cue, replied in the words of the catechism, "To pay *tides* to the lawful *pasterns* of the Church, sir."

"*Pasterns!* oh, you ass, you; pasterns! You poor, base, contemptible, crawling reptile; as if we trampled you under our hooves—oh, you scruff of the earth! Stop, I say—it's *pastors.*"

"Pasthors of the Church."

"And tell me, do you fulfil that commandment?"

"I do, sir."

"It's a lie, sir," replied the priest, brandishing the whip over his head, whilst Kelly instinctively threw up his guard to protect himself from the blow; "It's a lie, sir," repeated his reverence, "you don't fulfil it, What *is* the Church?"

"The Church is the congregation of the faithful that purfiss the true faith, and are obadient to the pope."

"And who do you pay your tithes to?"

"To the parson, sir."

"And, you poor varmint you, is *he* obadient to the pope?"

Kelly only smiled at the want of comprehension which prevented him from seeing the thing according to the view which his reverence took of it.

" Well, now," continued Father Philemy, " who are the *lawful* pastors of God's Church ? "

" You are, sir, and all our own priests."

" And who ought you to pay your tithes to ? "

" To you, sir, in coorse ; sure I always knew that, yer rev'rence."

" And what's the reason, then, you don't pay them to me instead of the parson ? "

This was a puzzler to Kelly, who only knew his own side of the question.   " You have me there, sir," he replied with a grin.

" Because," said his reverence, " the Protestants, for the present, have the law of the land on their side, and power over you to compel the payment of tithes to themselves ; but we have right, justice, and the law of God on ours ; and, if everything was in its proper place, it is not to the *parsons*, but to *us*, that you would pay them."

" Well, well, sir," replied Kelly, who now experienced a community of feeling upon the subject with his reverence that instantly threw him into a familiarity of manner which he thought the point between them justified—"who knows, sir ? " said he, with a knowing smile, " there's a good time coming, yer rev'rence."

" Ay," said Father Philemy, " wait till we get once into the Big House, and if we don't turn the scales—if the Established Church doesn't go down, why, there's no truth in Scripture.   Now, Kelly, all's right but the money—have you brought your dues ? "

" Here it is, sir," said Kelly, handing him his dues for the last year.

It is to be observed here that, according as the penitents went to be examined, or to kneel down to confess, a certain sum was exacted from each, which varied according to the arrears that might have been due to the priest.   Indeed, it is not unusual for the host and hostess, on these occasions, to be refused a participation in the sacrament until they pay this money, notwithstanding the considerable expense they are put to in entertaining, not only the clergy, but a certain number of their own friends and relations.

"Well, stand aside, I'll hear you first ; and now come up here, you young gentleman, that laughed so heartily a while ago at my joke—ha, ha, ha !—come up here, child."

A lad now approached him whose face, on a first view, had something simple and thoughtless in it, but in which, on a closer inspection, might be traced a lurking, sarcastic humour, of which his reverence never dreamt.

"You're for confession, of course ? " said the priest.

" *Of coorse*," said the lad, echoing him, and laying a stress upon the word, which did not much elevate the meaning of the blind compliance in general with the rite in question.

"Oh ! " exclaimed the priest, recognising him when he approached—"you are Dan Fegan's son, and designed for the Church yourself; you are a good Latinist, for I remember examining you in Erasmus about two years ago— *Quomodo se habet corpus tuum Charum lignum sacerdotis ? "*

" *Valde, Domine*," replied the lad, " *Quomodo se habet anima tua, charum exemplar sacer*dotage, *et fulcrum robustissimum Ecclesiæ sacrosanctæ.*"

"Very good, Harry," replied his reverence, laughing— "stand aside ; I'll hear you after Kelly."

He then called up a man with a long, melancholy face, which he noticed before to have been proof against his joke, and after making two or three additional fruitless experiments upon his gravity, he commenced a cross fire of peevish interrogatories, which would have excluded him from the "tribunal" on that occasion, were it not that the man was remarkably well prepared, and answered the priest's questions very pertinently.

This over, he repaired to his room, where the work of absolution commenced ; and, as there was a considerable number

to be rendered sinless before the hour of dinner, he contrived
to unsin them with an alacrity that was really surprising.

That a station is an expensive ordinance to the peasant
who is honoured by having one held in his house, no one
who knows the characteristic hospitality of the Irish people
can doubt.   I have reason, however, to think, that since the
Church of Rome and her discipline have undergone so
rigorous a scrutiny by the advocates of scriptural truth, she
has been much more cautious in the manner in which they
have been conducted.   The policy of Romanism has uniformly been to adapt herself to the circumstances by which
she may be surrounded, and as the unbecoming licentiousness, which about twenty, or even so late as fifteen years
ago trod so closely upon the heels of a ceremony which the
worship of God and the administration of sacramental rites
should have in a peculiar manner solemnized, was utterly
disgraceful and shocking—she felt that it was expedient,
as knowledge advanced around her, to practise a greater
degree of external decorum and circumspection, lest her
little ones should be scandalized.   This, however, did not
render it necessary that she should effect much reformation
on this point in those parts of the kingdom which are exclusively Catholic ; and accordingly stations, with some ex-
ceptions in a certain diocese, go on much in the old manner
as to the expense which they occasion the people to incur,
and the jolly, convivial spirit which winds them up.

About four o'clock the penitents were at length all despatched ; and those who were to be detained for dinner,
many of whom had not eaten anything until then, in consequence of the necessity of receiving the Eucharist fasting, were taken aside to taste some of Phaddhy's poteen.
Of course, no remorse was felt at the impiety of mingling
it so soon with the sacrament they had just received, be-
lieving, as they did, the latter to contain the immaculate
Deity ; but, indeed, their reverences at breakfast had set

them a pretty example on that point. At length the hour of dinner arrived, and along with it the redoubtable Parrah More Slevin, Captain Wilson, and another nephew of Father Philemy's, who had come to know what detained his brother who had conducted the auxiliary priest to Phaddhy's. It is surprising, on these occasions, to think how many uncles, and nephews, and cousins, to the forty-second degree, find it needful to follow their reverences on messages of various kinds; and it is equally surprising to observe with what exactness they drop in during the hour of dinner. Of course, any blood-relation or friend of the priest's must be received with cordiality ; and consequently they do not return without solid proofs of the good-natured hospitality of poor Paddy, who feels no greater pleasure than in showing his " dacency " to any belonging to his reverence.

I daresay it would be difficult to find a more motley and diversified company than sat down to the ungarnished fare which Katty laid before them. There were first, Fathers Philemy, Con, and the auxiliary from the far part of the diocese ; next followed Captain Wilson, Peter Malone, and Father Philemy's two nephews ; after these came Phaddhy himself, Parrah More Slevin, with about two dozen more of the most remarkable and uncouth personages that could sit down to table. There were besides about a dozen of females, most of whom by this time, owing to Katty's private kindness, and a slight thirst occasioned by the long fast, were in a most independent and placid state of feeling. Father Philemy, *ex officio*, filled the chair—he was a small man, with cherub cheeks as red as roses, black twinkling eyes, and double chin ; was of the fat-headed genus, and, if phrenologists be correct, must have given indications of early piety, for he was bald before his time, and had the organ of veneration standing visible on his crown ; his hair, from having once been black, had become an iron-grey, and hung down behind his ears, resting on the collar of his coat, according to the old school, to which, I must remark, he belonged, having been educated on the Continent. His coat had large double breasts, the lappels of which hung down loosely on each side, being the prototype of his waistcoat, whose double breasts fell downwards in the same manner; his black small-clothes had silver buckles at the knees, and the gaiters, which did not reach up so far, discovered a pair of white lamb's-wool stockings, somewhat retreating from their original colour.

Father Con was a tall, muscular, able-bodied young man, with an immensely broad pair of shoulders, of which he was vain; his black hair was cropped close, except a thin portion of it, which was trimmed quite evenly across his eyebrows; he was rather bow-limbed, and when walking looked upwards, holding out his elbows from his body, and letting the lower parts of his arms fall down, so that he went as if he carried a keg under each; his coat, though not well made, was of the best glossy broadcloth, and his long clerical boots went up about his knees like a dragoon's; there was an awkward stiffness about him, in very good keeping with a dark, melancholy cast of countenance, in which, however, a man might discover an air of simplicity not to be found in the visage of his superior, Father Philemy.

The latter gentleman filled the chair, as I said, and carved the goose; on his right sat Captain Wilson; on his left, the auxiliary—next to them Father Con, the nephews, Peter Malone, *et cetera*. To enumerate the items of the dinner is unnecessary, as our readers have a pretty accurate notion of them from what we have already said. We can only observe that when Phaddhy saw it laid, and all the wheels of the system fairly set a-going, he looked at Parrah More with an air of triumph which he could not conceal.

THE END.